There's Magic Between Us

Jillian Maria

To anyone seeking adventure: may you find it in big cities and small towns alike.

The universe is testing me.

We've been in Fairbrooke for less than ten minutes, but I already want to punch someone in the face. Specifically, the thirty-something guy behind the counter in this gas station.

Mom's picking through the snack aisle, and this asshole won't stop gawking at her like she's an endangered animal at the zoo. I glare at him as I fill up my cup with every flavor of slushy. He whips his phone out of his pocket and starts texting, his expression screaming *gossip*. My classmates are more subtle than this guy, and someone once tried to order Chinese food in the middle of algebra without the teacher noticing.

I kind of want to smack it out of his hand, but I promised Mom before we even left Chicago that I wouldn't start fights here. I pretend I'm interested in the stuff by the register instead. On the counter there's a basket full of plain gray rocks that are supposedly "good luck charms" you can buy for fifty dollars each. This seems both ridiculously expensive and intensely weird to sell at a gas station. But I've never been to Wisconsin before. How am I supposed to know how they do things here?

Even though I'm literally right in front of him, gas station guy doesn't look up from his phone until Mom approaches the counter with her snacks. When she does, he breaks into a grin that looks extra smarmy on his pale, patchily shaved face. "Charlotte, is that you? Thought hell would freeze over before I saw your face around here again!"

Mom offers a thin smile while I glower at him from over her shoulder like a bodyguard. If bodyguards looked like five-foot-two teen girls in overall shorts.

"Hello, Dale," Mom says in a calmer voice than he deserves. "I'm only in town long enough to drop off my daughter. Lydia's visiting Mom this week."

She gestures to me, and the guy—Dale—finally looks at me. His eyes widen, and I can practically see his final two brain cells banding together to calculate my age. "Your *daughter*? You mean . . ."

I bare my teeth in a grin. "The sixteen-year-old scandal that you guys gave my mom endless shit for? Yup, that's me!"

Dale gets a slack-jawed look that improves his pasty face significantly. Mom gives me a reproachful side-eye, but what does she want me to do? I'm not going to let him talk about me like I'm some sort of dirty secret. I'm *definitely* not going to let him talk about her like she needs to feel ashamed of anything.

His eyes focus on the things people like him always focus

on—the nose ring, the multiple ear piercings, the woven bracelets on my wrist. The pansexual pride bracelet is probably wasted on him since there's no way in hell he knows what those colors mean, but I've got a rainbow bracelet on the same wrist to help it along. God forbid anyone assumes I'm heterosexual.

"Hell, you're just like your mother, aren't you?" He doesn't say that like he thinks it's a good thing.

I lift my lips in the fakest smile I can manage. "Thanks for the compliment. Are you gonna give us our total or are you going to keep being an asshole?"

He doesn't answer right away, like he's trying to decide if I'm worth arguing with. I sort of wish that he would—the drive from Illinois to Wisconsin was long, and I'm restless. An argument would liven things up a little.

Unfortunately, he just sighs. "Five seventy-five."

Mom reaches into her purse, but I beat her to it. I pull a crumpled five and a handful of quarters out of my pocket.

Then I whip them over the counter at Dale.

It's not quite as effective as lobbing one of his stupid overpriced rocks, but one of the quarters *does* bounce off his forehead with a very satisfying *thwap*. Dale flinches back with a truly hilarious noise, somewhere between *oof* and *what the hell?*

"Keep the change!" I shout with fake, overblown cheer. I stomp out, determined to have the last word.

Mom doesn't follow me out right away. She's probably apologizing and promising to talk to me, all those good adult things mature people do. After several long slurps of my slushy, the bell dings, the door opens, and she passes me

3

without saying a word. I make a face and follow her to the car.

She lets the silence build as she pulls out of the gas station parking lot. But once we're back on the disturbingly empty gravel road, she sighs.

"Lydia . . ."

"I promised I wouldn't *start* fights." I jab the straw into my slushy for emphasis. "*He* started it."

Mom sighs again, softer this time. "Just . . . stop and think next time, okay? Pick your battles, doll."

I look at her, at the tight lines that only show up in the corners of her eyes when she's stressed, and I smile. "Ones for you are always worth picking, though." It's true. I won't let anyone give my mom shit. Not about how young she was when she had me, not about how she chooses to parent me, not about anything.

Mom smiles, and while those tight lines don't totally go away, they do get a lot smaller. "You know, back in high school, Dale was the *worst*."

I grin. I love when she gives up on being the responsible adult and just talks shit with me. "Oh yeah?"

"Yeah. He always had a mustard stain on his T-shirt? It's not like he wore the same shirt every day. Every one he owned just had a mustard stain."

We laugh, and the tension in the car disappears. I kick my combat boots up on the dashboard and watch as trees and the occasional farmhouse slip by. It's ridiculous how far apart everything is here. The sky seems to go on forever, an endless expanse of pink and orange and blue. It's so different from home that it almost makes me dizzy.

We turn at a stop sign, and the gravel road changes to dirt.

4

I'm being dramatic and I *know* I'm being dramatic, but I kind of hate the way it feels. Maybe all this rustic, unfinished business is beautiful to some people, but all it does is remind me of how out in the middle of nowhere we are. I won't be able to walk to the store or the movies if I get bored here. The little town we stopped in only had a diner. Oh, and a gas station run by an asshole. Can't forget that.

I grab my slushy and take a noisy slurp, trying to disguise whatever expression wants to come up on my face. I don't want to be a brat about this. It's *good* that I'm here.

"Don't get so excited, doll. I can feel your enthusiasm."

Out of the corner of my eye, I glance at Mom, her pink-glossed lips curved up in an understanding smile. I'm not surprised she can see right through me. But I force a smile anyway, like I can fool her.

"It's cool! I'm totally cool with being here."

"I know you are," Mom says, and I can tell she means it. "But . . ."

And because it's my mom, and I know she gets it, I give in. I grab the little lever on the side of my seat and fling myself back as dramatically as physically possible. "There's nothing to *do* here!"

Mom, full of understanding and compassion, laughs so hard that she almost shoots soda out her nose. I grin.

"*Seriously.*" I pull myself upright again. "I've been in Fairbrooke for like ten seconds and I'm already over it. I don't know how you managed seventeen years here."

Mom moved away after she got pregnant with me. I don't know the whole story, never really wanted to ask for the awkward details. But I know that my dad was never in the picture, and she's always hated Fairbrooke, even before me.

That's probably why she isn't staying, too. She told Grandma she's busy with work, and it's true, but I know she's relieved to have an excuse to not stick around. Hell, she didn't even want *me* visiting Fairbrooke. Which sort of makes two of us.

It's my own fault, though. I'd been on the phone with Grandma, and I mentioned visiting in that polite way you do where both of you agree it's a great idea and then never follow through. I didn't expect her to get so *excited*. She kept bringing it up to me, and to Mom, every time we called. And then Mom felt guilty enough that she basically had to let me come, if I wanted to come.

What was I supposed to do? I couldn't just say, *Sorry, Grandma, I was just thinking out loud. I'm about as serious about visiting you as I am about actually taking up guitar lessons.* That would be a dick move.

I try to put a positive spin on it. "I really am excited to see Grandma. It's been forever." When I was younger, she used to visit us in Chicago. But she can't travel or move around so well after breaking her hip. Since then, we haven't even been able to video-call because Grandma only has a landline.

Mom sighs, her eyebrows knitting together. "I am sorry I can't stay with you, though." She taps her fingertips nervously along the steering wheel. "I hope you won't be *too* bored."

The guilt in her voice tugs at my heart. I cover her hand on the steering wheel with mine. "Hey, it's cool. Grandma and I will be fine." I give her hand a little pat. "Assuming I don't die from shit cell reception and no Wi-Fi. You know."

Mom rolls her eyes, smiling a little. "Kids these days."

I grin. "Rotten, the lot of them."

We turn onto a long, winding driveway.

I've never been to Grandma's house, but I've seen the pale blue home at the top of the hill in pictures, so I recognize the dainty white accents and the swing on the front porch. With the sun just about to set behind it, it looks like something out of a postcard.

But it also looks small, even though it's two stories. Her yard is just so *big* by comparison. I don't think I've ever seen that much grass not covered in park benches and trash cans before. It stretches all around the house and slopes down in a gentle hill. At the bottom, it evens out and eventually hits a clear stream lined by tiny white flowers. A forest full of trees sits on the other side.

Mom hates that forest. She always talks about how awful it is, full of poisonous plants and feral animals. It doesn't *look* dangerous, but I don't really plan on testing that.

We pull up to the house, and Mom kills the engine. The wind chimes on Grandma's porch seem loud with it off. The only other sounds are the wind and bugs singing in the forest. I turn to the trees again. It's weird—I imagined them looking a lot creepier. Mom sure made them sound that way.

"Oh!"

Mom's voice pulls my gaze to the house in time to see Grandma walking off the front porch. I'm a little nervous, getting my first real look at her after so long. She had Mom late enough in life to make her actually old, even though Mom had me so young. I guess I'm worried she'll look frail and breakable and it'll make me uncomfortable.

But if anything, she looks *younger* than I remember, even

though she shuffles forward in careful steps that would get her knocked over in Chicago. Maybe it's because I was ten the last time I saw her in person. Even teenagers look old when you're a kid.

Her hair is long and gray but clean, tied back with a ribbon bright enough to compete with the vivid pattern of her long skirt. Even with its deep wrinkles, her face is alert and intelligent. Her sea-glass blue eyes are exactly the same shade as mine. They've got the same sparkle, too.

Grandma beams at both of us when she reaches the driveway. "It's so *good* to see you." Happiness radiates off of her. Trapped in a boring town or not, I can't regret this.

Mom moves to hug her first. "Hey, Mom. I'm sorry I can't stay."

It's crazy how alike they look. There are some differences, sure—Mom inherited Grandpa's brown eyes instead of Grandma's blue ones, and Grandma's hair has gone gray instead of staying Mom's chestnut brown. But they've got the same pointed nose, the same wide forehead, the same rounded cheekbones.

I inherited Grandma's blue eyes and Mom's round chin. But I have things that aren't from either of them. My hair is thick and curly instead of loose and wavy, and I have a button nose that no one in our family has. My skin is a few shades paler than both of theirs, more ivory than peach. I assume these are from the father who was never in the picture. I watch them hug, and for a second I feel like an outsider.

I know it won't last, though. Sure enough, Grandma pulls away and looks at me with a warm smile, and that feeling vanishes.

"Lydia, sweetheart! You've grown so much! And you've changed your hair—it looks lovely."

I smile, tugging on one blonde curl. My natural color, brown a few shades lighter than Mom's, shows at the roots, but I've been bleaching it since the summer before I started high school. The curls barely brush my shoulders, which is shorter than I wore them as a kid, too. "Thanks!" I go forward for a hug. "It's good to finally see you, Grandma."

She may walk like she's breakable, but her hugs are as warm and tight as I remember. I can probably manage a week of this.

Mom starts pulling my suitcase out of the trunk, but I wave her off. "I got this. You have to leave in like an hour. Don't waste catch-up time moving my sh—stuff."

Grandma laughs, her eyes sparkling. "So polite." She pats me on the head so my curls bounce. "Come on, Charlotte. I've made lemonade."

Mom hooks her arm through Grandma's and they go inside. I move to the trunk and start pulling out my stuff. There's a lot of it. A guitar I haven't played in years, books I never finished reading, a laptop I won't use without Wi-Fi. Grandma's old, and she gets tired easily. I can't expect her to keep me entertained all the time.

I've never been much good at entertaining myself. I've never needed to be, not with so much stuff to do right outside my apartment. Hopefully all of this junk will make this week bearable.

As I put the last of my stuff on the driveway, my gaze gets pulled to the forest again. I try to match up what I'm seeing with my mom's stories, but I can't do it. The branches aren't overgrown and rotting; they're full of bright leaves. The stream isn't muddy and stagnant; it's clear and babbling. The grass isn't yellowed and overgrown; it's bright green and inviting.

A light summer breeze ruffles my hair, wisps of blonde floating in the corners of my vision. I can smell the forest, all pine and fresh water and flowers—definitely not the rot and animal turds I imagined. The wind through the leaves sounds high and clear, almost like voices singing a bit too far away for me to make out the words. A smile tugs at my lips.

"Lydia? You coming, doll?"

I'm standing on the edge of the driveway, right where the dirt meets the grass. I'd zoned out so hard staring at the forest that I barely noticed myself move.

"Shit, I spaced out. Sorry." I hurry back to the car, hefting my duffel bag over my shoulder.

Mom hovers in the doorway. "Do you need help carrying that?"

I wave her back into the house. "Don't worry. I got it." And before she can argue more, I gather up the rest of my stuff and follow her inside, turning my back on the forest below.

I mean, no need to roll out the welcome wagon or anything.

My first morning at Grandma's house is almost disgusting in how perfect it is. Warm yellow light streams into the bedroom, filtered through gauzy white curtains. The open window lets in the sound of birds singing and the smell of sweet grass carried on the breeze. Even my pillow fits the aesthetic you'd find on one of those lifestyle blogs, white and dotted with cute little flowers that look hand-stitched.

I press my face into it and groan.

Okay, it isn't *that* bad. It's just so early compared to when I usually wake up. Somehow, the birds outside sound so much louder than the constant stream of chatter, cars, and music back home. There's no way I'm getting back to sleep now.

It doesn't help that I went to bed before I usually do. Grandma practically fell asleep at sunset. I tried my best to keep myself entertained, but there was really nothing else for me to do, so I went ahead and followed her example.

And I have a whole *week* of this to look forward to. I groan again, the special noise I reserve for watching storms from the apartment window or going into long standardized tests. Don't get me wrong, I love Grandma and I want to spend time with her. But thinking of all the time I'll have to spend by myself while she rests sort of makes me want to try my luck in the forest Mom hates so much. At least the possibility of getting eaten by a bear is sort of exciting.

I cross the room and lean outside, my elbows against the window frame. I've got a clear view of the forest from here. The flowers along the stream sway in the breeze, and the trees behind them stand sturdy and alive, soaking up the sunlight in a way that almost feels like they're inviting me to join them.

I don't realize I'm zoning out again until my fingertips catch on something, pulling me out of my thoughts. Looking down, I see that *someone* carved a picture of a dick into the windowsill. I laugh, turning back to the room. The sheets are changed, the posters taken down from the walls and most things stowed away in the closet, but the spirit of Mom's teenage rebellion lingers on.

I swap my pj's for overall shorts and a fresh T-shirt, making a token effort with my blonde curls before heading downstairs. The sound of sizzling greets me on my way down, and I grin at the smell of bacon.

I'm not expecting much more than that and maybe some toast when I reach the kitchen. But there's enough food in here to feed an army, it feels like. Pies and cakes sit on the counter, cookies cool on a wire rack, and several fresh loaves of bread sit on top of the stove. In the center of this chaos is Grandma, a smudge of pancake batter on the tip of her nose, wisps of gray hair falling over her forehead.

"Good morning, dear!" She pushes a plate toward me, gesturing to an array of breakfast items: pancakes with fruits and whipped cream in separate containers, scrambled eggs, bacon drying between grease-soaked napkins. "Help yourself. I made breakfast."

"Talk about an understatement." I laugh as I load up my plate, adorning a few pancakes with sugar-soaked strawberries. "Are people coming over? 'Cause, like, I've got an appetite and all, but I'd have to stay for a month to plow through all this."

Grandma shakes her head with a smile. "No, no, most of this is for town. It's a little tradition we have. Once a week, we meet up and swap things."

"Oh! That's cool." It probably doesn't sound as sincere as I mean it. In my defense, the food looks very good, and it's incredibly distracting. I grab whipped cream and doodle a heart on my pancakes.

"Would you like to come?" Grandma smiles at me when I look up from admiring my handiwork. "I'm sure it's not as exciting as what you're used to, but it would get you out of the house."

I think about it. The town is depressingly small, but at least it'll be full of people. Sitting alone in this house would be the opposite of that. Besides, I did come here to hang out with Grandma.

I hum like I'm still mulling it over, grinning so Grandma knows I'm kidding. "I guess I'll go. I'm gonna need payment in the form of cookies, though."

Grandma laughs. "Deal."

I carry all the food out to the car after breakfast, although I let her arrange it. I'd probably wind up smashing the cookies or smushing down the bread or something if I tried. The car smells delicious when I haul myself into the passenger seat.

Grandma drives ten miles under the speed limit, which is pretty impressive considering how low it is already. I sit on my hand when I catch myself drumming my fingertips against the dashboard.

"So you bake this much every week?" I ask, mostly to distract myself from the fact that I could be *walking* faster than this.

Grandma nods, smiling. "Yes, it's something we've done for years now. Our houses are very far apart, so it's a good way for us to see each other when we're not in town meetings."

"Do people actually *have* those?" I try to imagine it. Can everyone in town really fit into a single room? You'd need a stadium to make that work back home, and even then, it would be overflowing.

"Oh, yes." Grandma doesn't roll her eyes, but with that sort of tone, she doesn't need to. "More often than I'd like. Some people call them over the pettiest problems."

"*Ethel's grass is a quarter-centimeter too long!*" I screech in my best impression of a crotchety old-lady voice before realizing Grandma maybe isn't the person to really appreciate old-lady jokes. But she just throws her head back and laughs. I guess my inability to think before I speak hasn't landed me in shit quite yet.

"Something like that," Grandma says as we turn onto the main road. Although calling it that is pretty charitable. The actual "town" of Fairbrooke is so small that we could drive past it in the time it takes to sneeze—if, you know, we were driving at the pace of a normal person. Instead, Grandma's creeping lets me take in just how *boring* this place is.

I'm not being fair, because it's not like the town is totally disgusting. The general store has a wooden porch complete with a rocking horse, and what I think might be a church has a cute little bell tower. But most of my impression is peeling finish on wooden walls, ramshackle shingles and dust, and, most of all, emptiness. Every parking lot except one looks completely deserted.

It's this lot that Grandma pulls into, next to a grungy-looking diner. In the window, a neon *OPEN* sign flickers. For a second I'm surprised Grandma found a place to park so close. But this isn't home. You don't have to drive around the block four times to find a spot.

Small-town living has *some* charms, I guess.

I help Grandma unload the car, and we walk inside. It's like every small-town diner I've ever seen on TV, only more run-down. The ghosts of coffees past stain the countertops, and the booth Grandma directs me to has a large tear along the other side of it, spilling foam from its cheap red casing.

At least there are people here. Not many, but it's a small enough space that it feels like a crowd. It's not what I'm used to, not what I love. But at least it's *something*.

The tables and booths are packed with things to trade. Some of them have food like Grandma's, while others have clothes or different things. One woman looks like she's trading wood carvings, and another guy has jewelry.

Some people sit and shout in place. Others walk table to table. But everyone's talking to each other, so it's weird that, at first, no one even says hello to us. The back of my neck prickles like someone's staring, but I don't catch anyone's eye when I turn around.

Finally, a woman with crow's feet and the most stereotypical *can-I-speak-to-the-manager* haircut approaches. "Good morning, Dorothy." She does her best to ignore me entirely, her gaze trained on the bread.

Grandma either ignores or doesn't notice this, just smiles her warm smile. "Good morning, Georgia. This is my granddaughter, Lydia."

Forced to acknowledge my existence, she presses her lips into a thin smile. "How sweet." She talks like I'm a toddler offering her a chewed-up carrot. "It's nice to meet you, Lydia."

"I can tell," I say, because my filter eroded at some point in middle school and hasn't grown back since.

Grandma cuts in, clearly trying to ease the tension. "Your usual?"

Georgia just shakes her head and hurries away. I guess I ruined *that* deal. Grandma sighs.

"Sorry," I mutter.

Grandma looks at me and smiles. "You're your mother's daughter, alright."

I *try* to play nice with the next people who come by. They at least trade with Grandma, but they still ignore me unless she introduces me directly. She tries her best, even cuts me a slice of rich chocolate cake to eat and trades the rest away to several people. But I can tell she regrets bringing me.

Finally, all of Grandma's food is either traded away or just plain gifted. I'm helping her pack up when a woman approaches. She's pretty much the quintessential old lady, blue-rinsed hair in short curls. She'd look like the sort of person to offer cookies if her expression wasn't so guarded. "Dorothy, can I borrow you for a moment?"

Grandma smiles. "What can I help you with, Etta?"

"It's town business. Regarding last week's meeting." Etta's eyes dart to me, then away. "Maybe we should talk outside?"

Grandma just gives me an apologetic smile. "Do you mind, dear?"

I wave her off, biting back a quip about how painfully obvious Etta is being about not wanting me around. "Don't worry about it. Gotta make sure everyone's grass is the proper length or whatever, right?"

Etta stares at me, mystified, but Grandma hides a smile behind her hand. Worth it.

I watch them head out the front door, then turn my attention back to my cake. But it's not the same without Grandma sitting here with me. I jiggle my foot hard enough to shake the table. At first, I'm not sure why I feel so weird, but then I figure it out. It's the townspeople.

Whatever fake-polite bullshit the others were holding up for Grandma's sake, it's done now. They're all silent or whispering to each other, and when I catch their gazes, they don't even bother to look away.

I grimace, and the next time I catch an old lady gawking, I give her a tight grin before she can tear her eyes away. "Take a picture. It'll last longer." My voice is the loudest thing in the place. But whatever. If they're not going to bother pretending to be polite, then neither am I.

This is so different from home. No one stares if you're new there because there's new people everywhere. You never have to worry about being the loudest person around because the city's always louder.

I pull out my phone. Still no Wi-Fi, but I do have weak cell reception, which is more than I can say for Grandma's house. My first thought is to try and call my mom, but she's at work. Instead, I open a group chat and type, *Is it wrong to punch an old lady in the face????*

After a few confused responses, I have to explain where I am. I either forgot to tell them I'd be away from home this week or they forgot I told them. It could be either. I hang out with these people, but I'm not sure I'd call them friends. We don't really talk about ourselves, anyway. I'm not sure I could remember even a single last name.

Texting helps, but not much. I can't stop bouncing my leg and glancing around, glaring whenever I lock eyes with someone gawking at me. What are they doing, anyway? Studying the way I eat my cake or hold my phone? Maybe they need things to discuss later, like my group chat is currently discussing some drama I missed. I huff and send a line of applicable emojis, wishing I could've been there to see it happen.

Finally, I can't take it anymore. Leaving the diner will totally ruin my cell reception, but it's not worth this bullshit. I'll wait for Grandma in the car. I send a final, *Going back into the dead zone,* complete with a bunch of skull emojis, and get to my feet.

Before I can reach the door, a voice stops me.

"You're Charlotte's girl, aren't you?"

I turn. A guy in a grease-stained T-shirt and a trucker hat sits at the counter, staring me down. I cross my arms over my chest. "How'd you guess?"

"You got your grandma's eyes." His eyes are a dusky gray, not quite milky, as they lock onto me. "And your *mother's* attitude."

I give him my best fake smile. It's getting a workout in this place. "You're not the first person in Fairbrooke to give me that compliment." The guy's face twists, and my fake smile turns into a grin. I'm kind of glad someone finally screwed up enough courage to actually say something instead of just staring.

The old guy huffs. "Dale told me all about you."

I roll my eyes. Gas Station Dick strikes again. "Word travels fast in small towns, doesn't it?"

The old man leans forward, but I don't back down. If he's trying to scare me, he's doing a shitty job. "Travels even faster when it's about trouble like you."

I grit my teeth. "Oh, yeah, I'm the worst, huh? Out here causing all sorts of trouble, by, sorry, what was it again? Sitting in a diner? Eating a cake? Breathing without permission? Shit, you've got me. I'm a total delinquent. Might as well lock me up now." I hold out my wrists like I'm actually inviting him to slap handcuffs on me.

There's no way in hell I'd let him lay a finger on me, but whatever.

He doesn't touch me, though. He just leans back in his

chair, shaking his head. "Kids these days."

Mom said the same thing as a joke. If she were here, we'd be laughing at this jerk the second we walked out. Loneliness rushes through me, but so does anger. I focus on that. "Yeah, kids these days, not putting up with bullshit just because some guy's got white hair and thinks he knows everything. Where do we get off?" I spin and walk toward the door, but the guy's voice stops me.

"You been in the forest yet?"

I turn to face him again. I'm not sure what to expect— maybe a glare, or a smirk as he messes with the city girl. But his face is stony still and gives nothing away.

It makes me curious enough to continue. "What the hell does the forest have to do with anything?"

He shakes his head. "Forest is full of trouble. That's all you Barneses are. Family full of trouble."

I open my mouth to ask more, but then the bell dings over my head and Grandma runs into me. "Oh, Lydia! Good timing. Are you ready to go?"

"Yeah . . ." I glance back at the counter. But the guy's gone, stalking off to the bathroom. Maybe he doesn't want to deal with another trouble-filled Barnes.

Grandma watches him go. "Was Clyde bothering you?"

"Eh." I shrug, making sure my voice is loud enough for him to hear. "I wasn't bothered." Because I'm not. Assholes like him don't have permission to make me feel anything.

"Good." She drapes an arm over my shoulder. "Let's go."

We head back to the car. I'm quiet for most of the drive home, too caught up in my own thoughts. Everything gets under my skin—the way no one approached Grandma's table, the way eyes would lock on me. Mostly, I can't get Clyde's words out of my head.

Finally, as we turn into her long driveway, I can't hold it in anymore. "Grandma, what's up with the forest?"

Grandma presses her lips together. The wrinkles deepen in the corners of her eyes. "Why do you ask?"

"Clyde said it was full of trouble. Our family, too." It occurs to me too late that blunt honesty maybe isn't the way to get the answers I want. But I hate lying, and I've already gone this far. "What is everyone's *deal* here, Grandma?"

Grandma sighs as we park. "That's a long story, dear. And I'm really too tired to tell it right now. These trades always take a lot out of me. Do you think you can entertain yourself for a few hours while I rest?"

"Oh. Yeah, sure." Is she trying to get out of the conversation? Part of me hopes not. I don't want my family keeping secrets from me.

Anyway, she does look tired as we get out of the car. "Thank you, dear." Grandma smiles and pats me on the head.

And as soon as we're inside, she heads to her room.

Family full of trouble, huh? Might as well live up to the name.

I start to get restless about five seconds after Grandma goes to nap.

It's not like I don't try. I pace from room to room, looking for something to catch my interest, but nothing does. I try to sit in the bay window and read, the way you're supposed to enjoy peaceful time, but I spend more time bouncing my foot and staring out the window than I do focusing on the page.

My leg cramps up after too much of this, and I groan, silently admitting defeat. Sitting and enjoying the quiet is never going to be my thing.

I drag my guitar out onto the front porch, plopping down on the swing there. Plucking at the strings at least helps, but I only ever learned basic chords. I run out of material fast.

Which is when I turn to the forest.

I probably wouldn't even be sparing it a second glance if it wasn't for Clyde and his bullshit. Then again, maybe I would. It seems like whenever I zone out, it's where my attention naturally goes. Something about how the leaves constantly seem to be moving, maybe.

I squint at the trees. "What the hell is *your* deal?"

The leaves rustle, like a response.

I set aside my guitar and stand. There's nothing in a dumb forest to interest me, but walking to the stream that separates the trees from Grandma's yard kills about ten seconds, so it's better than nothing. Maybe I can walk along the bank or something. The stream's way too wide to cross, so there's no way for anything to get me—and no way for me to get in, even if I wanted to.

At least that's what I think. But then I see the bridge.

I jog over to make sure it's not just a tree that fell across the gap or something. But it's not. It's small and wooden, with railings that come up to my waist. Definitely there on purpose, which makes no sense. If the forest is so dangerous, why build a bridge in the first place? And why is it still so sturdy, not rotting or overgrown? Grandma pays someone to keep her yard looking decent, but I don't know why they'd bother with a bridge no one uses.

So why don't you use it? I try to shake off the thought. I don't care about nature. Wandering around a bunch of trees doesn't sound like my idea of a good time. But neither does sitting on a porch or in an empty living room. I definitely don't want to go back to that stupid town.

Clyde's words bounce around my head. *Forest is full of trouble. That's all you Barneses are. Family full of trouble.*

Okay. I'm a little curious. The bridge sort of implies our family went into the forest at one point, and Clyde sure as hell made it sound that way. But there's no way Mom wouldn't have told me about it. She's told me all her stories.

I step onto the bridge, more cautious than I'm used to. But it holds my weight fine. And it's actually not so bad. Even from this far away, the branches on the other side of the river reach out, shielding me from the worst of the sun. I hold out my arms and stare at the patterns the light through the leaves makes against my bare skin.

I'll give the forest this—it's not still, and it's not silent. It's not *home*, not even close, but it feels alive in a way that's familiar, a way the diner just wasn't. I lean against the railing and peer into the water. It's clear enough that I can see right to the bottom, the pebbly floor distorted by the current.

It's a little easier to breathe here under the branches. My annoyance from the diner rushes away in the stream.

Leaves rustle, and I turn my head toward the forest without really thinking about it. A smile tugs at my lips. The forest isn't as fun as home, isn't as good as home, but I can't deny that it smells a lot better.

I sort of expected the forest to look grosser on the inside, but it doesn't. A path of bright green grass winds away from me, the only flat earth I can see. The rest is dominated by tall trees and all different sorts of plants. It's a beautiful kind of chaos.

Wedged between a pine tree and one with bright green leaves, there's a little patch of bright purple flowers that looks very social-media-worthy. I wouldn't even have to step off the path to take a picture. Next time I have service, I could text it to the group chat with a joke about how I became one with nature for five whole minutes.

And that's all it takes to get me to step into the forest my mom hates, the one that's so "full of trouble."

But it's not a big deal. I can still see the bridge, so I can run if anything shows up. I'm even responsible enough to keep an ear out for any movement. There's nothing but birds singing and wind snaking through the branches as I kneel to snap my picture, warm grass tickling my bare knees.

I look up, and an awful, twisted face fills my vision.

"Oh, what the *hell*?" I crab-walk backward, ready to run. Then I realize what I'm actually looking at.

A kid hangs upside down above the flower patch, skinny knees locked around a branch. As my heart tries to remember how to beat, he drops onto the path in a move that's too graceful to be an accident. He rolls in the grass, laughter echoing off the trees.

"Jesus. Yeah, yeah, okay. You got me." I laugh a little, too, mostly letting go of excess adrenaline. It was a little too fast to actually get scared, but with his long dark hair hanging and his upside-down grin, he did look like something out of a horror movie.

He doesn't look like that as he stands, though. Just a kid in a grass-stained tunic shirt and olive-green pants rolled up his shins. Even when he stops laughing, brown eyes just a few shades darker than his skin sparkle.

"What are you doing here, anyway? I'm pretty sure this isn't the sort of place for a kid to be hanging around." Not that

I'm one to talk. But at a lofty sixteen years old, I have at least eight years on this kid, if not more. "Haven't you heard the forest is full of trouble?"

He laughs again. "What *kind* of trouble?"

"I don't know, actually." I stand up, brushing dirt from my overalls with the hand not holding my phone. "Any ideas? You're the local around here, I'm guessing. What kind of trouble should I be expecting?"

His grin widens. "Something like this."

He snatches the phone out of my hand and runs down the path.

"Hey! You little shit!" I rush after him. He's faster than me, and he seems to know where he's going. If he ducks into the trees, I'm pretty sure I'll never be able to keep up with him. But he doesn't do that.

Instead, he keeps stopping and glancing over his shoulder, making sure I haven't lost him or given up in frustration. He wiggles the phone over his shoulder, grinning.

He's not trying to steal it at all. The little brat is messing with me.

"Okay, you've had your fun. Come on, you goddamned gremlin." The kid flashes me an obnoxious grin and ducks into the trees with a ballet-like twirl. I swear, jogging after him.

It's a little harder to follow him through the trees, but he waits for me, always just out of reach. Sometimes he pauses, whistling cheerfully, and once, he actually winks at me as I squeeze between too-tight tree trunks. I don't really bother talking sense into him. I can't outrun this kid or outsmart his knowledge of this place. That means I have to outlast him.

Branches snap beneath my feet as I wrestle my way

through a particularly thick patch of trees so close together that bark scrapes against my skin as I squeeze through. The kid waits on the other side, sitting on a branch over my head.

"You're a little asshole, you know that?" I shout up at him.

He giggles and jumps, landing on the other side of some tall grass. I push through, expecting more trees and a grinning kid. What I get instead is a clearing, empty except for a cluster of crumbling houses.

"What the *hell*?" I blink rapidly, like maybe I got annoyed enough to start hallucinating. But the houses, dozens of them, are still there when I open my eyes. The rotting wood is a far cry from the well-kept bridge at the stream. Most of them have busted windows and vines growing up the sides.

The kid is gone. But after a few seconds, I see he's left a present. My phone sits in plain sight on the crumbling railing of a front porch. I scoop it up, looking around. "Kid?" My voice echoes against the empty houses. It's a little creepy, honestly. I've seen abandoned houses before, sure, but this many at once makes it feel like a ghost town.

Who used to live in these things? Who would live here, in the middle of a forest?

It occurs to me that *I'm* in the middle of a forest. And did I think about how I was going to find my way back to Grandma's while I chased that damn kid? No, no I didn't.

"Son of a bitch." I twist my fingertips in my curls and tug, like I can jumpstart the part of my brain where my self-preservation lives. Alright. I've gotten myself out of stupider things before, and I'm sure I'll get myself out of this. Even though I know without looking that I'm not going to be able to use my phone's GPS out here in the middle of nowhere.

I close my eyes, listening to the leaves, the wind, the stream . . .

The stream! If I get there, I can follow it back to Grandma's house. How long can it be? I could walk through this entire town if I really wanted to, and the forest is only a small part of it. I start toward where I think the stream is, twigs crunching underfoot as I make my way through the trees.

I grin as the sound of the babbling stream starts to get louder. Not bad for a city girl. I didn't even fall into a pit of quicksand or have to outrun a moose or whatever. It's almost weird how different this place is compared to how Mom made it sound. Maybe it was worse when she lived here.

The trees turn long and skinny, so packed together that I've got to turn sideways to squeeze through them in some places. I grumble as I pluck a branch from my curls. At least the stream sounds like it's getting closer.

But while I strain my ears for the stream, I hear something else. Behind me, there's the sound of twigs crunching. It almost sounds like someone's following me. And considering how silent the kid was, I don't think it's him.

I turn, squinting into the trees behind me. "Hello?"

The sound comes again, but there's no answer. Honestly, it's probably just a squirrel. Or the wind. Smiling at myself for getting spooked, I speak into the air. "Look, if you're an axe murderer, you should know that my head is really hard, not made for axes at all, and—"

I don't actually realize I'm still backing up until my foot hits empty air instead of ground.

There's no time to think. In the time it takes for me to realize I'm fucking *airborne*—what the *fuck*—I'm already acting. There's a wall of dirt in front of me and I reach for it, palms scraping until they catch against something. My fingers close around a branch and cling like my life depends on it. Which, you know, it might.

"Shit, shit, *shitshitshit!*"

I'm clinging to the side of a cliff. I managed to fall off a literal actual *cliff*. Below me, the stream babbles along its merry way, taunting me with the possibility of a broken leg if I let go.

My combat boots scrabble against the wall, making little clouds of dirt. My arm muscles are already starting to shake from having to hold up my entire body weight. I lunge forward.

I actually manage to get one arm up and over the cliff edge. I dig my fingers into the earth, but I don't have enough momentum to pull myself up. I slide backward, taking a handful of grass and dirt with me as I go. My heart hits my throat and I open my mouth to scream—

And a hand closes around my wrist.

My scream cuts off in an undignified squawk, but I don't have time for embarrassment. I don't even have time to wonder who owns the hand I'm clinging to. I'm in primal, lizard-brain survival mode, and all I care about is scrambling back onto safe land. Which I do, with the stranger's help. I fall face-first into the grass.

Holy shit. The thought cycles through my mind as I try to remember how moving works. My chest heaves and my muscles shake. It isn't until I snuff in a nose full of dirt that I sit up, my brain finally making contact with my mouth.

"Holy *shit!*"

There's a soft noise off to the side, and I remember my rescuer. I look over to see a girl around my age clinging to a tree with one arm. Her eyes are dark, although that could just be because her pupils seem to be swallowing them whole as she stares at me. Her narrow features are slack with shock.

It's probably not the best time to notice that she's pretty cute. I do it anyway.

I clear my throat. "Well, hi there. Sorry to . . . drop in on you." I grin. It probably looks a little manic on my sweaty, dirty face. "Get it? Drop?" I point down at the rushing stream below, which I did, indeed, come very close to dropping into. I've got the racing heart to prove it.

The girl stares at me, slowly reaching up to push her straight black hair away from her face. It swings in a glossy sort of way above her waist. "Are you . . ." She coughs. Her voice is wispy and soft. "Are you *joking*?"

I grin wider. I couldn't stop even if I tried. "A little."

"You shouldn't." Even though it's still quiet, her voice is firm and full of certainty. "You could've *died*."

That sounds a little dramatic to me, but seeing as how she just saved my ass, I'm not going to push it. "Well, thanks for saving me then." I offer her a hand. "Lydia Barnes. I'm here visiting my grandma for the week."

She stares at my hand for a moment—an uncomfortably long moment, actually. Then she takes it. "Eden Yu."

She doesn't shake it, just leaves our palms pressed together like that. Her hands are very warm. Cleaner than mine, with long fingers. Heat rushes to my cheeks. *What is* with *this girl?* I move our hands up and down in an awkward, one-sided handshake before letting go. "Nice to meet you. Well, you know, besides the whole cliff thing."

Eden blinks. "Right."

She stands. She's tall but not quite gangly, wearing a button-down brown dress that just barely reaches her knees. It suits her even if it is a little old-fashioned. Her collarbone peeks out of the top, and the lace hem makes sun patterns against the gold-toned skin of her legs.

"Well then." She shifts her weight from one foot to the other. "Goodbye." And then she actually turns and starts to walk away.

"Hey, wait!"

She pauses, glancing over her shoulder. Confusion clouds her features, like *I'm* the weird one here. "Yes?"

"Um . . ." Now that I think about it, I don't really have a reason to want her to stay. I just know my heart is still hammering and I sort of want to barf. "Do you live around here?"

Eden frowns. "Yes. Is that all?" Her voice is sharp and annoyed.

I huff, echoing her tone. "Yeah. Sure. I'm *fine*, by the way." Not that she *asked*. What is this girl's *problem*? Maybe I'm being too harsh on her—she did help me, after all. But still. She seems to think I almost died. Don't you check in on someone after that? *I* would, and I'm not exactly known for my mastery of grace and tact.

"Okay. Good." And before I can say anything else, she squeezes through the trees and disappears.

I stay sitting on the ground for a few moments, staring after her. Between her and the kid, does anyone normal actually wander into the forest? Maybe only weirdos go into

31

a place that's "full of trouble."

That probably says something about me. I choose not to unpack it.

I stand. My muscles are a little wobbly, but other than that, I'm okay. I peer over the cliff at the rushing stream below. *You could've died.* I laugh a little. She was definitely being dramatic. I've fallen from higher and been totally fine.

Jumping down there doesn't sound fun, though. I turn, figuring I can follow the edge of the cliff until it lowers and meets up with the stream like it probably does.

And that's when I hear the piano.

I pause, straining my ears. At first, I think it's a bird or something, because it's not a proper song with chords and stuff. But it doesn't sound like a bird. It *sounds* like someone's pressing random keys on a piano, a jumble of notes that's a little different every time.

It's coming from the same direction Eden went.

And Eden made it clear she wanted nothing to do with me. So the smart thing would be to ignore whatever she's doing and walk away.

I'm not, as you might have noticed, known for doing the smart thing. I push through the trees after her.

Curiouser and Curiouser. Translation: bullshit and what the hell?

I step out into a wide-open space, squinting against the sun. It takes a second for my eyes to adjust and another second for me to make sense of what I'm seeing, because it's just so weird.

A piano sits in the center of a large, green field. It's one of those old-fashioned upright ones, made of dark wood with ivy crawling up a side. Eden sits on the bench in front of it, her eyebrows drawn together and her lips pressed into a tight, frustrated line.

She plays a run of notes, pauses, then sighs, scrubbing at the bridge of her nose. The corners of her eyes go pinched and tired like Mom's after a long shift at work.

"What are you doing?" I ask.

Eden's fingertips mash out a startled jumble of notes. She spins to face me. "What are *you* doing here?"

"Well. I heard you?" It feels sort of lame when I say it out loud.

"I thought you had a grandma to visit."

"She's resting." Still, probably. I take a step closer.

Eden turns her body to face the piano again but keeps talking to me over her shoulder. "She wouldn't like you in here."

"Because people don't like the forest?"

"Yes."

"Do you know why? No one's telling me anything."

Eden's face scrunches up, like she can't believe I don't know. Or maybe like she can't believe I'm wasting her time by asking her. "I'm too busy to worry about that."

"Busy with what?"

"With this." Eden gestures at the piano, exasperation creeping into her voice. "Do you mind letting me get back to it?"

I throw up my hands in defeat. "Okay, okay! Whatever." I'm not sure what's so goddamned important about pressing random notes on a piano, but even I know when to stop sometimes. This time, anyway. Eden's not really being subtle. I can almost appreciate it. Too often I don't know where the line is, but Eden's painted hers in neon colors.

She focuses on the keys, not bothering to see if I actually leave or not. I don't. I'm not sure why. Something about what she plays bugs me. It's familiar, even though she plays one or two notes differently every time. I keep listening, because I know it's gonna annoy me until I figure out why.

And finally, at one run of notes, I do.

"Oh! That sounds kind of like a lullaby my mom used to sing."

I want to call the words back the second they're out of my mouth. Eden's hands go still over the keys, and when she spins around, I'm pretty sure it's because she's going to yell at me to leave her the hell alone already.

But she doesn't yell. She doesn't even look angry. Her expression is blank, so different from her obvious annoyance before. "Sing it."

"What?"

"Sing it for me."

"A 'please' wouldn't kill you, you know."

Eden sighs, and that old, exhausted look creeps onto her face again. "Forget it. I shouldn't be asking for help, anyway." She turns her back to me.

Pride tells me to walk away, but now I'm curious. I stomp forward. "*Jesus!* Fine, fine." It's been years since I've heard the lullaby, but I can still remember it in Mom's rough and scratchy voice. I open my mouth and sing.

"In the darkness of the wood I found you,
"I stole you away.
"Now the song of the trees will surround you,
"For all of your days."

It's sort of creepy now that I'm old enough to actually think about the lyrics. But I guess all lullabies are sort of creepy, what with babies falling out of cradles and all that. Anyway, it doesn't feel creepy here. Not with the leaves and the grass and the distant stream providing the backing I never knew it needed.

Eden sits there for a long moment as the final notes hang in the air. Then she spins around, playing the tune of the first line perfectly on the first try. "That makes sense." Her voice is so soft I have to strain to hear it. She plays the whole tune, back bent over the piano. I step closer. She doesn't even seem to notice.

When she finishes, I swear something inside of the piano shifts, making a hollow knocking sound. "What the hell?"

Eden doesn't look at me. She's staring at the piano with an expression so raw and open and *pleading* it's almost uncomfortable to look at.

She plays the run again, tries to sing with it. But her voice cracks and wavers, sometimes giving out on her for whole syllables. She clears her throat.

"Come on," she says. And I don't even think. I just start singing along with her playing.

"In the darkness of the wood I found you,

"I stole you away.

"Now the song of the trees will surround you,

"For all of your days."

At the third line, the top of the piano opens. And at the fourth, a pale wooden stick floats out of it.

I open my mouth to ask something along the lines of, *What the hell?* But I don't have time. Eden leaps up, and the second her fingers leave the keys, the lid slams shut and takes the stick with it. "No!" She stands on the bench and slams her fist against the now-closed lid. "No, that's not *fair!*"

"Um . . ." I look around, half expecting a camera

somewhere, because this feels like some kind of prank. But no one shows up. I'm pretty sure I can't just leave her like this, even though part of me sort of wants to. I didn't sign up for whatever weird nonsense is happening here, and it's not like Eden's been nice.

But still. I go over and look up at her, rapping against the wooden side of the piano.

"You good?"

She steps down from the bench, sitting heavily. She stares into the trees. "I was so *close*."

"Right." Like that's even an answer. "You're trying to get that stick thing out of the piano?" Eden nods. I consider asking why, but she kind of looks like she's creeping into total freak-out zone. It's probably better to focus on solutions. "Okay. What if we try again, except this time I grab it while you play?"

Eden opens her mouth, then closes it. She turns away. "I shouldn't."

"What?"

"I didn't *ask* for your *help*." That angry, jagged edge is back in her voice.

My own voice rises to match it. "Well, shit! Fine! Have fun, I guess." This town is so goddamned weird. Am I going to meet a single normal person I'm not related to? I spin around and start to stomp off.

I'm at the tree line when Eden's voice pulls me back. "Wait!"

Against my better judgment, I turn. Eden sits at the piano, gripping the edge of the bench so hard her knuckles turn pale and bloodless.

"Okay," she says. "Okay. *Please.*"

I still sort of want to stomp off into the forest and leave her to deal with this on her own. Except she looks so *upset*, shoulders shaking and lips pressed tight together. Kind of like she might start crying, I realize with growing alarm. That would be bad. I'm pretty sure I'd feel like an asshole if that happened.

And okay, she's super cute and I'm a useless pansexual who sort of likes the idea of helping a damsel in distress. Sue me.

I hurry back over, grass squeaking under my boots. "Shit. Okay, okay, don't get all leaky on me. I'm bad with tears."

Eden looks down at the keys, color sparking in her cheeks. She scowls. "I'm not crying."

"Good, don't start."

I stand by the piano. A shiver runs up my spine, the air sitting weird against my skin, kind of like it does before a rainstorm. But the sky is bright blue. Eden puts her fingers over the keys and looks up at me with those dark, serious eyes. "Ready?"

I swallow. What have I gotten myself into? "Yeah."

She nods at me and plays along while I sing.

"In the darkness of the wood I found you,

"I stole you away.

"Now the song of the trees will surround you,

"For all of your days."

My voice rolls through the field. It's not pretty, but it gets the job done. Eden matches me note for note.

When the final line comes, I'm ready for the floating stick, which is not a phrase I ever imagined I'd use. I reach out and pull hard, expecting it to be stuck in there with some invisible wire or something. But it comes out so easy I stumble back. Maybe there were some magnets or something in there to make that happen.

I'm not sure why anyone would put magnets in a piano, but I'm not sure why someone would put a stick in a piano, either. Or get so intense about rescuing said stick they almost start crying. Really, I'm just full of questions.

The song ends, and the lid slams shut. But the stick is in my hands. It's the length of my forearm and made of pale wood, like something that would wash up on a beach. Weird, nonsensical carvings spiral all around it.

Eden stares at me like I just pulled a rabbit out of a hat. Or a stick out of a piano, I guess. I hold it out with one hand. "Uh. Here."

She reaches out and takes it, cautious like she thinks I'm going to rip it away from her. She stares at it for a long moment. Her jaw hangs open a little.

Then she *beams*, and my stomach does a little somersault. Shit. Well, this wouldn't be the first time I've gotten a crush on a prickly loner with a cute smile. I'm disgustingly predictable.

"So do I get to know what's so important about that thing?" I flop onto the bench, leaning against the wooden edge of the keys. I don't want to ruin the moment by mashing my elbow into them. But apparently I do anyway, because Eden leaps to her feet, holding the stick to her chest.

"It's a long story."

"I've got time."

"I don't."

She says it casually, without the bite from before. Like she's just stating facts. But the fact is obvious: she doesn't want me around.

Which doesn't matter. I don't know her. I don't care. I just think her smile is pretty. That doesn't have to mean anything.

"Well, alright then. Glad I could help." I start for the trees again, meaning to get back to Grandma's house. Wherever the hell that is. "Shit."

"Is something wrong?"

I turn around. Eden faces me, chin tucked to her chest and eyes wary, stick still clutched in her hands.

"Sort of. I got a little lost. I'm not sure where my grandma's house is from here."

"What does it look like?"

"Pale blue, top of a hill." I gesture with my hands while speaking. "White porch with a swing and vines growing up the pole. A pretty garden."

"I know where that is." Eden stands. "Follow me."

She walks right past me. For a second I just stand there, because her helping me is the last thing I expected. She's at the tree line by the time I catch up. "Whoa, hey, I don't want to interrupt."

Eden doesn't say anything about how it's fine or how it's no trouble at all or how she's not busy. She doesn't even say it's in thanks for helping her. She just leads me forward.

And even though all I can see is the glossy curtain of her hair, I swear I hear a smile in her voice.

"Well. It would be bad if you fell off a cliff again."

5

Are we sure this isn't an elaborate "haze the city girl" prank?

I glance up at the sky. The shadows through the leaves are too long for early afternoon. If I had to guess, I'd say it's around dinnertime. I've been here longer than I thought.

Eden's still walking a few paces ahead of me, so I hurry to match her before talking. "Thanks for the help. I'd probably worry Grandma if I stayed in here too late." I didn't even think about that until now, to be honest. Mom's chill when I disappear, but she's used to it. I should've left Grandma a note or something.

Eden shrugs. "We're even now." She tightens her grip on the stick in her hands.

To be fair, she did technically help me first with the whole cliff thing, but whatever. I stare at the stick again. There's

41

something familiar about the carvings around it, like something I saw in a dream.

"So are you gonna tell me about that thing? You're not busy now."

Eden sighs. Her face pinches, shadows growing across her narrow features. The silence is long enough that I start to itch, but she breaks it before I do. "You're not from around here."

I study her expression, like there's a real answer to my question hiding in that crease between her eyebrows. "Um. Yeah. So?"

"So you wouldn't understand."

I laugh. "Oh, *come on.*"

"It's the truth. This place isn't like other places." Eden's quiet voice is firm and matter-of-fact.

"So what? Chicago isn't like other places, either. But I don't get all weird whenever someone asks about the bean."

"The *what?*"

"It's this giant silver statue that's . . . Hey, don't change the subject!" I flap a hand at her. "Come on. I helped you get the stick thingy. Don't I at least get to know why it was so important?"

Eden gives a long-suffering sigh, but there might be a smile threatening the corner of her lips. "Thingy, huh?"

"Thingy. Doohickey. Thingamabob." I wave airily. Eden snorts out a reluctant laugh, hiding it behind her hand. I grin. "Whatever it is, I wanna know about it."

"Well." Eden runs her fingertips along the weird carvings. The sunlight seems to make it sparkle a little, like there're flecks of gold embedded in the wood. "This isn't an ordinary stick. It's fae."

"Huh?"

"Fae. As in made by faeries."

I laugh, waiting for her to drop the deadpan bit and tell me what this thing really is.

But she doesn't drop it. Instead of showing off that cute smile again, she scowls. "Well, you *asked*."

I stop laughing. "Wait. Are you *serious*? I really, genuinely thought you were joking."

"You should never joke about faeries."

Discomfort twists my gut. I didn't expect her to get so *serious* so fast. "Why, because they might be listening?" I look around. "Oh, shit, are they like really tiny? Hiding in the flowers or whatever?" I sort of hope the joke will get Eden to loosen up.

It doesn't. If anything, she frowns even more. "No. Don't be ridiculous."

I throw my hands up. "Well, *excuse* me! You're talking about faerie magic, and *I'm* the ridiculous one?"

Eden opens her mouth to respond, but a male voice booms through the trees, cutting her off.

"Is that really so hard to believe?"

I tense, hands curling into fists as I spin in the direction of the voice. About five feet from us, a man leans against a tree, grinning. Long dark hair spills over his shoulders, and his grin seems impossibly white against his dark skin.

Behind him is a familiar bridge. Grandma stands in the well-kept grass on the other side. Her eyes widen when she sees me.

"Lydia!"

"So this is young Lydia." The man approaches. He towers

over me, which isn't that hard to do, and over Eden, which is maybe just a little more difficult. "You have your grandmother's eyes. But not, apparently, her sense of wonder."

"*Right.*" I look over his shoulder at Grandma. "You gonna make the introductions?"

There's a pause before she answers, calling from her side of the bridge. "This is Florian. He's an old friend."

I frown. He looks around Mom's age, maybe a few years older. Not really old enough to be an "old" friend of Grandma's.

He smiles at me, all bright and knowing. "Now, did my ears deceive me? Or did a Barnes scoff at the idea of fae magic?"

I blink up at him. "Uh. Yes?"

Florian *tsks*, shaking his head. "You should know better, young Lydia! There are stranger things in these forests than a bit of magic." His gaze drifts over my shoulder. "You, for example, could be quite the surprise for many. Is that what unnerves you so?"

I glance over my shoulder. Eden's been so silent I practically forgot about her. She's standing frozen, shoulders rigid, arms stiff at her sides. Her face is tight and pinched with fear.

"Whoa, is everything okay?" I put a hand on her shoulder.

Grandma calls over the bridge, her tone gentle. "I won't tell anyone you're in here, if that's what you're worried about." Beneath my grasp, Eden's shoulders tense up even more. Maybe her family's got some shit against the forest like Clyde?

Wow. You wouldn't guess it, but Eden's sort of a badass.

"I . . ." Eden frowns down at her feet.

I nudge her shoulder a little. "Hey, don't worry. Grandma's cool."

Grandma makes her way onto the bridge in slow, careful steps. She stays on the wood, one hand braced against the railing. "I don't feel the same way the others do about the forest. If I'd . . ." She trails off with a kind smile. "Well, I won't give you away, dear. That much I can promise."

Eden finally relaxes. She doesn't quite look Grandma in the eye, but she lifts her head at least. "Thank you."

"Okay," I butt in. "Is anyone going to tell me what the deal with the forest is, or am I just gonna get weird cryptic clues all week?"

Florian grins at me. "No clues, young Lydia, merely facts! Facts that you see as fiction."

"Florian." Grandma's voice is sharp like a warning, but I don't look at her. I focus my attention on the guy in front of me, hands on my hips.

"Are you seriously trying to convince me that magic is real?"

"That depends! Can you *seriously* tell me nothing you've seen here has convinced you otherwise? Surely you've noticed this isn't a normal forest."

"I'm not exactly an expert on normal forests." I guess the thing with the stick was weird. And now that I think about it, maybe the cliff was too big for this place. And it's a little strange that bugs aren't swarming me. I haven't even gotten dive-bombed by the forest equivalent of pigeons. I *hear* bugs and birds, but I don't *see* any.

But just because *I* haven't come up with an explanation

doesn't mean the explanation is *magic.*

My disbelief must show on my face, because Florian shakes his head. "So skeptical. Maybe this will convince you."

And with a grin and a snap of his fingers, he . . . *shrinks?*

It's impossible, ridiculous, crazy. But it's also happening right in front of me. Florian's no longer towering over me. He grins *up* at me instead, his features rounder and more childish. He looks like the kid who stole my phone.

He *is* the kid who stole my phone.

I just watched a grown-ass man turn into a kid.

I blink. I stare. I consider several possibilities.

Possibility one: I've lost it. I reject that one quickly. If this is a hallucination, it's weirdly specific.

Possibility two: Someone's drugged me. But while the people in town were assholes, they didn't really strike me as the drug-a-teenager brand of assholes. Even if they were, when would they have gotten a chance to do it?

Possibility three: Magic is real.

It's the most ridiculous possibility yet. It shouldn't be the one that makes the most sense. But it does. And I don't think I can really deny it, considering the fact that Florian is still staring at me with his mischievous kid face.

"Okay!" I shout, throwing my hands up in the air. I want to sit down. Or scream. Or something. I don't know. I just watched a dude shrink and apparently pulled a magic stick from a piano. I don't know anything anymore.

I flop down on the bridge, completely by choice. Definitely not because my legs just gave out from under me. That would be lame.

There's a warm hand on my shoulder, then Grandma's

reproachful voice at my back. "Florian, you shouldn't have done that."

"I'm fine!" *Fine* is maybe not the best word to describe me, but I'm definitely *not* scared. I don't get scared—especially not in front of cute girls, even when said cute girl is still staring at Florian. But she doesn't look shocked.

"You knew about this?"

Eden turns to me. "I *told* you about fae magic."

I can't really argue with that. I face Florian instead. "You're a faerie. Seriously?"

Florian grows to his full height, which is only a little bit less disorienting now that I know it's coming. "Indeed I am." He pushes his hair back, revealing the pointed tips of his ears. "Although the other faeries might disagree with that assessment, were they still around to hear it."

Maybe I should be more curious about that, but I'm still sort of processing the whole ear thing. I flop back on the grainy wooden surface of the bridge, legs dangling into the grass. "Holy *shit*! I mean . . . holy shit. Faeries are real. *Magic* is real." I cover my face with my hands, starting to laugh. "How could I not know about this? How . . . Wait." I whip into a sitting position, spinning clumsily to face Grandma. "Why didn't you tell me?"

The shadows shift across Grandma's face as it falls. "I'm sorry, Lydia. I promised your mother I'd keep it a secret. I never expected you to come in here."

This brings me up short. "What? Mom doesn't keep secrets from me."

"Oh dear." Florian's booming voice sounds a little subdued. "Does her heart still bear those scars?"

Grandma sighs, kneeling with a wince to get at eye level with me. "Lydia, your mother . . . had a very bad experience in this forest. It left her biased, even though the place itself isn't dangerous."

"And as for the one who hurt her here, he's long gone," Florian adds.

It feels like I finally hit the bottom of that cliff. I don't even want to think about what they're implying. I mean, I'm not the most cautious person on the planet, but I know what can happen in big cities *and* small towns. I know to always carry pepper spray in my purse, and I didn't take that self-defense class just because it's fun to punch shit.

I stand up and start to pace. Maybe the thought won't stick to me if I move fast enough. Maybe I won't have to think about it. "So—" My voice cracks, and I try to disguise it with a cough. "So . . . this forest. It *isn't* gross and awful and weird? It's never been?"

"No, dear." Grandma's voice is gentle as she uses the bridge's railings to pull herself to her feet. "Our family has always visited the forest."

"Too bad you don't come and visit it as often as you once did, my dear." Florian's eyes are sparkling again, his smile bright.

Grandma's answering smile is gentler, more wistful. "I doubt I'd be able to find my way back if I did."

Florian hums. "Well, then, you'll just have to follow me when you're less concerned about getting back." That sounds a little morbid to me, but by the way Grandma laughs at it, I guess it must be an inside joke. "Until that day comes, dear."

He bows dramatically to Grandma, turns and nods to me,

and then offers a nod to Eden, who is *still* standing there. And then he disappears into the trees. Like, literally disappears. More magic I can't ignore.

Grandma sighs. I turn to face her, and she shakes her head. "Lydia . . . My promise to your mother was the only way I could convince her to allow you to come here." A soft smile lights up her face. "But for my sins, a part of me is happy you discovered the forest anyway. I wouldn't feel right telling you more about it or encouraging you to come here again. But if you were to seek out more information, or come here on your own, I couldn't dissuade you from doing that, either. Do you understand?"

"Right. Yeah, okay, I get it." Basically, she's cool with me coming to the forest again as long as I don't ask permission.

Grandma smiles, warmth creased in the corners of her eyes. "Alright then. I'll be waiting for you back at the house." Her gaze shifts over my shoulder and lands on Eden for a moment, then glides back to me. "Goodnight."

She makes her careful way back up the hill, leaving Eden and me alone.

There's a beat of long silence, and I don't know how to fill it. My brain is still swirling with thoughts of magic and faeries and *Mom*. The third thing isn't very fun at all, so I decide to focus on the first two.

"I'm sorry for laughing at you," I say, sincere this time. "I had no idea . . ."

"It's fine."

The silence sits heavy between us. Finally, a question occurs to me, and I blurt it out. "Wait. Are *you* a faerie?"

Eden blinks, mouth dropping open in shock. Then she

laughs, one hand curling against her mouth. "No." She tucks back her silky hair to reveal blunt, normal ears to prove it. "There aren't any more faeries in the forest. Florian is the last one."

"Really? Where did the others go?"

"There . . . was a war. Between faeries and humans." She twirls the stick in her hand, looking down. Maybe she doesn't want to tell me any more after getting a front-row seat to my family drama.

But she's clearly invested in the stick, and people like to talk about things they're invested in. I try that route instead. "So . . . magic stick, huh? What's it do?"

It's the right choice. The words fall out of Eden's mouth immediately, before she has time to question them. "Nothing *yet*. It's only one part of the treasure."

"A treasure. Seriously? That is so cool!" The word sparks something in me. I've never heard someone talk about treasures outside of movies.

Eden smiles a little, almost in spite of herself. "It's part of a staff. One that belonged to the leader of the faeries a long time ago. It shattered, but if you gather all the pieces . . ." She blinks, looking up at me like she's just remembering I'm here. "Well. It does magic."

"*Dude.*" It's all I can think to say. "Is that the first one you've found?"

"No, this is the fifth. There are seven in all."

"No shit, Eden! That's some dedication." I walk closer to her, looking down at the stick. I brush my fingertips over the carvings. Eden's hands tremble a little bit, but she doesn't jerk it away like she sort of seemed like she wanted to. "What's

50

with the writing?"

Eden blinks. "How did you know it was writing?"

"Huh? Oh." I didn't even think about what I was saying, honestly. I shrug. "Lucky guess?"

Eden shifts her weight. "Well, it's a clue. In fae language." She squints at it, reading. "It says something about . . . a stream? No, the *sound* of a stream." She purses her lips. "It says to follow the sound of the stream and not to be fooled by what things appear to be."

"What does *that* mean?"

"It's a riddle. A *translated* riddle." She frowns at it, all thoughtful. "I have a few ideas of where to start looking."

"Cool! Can I come?" I ask without thinking. It's the same sort of impulsive comment as the one that got me to Fairbrooke in the first place. But what the hell? When else am I going to have the chance to hunt magic treasure?

Eden looks uncomfortable, though. "Don't you have anything better to do?"

"I mean, I'm here for the week to hang out with Grandma, but when she's asleep? No, I really don't have anything better to do." I raise my eyebrows. "But, like, if you don't want me around, just tell me. Don't get all tactful on me now."

Eden shakes her head. "It's not that. It's just . . ." She pauses, face all scrunched up in thought. Finally, she nods. "Okay. You can help me look this week."

She doesn't sound hyped, exactly, but maybe that's just her personality. I'll take what I can get. "Awesome!" I pull out my phone. "What's your number? I'll text you when Grandma takes a nap or whatever and we can meet up."

Eden shakes her head. "I don't have a cell phone."

This takes me by surprise, but I guess it makes sense. Grandma doesn't have a cell phone, either. "Right. Okay then. Um . . ."

"I can be here at 1:00 p.m.," Eden offers. "I'll wait a half hour. If you're not here, I'll assume you aren't coming."

If I'm being honest, the time constraints sort of make me itch. I don't really like set plans. But it doesn't seem like I have a choice. "Okay. And, like, if I can't make it, I'll at least come and tell you so you aren't wasting your time."

Eden nods. "Alright."

For a long moment, we just stare at each other. It's like neither of us can figure out how to walk away.

Finally, Eden breaks the silence, turning her back. "I'll see you tomorrow then."

"Yeah," I say. "See you."

Eden walks down the forest path, her long shadow trailing behind her. I watch her until she disappears into the trees, and then I cross the bridge and walk up the hill toward Grandma's house.

6

Am I gonna find a unicorn next?
Actually, that'd be pretty sweet.

I spend a good chunk of my night awake. Still trying to wrap my head around all this faerie stuff, I guess. Just the idea they exist at all is still sort of wild. The fact that the forest across the stream is full of faerie magic is almost too much to handle.

I also think about Mom more than I'd like. I don't want to dwell on whatever she went through. But that pretty much leaves me with being angry at her for lying, and I don't want that, either. It's not like we've never argued. We live together and we're both stubborn as hell. But those were little fights, the kind we'd forget by the next day. I've never gotten mad at her in a way that sticks, and I don't want to start.

But she *lied*.

Eventually, I do fall asleep. And when I wake up the next morning, I'm determined to shrug off all that negative stuff. It's a new day and a chance to be a new person—one who is totally cool and chill and not at all wondering if her entire world is a lie.

I get ready for the day, scrubbing my face and tossing on a graphic T-shirt and jean shorts. I pause by the bedroom window to look out at the forest. This afternoon, I'll be meeting Eden there. That feels like an easier thing to think about.

Eden's complicated. Complicated and different than me in a lot of ways. But I keep thinking of the way she smiled in that clearing, the way the sun seemed to shine a little brighter in response to her happiness.

Then I laugh at myself, because what else are you supposed to do when you're thinking poetic thoughts about a girl you met yesterday?

I head downstairs. Grandma's in the center of the kitchen again, but it's a lot emptier today. I sit at the counter, kicking my legs back and forth. "Morning, Grandma."

"Good morning, dear." She slides a bowl across the countertop in my direction. "You're just in time for breakfast."

Sliced bananas sit on top of a bowl of oatmeal. It's surprisingly delicious for what I always assumed was just warm mush, full of cinnamon and other rich spices I couldn't even name. "Is the oatmeal magic, too?" I ask around a bite, my mouth half full.

Grandma shakes her head. "No. Yesterday's exchange took up most of my magic, I'm afraid. You'll have to wait."

I gasp and immediately spend several moments hacking

warm oatmeal out of my lungs.

"I'm sorry—*what?*"

"Oh. Oh, dear." Grandma looks down. "I assumed your friend told you about magic and that's why you were asking."

"Not that *people* can do it." I gesture so wildly with my spoon I almost send oatmeal flying at the wall. "Unless *you're* a faerie? Oh my god. You're my faerie godmother. My faerie *grandmother*."

"Lydia—"

"Wait, does this mean Mom's half faerie? Am I a quarter faerie? Not gonna lie, I've been taking this pretty well so far, but if you tell me—"

"Lydia!" Grandma finally breaks through my babbling. "No, dear, you and I are both completely human. Some people just have certain abilities. Nothing so dramatic as fae magic, though." She pauses, then adds, "For me, it's baking intentions into things. Simple intentions, like good luck or health."

"Oh. So you're a *witch?*" Grandma nods. I take a deep breath, taking this in. "Can *I* do magic? Can Mom?" Unease churns in my guts. The idea of doing magic is kind of cool, but the idea of Mom hiding magic powers isn't.

Grandma shakes her head. "No. Magic is often inherited, but it can skip generations occasionally. Your mother was born without it, and she would have noticed if you had any by now. She knows the tells."

I relax a little, my want for no more lies outweighing my want for cool powers. Am I going to have to deal with some new life-shattering revelation every day here? Maybe there are witches in Chicago, too. Why not? Let's toss some werewolves and vampires into the mix, make it a party.

"Are you okay, dear?"

I realize I'm jiggling my foot hard enough to slam it noisily against the side of the counter. I curl my leg up and sit on it to make myself stop. "Yeah, no, it's just . . . this is crazy! This is all crazy."

Grandma makes a sympathetic little hum and sits next to me. And just like that, the floodgates open.

"Like, okay, I've never been like a diehard skeptic or anything. There's this girl I hang out with sometimes who is like super into astrology and crystals and junk and I never give her shit for it. And, like, I'm totally open to the idea of ghosts and stuff. Once I spent the night in a haunted house on a dare. But this? This is some next-level shit. I can't believe that it's all just . . . existed all along and no one's ever told me about it."

Grandma gives me a knowing look. I guess I'm not being subtle. I sigh.

"I can't believe Mom didn't tell me about it." My shoulders slump. "I *get* why. But that doesn't change the fact that she didn't tell me." I look down at my oatmeal. Hearing the words out loud makes them sound petty somehow. "Is it awful that I'm mad at her?"

Grandma puts a warm hand on my shoulder, smiling. "Feeling is never awful. It's what you do with those feelings that counts." Her smile fades. "At any rate, I suppose I owe you an apology for not being honest with you."

"I mean, you *were* just doing what Mom asked you to do." To be honest, Mom lying hurts a lot more. I love Grandma, but I don't know her like I know Mom. Grandma and I haven't stayed up all night venting to each other and sharing hopes and fears.

56

But all of this is getting a bit too real. I swirl my oatmeal with my spoon and try to move on. "So all that stuff you were giving away yesterday was magic? Were the other people giving away magic, too? Or am I not allowed to ask about it?" I try not to sound too bitter about that.

Grandma sighs. "I suppose there's no harm in telling you this much now. Fairbrooke has always been home to people with certain talents." She frowns a little. "I suppose that's why your mother was so eager to leave."

"Wow." On top of everything else, this doesn't make too much of a dent in my already sizable existential crisis. "Wait— is that why that gas station asshole was selling rocks for fifty dollars?"

Grandma wrinkles her nose. "Dale. Most of us don't sell our magic. Personally, I find it immoral to put a price on our power, much less sell it to those who don't understand it enough to use it to its full potential. But perhaps that's my age showing."

"Nah, I'm pretty sure he's just an asshole."

Grandma smiles a little. "I suppose he might be, at that."

It's a relief to be actually talking about this stuff. I grin. "He was a total dick to Mom. You should've seen his face when I came for him."

"I could imagine."

"I sort of threw some quarters at him."

"*Lydia.*" Grandma tries to keep a straight face, but her eyes sparkle the same as mine, a dead giveaway she's hiding laughter.

"He deserved it!" I lean back, wrinkling my nose. "I hope I don't run into that asshole again. Not like I'm going back into town. And he doesn't seem like the type to go into the forest."

Grandma makes a face, and I remember her comment to Eden yesterday about how she wouldn't tell anyone she was in the forest. At the time, I thought it meant Eden's family wasn't cool with it. But maybe it goes further than that.

"Wait, is *everyone* in town weird about the forest? Why?" If they're all witches anyway, I don't see why they'd get all up in arms about a magic forest.

It takes a while for Grandma to answer. When she finally does, it's with a tight-lipped smile. "That's complicated, dear. And telling you that would be breaking my promise."

"Oh." I don't like it, this reminder of Mom's lies.

Grandma's expression softens. "Maybe your friend will tell you more."

"I don't know if I'd call Eden a friend."

"Oh, is she something more?"

"*Grandma!*" I let out a very undignified noise, all thoughts of townspeople and Mom forgotten. "It's totally not like that. I hardly know her." Sure, there's a lot to like about what I do know about her—that she's complicated enough to be interesting, that her smile does weird little giddy things to my chest. But I don't need to tell Grandma that.

Her smile makes me wonder if she already knows, though. "Just an observation." Her tone is light and airy and all too innocent. "It's been a while since you mentioned anyone special. I know you were seeing that girl . . ."

"Olivia? That was like forever ago." Okay, maybe last year doesn't qualify as forever, but it sure does feel that way. We dated a few months during my freshman year.

"There hasn't been anyone since then?"

"No." Technically there was Devin, but that wasn't so much *dating* as it was *awkward fumbling to second base.* I might be an open book, but there are some things you just don't tell your grandma. "I'm sorta bad at the whole relationship thing."

Grandma takes this more seriously than I meant it. "What do you mean?"

"Well, you know." I give a vague hand gesture. "Relationships are a lot of work. Who has time for that?" I grin. "Besides, I'm a free agent. Can't be tamed and all that."

It's easier to think of it as my choice to be single. And at the end of the day, it is my choice. I refuse to be anyone less than myself. If some people think that makes me a flake, or an asshole or whatever, that's fine. When we broke up, Olivia claimed I never cared about her. "*You don't take anything seriously,*" she'd said. But the truth is, she just didn't get me. A relationship like that wouldn't have worked.

Besides, I *do* like things better this way. I'm way more interested in adventures with cool people than the gushy feelings-talk relationships seem to need.

Adventure is exactly what's waiting for me with Eden. I stick my tongue out at Grandma to punctuate my point. "*Anyway.* Cute as Eden is, I don't think we'll have a lot of time for flirting with all the treasure-hunting we're going to be doing."

Grandma raises her eyebrows. "Treasure-hunting?"

"Yeah! Eden's looking for these . . . magic stick things? Apparently there are seven of 'em and they get put together to form—"

"A staff," Grandma finishes for me. She shakes her head.

"That's a good idea, but I'm sorry to say I don't think those exist."

"Huh? Yeah, they do. We found one yesterday, and she's found like four already? I think?"

Grandma doesn't answer for a long moment, so long that I worry I've crossed a line again. Finally, she blinks, shaking her head. "Well, that's . . . surprising. How is she finding them?"

"There are these clues written on them. It's in some weird elf language, or fae or whatever, but I guess she knows how to read it?"

"Written fae language is easy enough to learn." Grandma frowns. "But on the staff pieces . . . You're sure?"

"Yeah. I saw them on the one we found yesterday myself."

"So strange . . ." Grandma shakes her head but smiles at me. "The forest keeps its secrets until they're ready to be revealed—and not a second sooner. Eden must be a remarkable girl to be the one to find them."

I smile a little. She seemed rude at first, but now I see she just didn't want to get distracted. It's actually a little impressive, when I think of it like that. I could never be that focused on anything.

"Yeah. She is." It takes me several beats of silence to realize Grandma is smiling at me. "What? What's with that face?"

"Oh, nothing." She's back to that light, fake-innocent tone. "Just that you might want to rethink your position on relationships."

I laugh, mock-throwing my spoon at her, and very

carefully do *not* think of how Eden's dark eyes reflect the sunlight or how her silky-looking hair might feel underneath my fingertips.

7

Guess we're not sticking to the rivers and the lakes that we're used to.

Grandma lies down for a nap at a suspiciously specific time, so I'm free to go hang out with Eden.

I walk out into bright sunshine. The wide-open space feels a little less awful now that I know there's actually something to do here. It puts a little bounce in my step as I head down the hill to the bridge.

Eden waits on the other side, arms crossed over her dark blue blouse. She raises her eyebrows when she sees me. "You're here."

"Yeah, I said I would be." Not like that means all that much with me, but Eden doesn't know that.

"You did. At one."

I glance at my phone. It's 1:03. "Well, you said you'd wait a half hour."

"Yes, and here I am."

I frown as I step into the shade of the trees. "So am I. Are we doing this treasure-hunting thing or what?"

Eden shrugs and spins on her heel to start walking, brown skirt swishing back and forth just past her knees. I have to jog to keep up.

I don't know whether I'm annoyed or amused. Eden's something else, that's for sure. But I can't doubt that she wants me around. If she didn't, she would've said something. Or just not shown up to wait for me. It's already obvious she doesn't care about sparing my feelings.

I already sort of appreciated how blunt she is, but I do even more now. I mean, I just found out the most honest person in my life has been keeping a huge secret from me. It's sort of comforting to be with someone who doesn't have any interest in lying to me.

I pick up the pace until I'm walking side by side with Eden on the path. "So where are we heading?"

"I looked at the map and figured out a few places where the stream is especially loud." Eden doesn't look at me as we walk forward. "Those will be good places to start, since the clue specified the sound of the stream is important."

"Cool. You have a map?"

"Yes."

"Is the forest really that big?"

"Yes."

"How big is it?"

"Big."

"You're a hell of a conversationalist, you know that?" Part of me immediately wishes I could take the words back. But, hell, I'm trying here. I don't know why she bothered to let me come along if she wasn't going to try, too.

Eden makes a face. I've seen her scowl, so I know it's not quite that, but it's close. "I don't have a lot of opportunity for conversation." It's hard to tell in the sunlight with her golden complexion, but I think she's blushing.

Well, shit. I didn't mean to embarrass her. "Sorry. That was sort of a dick move." Eden doesn't respond. I keep trying. "My mouth gets away from me sometimes."

Eden finally breaks, shaking her head with a sigh. "I suppose I haven't exactly been the most tactful, either. Like I said, I don't get much conversation."

"Do you really spend that much time alone in here?"

"More than I want to admit to."

Part of me wonders if all this treasure-hunting is really healthy. Then again, what else is there to do here? It's not like there are loads of cool people for her to talk to. I'm pretty sure she's the only one under thirty in Fairbrooke.

That makes me feel a little bad for her. Maybe that's the reason she decided to let me come along. Maybe she's bored out of her skull and needs to hang out with someone her own age for the week.

So I shoot her a wink. "Well, consider me your conversation practice then."

"Does this really count as practice?" Eden looks at me, eyebrows raised. "It is, after all, a real conversation."

"Are you actually this literal or are you just screwing with me?"

"Maybe a little of both."

"A joke!" I press a hand to my chest in mock surprise. "I knew you had it in you."

Eden finally cracks a smile, huffing out a breath that isn't quite a laugh. I sort of want to hear her real one. It's not really a *goal* for the week, just a sort of secret, nonurgent mission.

"Here we are." Eden's voice pulls me out of my thoughts. The stream's steady trickle somehow turned into a dull roar while I wasn't paying attention. It's been getting louder, I realize now, but it happened so slowly I didn't even notice. It doesn't help that I can't actually see it.

The sound comes from the other side of a gray wall made of rock, covered in patches of ivy and moss. It's too flat to climb, but Eden pushes aside a curtain of vines, and sunlight spills in from the other side. With what might be a smile, she gestures forward.

I walk through—and stop in my tracks.

Shock scrambles my thoughts so hard that, for a second, all I can register is the size of what I'm looking at. Slick, jagged gray rocks tower all around me. They stretch into the sunlight, so tall my eyes blur to look at them, taller than any of the trees, taller than skyscrapers, even. A waterfall cascades over the edge of the highest one, crashing down into a stream that bubbles cheerily past our feet.

But the really cool stuff here has nothing to do with Mother Nature flexing. It's man-made—ladders to climb up higher, steps carved into the rocks, rope bridges strung from stone to stone. It's like the world's most amazing obstacle course, the sort of place parkour nerds see in their dreams. I immediately want to climb all over everything, but shock keeps me rooted to the spot.

"Holy shit!" I gape up at everything, trying to take it in.

"It is beautiful, isn't it?" Eden's smiling in a funny sort of way. She's also looking at me. I definitely, totally do not read anything into that. It's the same look I give people when they see my city for the first time. It's nice when a stranger appreciates the things you see every day.

"Totally. I can't believe it's *real*!" It's the size that gets me more than anything. "How didn't I see this from outside?"

Eden shrugs. "The forest keeps its secrets."

Grandma had said something similar, but now I get it in a way I didn't before. "Right. Still getting used to the whole magic thing." Holy shit. I'm searching for literal magic treasure in an actual magic forest. Excitement smacks into me like a freight train. I want to climb every inch of this place. I bounce on the balls of my feet. "Where do we start?"

"Does anything look out of the ordinary to you?"

Yeah, all of it. But I get what she means. "Nowhere that has super-obvious magic stick vibes."

Eden nods. "Let's look around."

We start moving. Eden apparently has a method, because she stays in spots for a long time, scanning them for something. I don't have the patience for that, so I just go wherever I want. This seems like a good way to search for magic treasure to me. Shouldn't magic pull me in or something?

Eden glances up at me as I try to scale one of the smaller stones, the toe of my combat boot wedged in a crack. "Be careful."

"I'm fine." I wave a dismissive hand at her, which almost makes me lose my balance. I cling to the rock face and heave myself closer to the top.

"You could fall."

"Then I fall! Not the first time."

"I believe that," Eden says dryly. "Still, be careful. I don't want you to get hurt."

I manage to haul myself to the top of the rock. I sit there, legs dangling over the edge. "My heart is aflutter from all of this consideration, but seriously, Eden, I'm fine. See?" I spread my arms out. "You don't have to rescue me this time!"

Eden shakes her head, smiling. "Alright then." She turns back to the small cave she was searching. She has to bend over to look into it, one hand braced on the rock wall. Her hair falls over her face in a glossy curtain, and the hem of her skirt rises to show the backs of her knees. My gaze travels up.

Oh my god, chill. I look away quickly. Eden's cute, and I can recognize Eden's cute, but there's a fine line between *cool* and *creepy*, and spending any extended amount of time checking out her butt feels like it's probably at least straddling that line.

I scan the horizon for clues instead. From this vantage point, it's a little easier to see higher up. I don't have to crane my neck so hard, anyway. My gaze travels over to the waterfall. A small chunk of it is out of sync with the rest, like one of those sliding puzzles with one square out of place.

"Hey, Eden, look at that."

Eden stands up straight, shielding her eyes against the sunlight. "What?"

"See the waterfall? Close to the top. It sort of zigzags or

something."

"Hm. You're right. I see it." She frowns, lips pursed. "It doesn't look natural."

"Well, what are we waiting for?" I jump down from the rock. Eden lets out a startled noise as I land on the ground.

"Are you alright?"

"Yeah, why?"

"That had to hurt your ankles."

"What? No, I'm totally fine. It wasn't even that high!" Eden gives the top of the rock a dubious look. I scoff. "Eden, are you afraid of heights?"

"I'm not afraid of heights! I am reasonably wary of heights!"

I laugh before I can help it. Eden gives me a flat look but doesn't seem as annoyed as she might have gotten before.

"And right now, my reasonable wariness of heights is saying we shouldn't try to get all the way up there."

"Oh, come on. There are stairs and ladders and stuff! We'll be fine."

Eden shoots a wary glance up. "There's no ladder into the waterfall."

"Well, no. But, uh, look. There's a ledge right there next to it." I point at a little rock shelf to the right of the waterfall, just a bit above the weird glitch thing. A ladder leads right to it. "We'll be able to see it better, at least."

"Well . . ." Eden sighs. "Alright. I guess it's the best lead we have right now."

"That's the spirit!" I pick some stone steps and start walking.

"Do you know where you're going?"

"It'll be fine. Come on!" I'm not sure exactly how to get to the ladder, but there are bridges and ladders and stairs all over this place. We'll get there eventually. Besides, I've got a really good feeling about these stairs.

Eden sighs in a long-suffering way, but she follows me. I grin. Maybe I'm a good influence on her.

"So how long have you been treasure-hunting?" I ask as we cross a rickety bridge.

Eden clings to the guard rails as it swings back and forth under our footsteps. "A little over a year."

I frown a little as we step back onto solid land. "I thought you said it took you a year to find the last treasure? Were the first four, like, super easy or something?"

"Oh." Eden's eyes widen just a little. "No. I found the fourth one right when I started looking, but that was only after . . . after my parents did a lot of the work. And they're the ones who found the first three."

"Huh." I sort of thought her family didn't like the forest. Why else would she have been so worried about someone finding out she was in here?

I'm about to ask, but then I notice Eden's expression. Her shoulders are tense, her hands curling in and out of fists. And her dark eyes are *sad*. If I ask, it will probably only make her sadder. Or she could close up and go back to those short answers from before. I don't want that, not when she's just starting to open up.

So instead, I say, "Well, still. I think spending a year on something's pretty impressive."

To my relief, Eden's shoulders relax. She smiles a little. "Really?"

"Totally. I don't think I could do it. I've never stuck with anything longer than a month." I laugh a little, the sun hot against the back of my neck. "Shit, when I put it like that, I sort of sound like a total flake." I mean, I *am*. But Eden doesn't have to know that.

Eden looks at me, head cocked to the side. "Yet here you are."

And I guess that's true. But this isn't Chicago, where there're all sorts of cool things competing for my attention. I shrug. "A week's a lot easier to stick to, especially in a town this boring. Even if it is full of witches, apparently." I blink. "Wait. Can you do magic, Eden?"

"Well, *anyone* can do magic, provided they have the proper tools and the knowledge to use them. I've been researching the fae staff enough that I'll be able to use it once I find all the treasures. But I'm not a witch with natural powers, if that's what you're asking."

Like Mom. Like me. The feelings that information stirs up are honestly too embarrassing for me to look too close at.

We cross one more bridge, and then we're to the ladder that leads up to the ledge. I gesture at it, leaning my shoulder against the wall. "After you."

Eden shoots me a bemused smile and climbs up the ladder in slow, careful steps. I hop from one foot to the other, waiting for her to finish. If I tried to climb up while she was still on the ladder, I'd probably run into her.

When I do finally climb up and reach the top, Eden is sitting there, leaning against the rock. She glances at me. "I don't think there's anything over there. There's a little space behind the waterfall, but there's no way to access it."

I squint against the spray of the water. She's right about there being no easy way to get to the waterfall, but I don't think she's right about nothing being there. The rock on the other side has two pegs, the same kind all the bridges have. I point. "But look there! I think there used to be a bridge." A pretty short one, by the looks of it. It's only two steps away, three at most.

Eden pauses, peering into the spray. Finally, she nods. "I see it. But that seems like a moot point. We can't get over there."

I get what she's saying. But they wouldn't have built a bridge to nothing. And that means, hypothetically, the treasure could totally be behind the waterfall. It would suck if Eden spent years looking only to realize it was in the very first place she checked.

This seems too complicated to explain, so I jump instead.

"Lydia!" Eden's alarmed voice follows me as I cross the gap. Mist from the waterfall sprays my face for a second before I land hard in the dirt, tucking myself forward so I don't fall off the other end. That would be embarrassing.

I think Eden says something else, but I can't hear her over the roar of the waterfall. Which I'm now behind. I look around. Someone's built a whole little room back here, filled with blankets and a few books and even a patterned rug on the stone floor. A stone bench looks off to the side, facing a perfect view of the sun hanging over the trees.

I go back to the edge, cupping my hands to shout at Eden. "Hey, it's really cool over here!"

Eden shouts, "How do you intend to get *back*?"

Oh, shit.

"Hold that thought!" I peer around the room. There's some stuff at the far end, including, to my relief, a ladder that looks long enough to stretch across the gap. Someone's taped a piece of paper to it that says *Emergency Exit* with a little smiley face.

I drag it over and brace it against the pegs. It falls across the gap perfectly. "Problem solved!"

"There's no way you knew that would be there."

"But it is!" I wave her over. "Come on. You should check this out."

Eden grumbles something I don't think I'm supposed to hear. She *does* climb over, though. I grin.

On the last rung, she slips. Her hands shoot out and find my shoulders to cling to. I grab her waist to steady her. "Whoa! Be careful."

"*You're* one to talk."

"Touché."

We stand there, looking at each other for what might be the world's longest second. I don't exactly let my hand linger on her waist, but I don't exactly pull away, either—my fingertips just barely brush her side. And in that moment, Eden stays, too. Her eyes lock with mine.

Then the moment's over. Eden looks away hurriedly, pushing her hair back with one hand. She steps past me, and a grudging sort of wonder spreads across her face. "I've never seen this place."

I grin at her. "See what happens when you take a little risk?"

"Yes." Eden gives me a flat look, but there's a smile threatening the corners of her lips. "And that means I can also see all the ways that could have gone very, very poorly for you."

"I think you mean, 'Thank you, Lydia. I want you to keep doing awesome cool stuff in the name of treasure-hunting.' Don't worry, I will."

"Please, no."

"It's too late! I'm your self-appointed risk-taker."

Eden hangs her head and groans. "You're going to give me a heart attack, Lydia." But then she laughs—*really* laughs.

Mission accomplished.

Nothing left to do but get a little nosy.

After all that, we don't find treasure behind the waterfall. At least Eden and I chat while we look. Maybe I'm imagining things, but I think she's answering a little faster by the time she leads me back to Grandma's bridge.

We pause there, the stream rushing clear and gentle at our feet. I kick at the ground. "So . . . same time tomorrow?" I almost surprise myself with how much I'm looking forward to it. Even if we didn't find anything yet, hanging out with Eden is genuinely really fun.

Eden smiles. Like her words, it comes faster than it did before. "Yeah. I'll see you then, Lydia."

She heads back into the forest, and I cross the bridge into

Grandma's yard. But part of my brain is still back there, stuck on Eden's smile. Her voice. Her laugh. The way the sunlight shines on her glossy black hair.

I fight back a wince. Like, damn, I'm not that far gone. I'm not gone at all, actually. I just think her smile is pretty—that's it. I guess I do sort of want to find out if she's into girls, though. It's always good to know if your friends are some flavor of queer or not.

And I want Eden to be my friend. Maybe it'll only be for a few more days, but that's not so weird. I make friends with tourists all the time. This is the same thing, only I'm the one who's leaving at the end of the week.

Grandma's in the kitchen when I get back to the house, stirring a pot of red sauce. She looks up at me and smiles. "Lydia. You're just in time for dinner."

I sit at the counter, propping my elbows on the polished surface. "Oh, shit, it's that late? I'm sorry." I'm here to visit Grandma, not flirt with pretty girls in the woods. Or, well, make friends with pretty girls in the woods. Whatever.

But Grandma waves me off. "You're your mother's daughter. I'm more than used to it."

It's still *weird* to think of Mom here. I've always loved it when people point out how similar we are, but now it sort of makes my gut twist.

Maybe some of that shows on my face, because Grandma gently directs the conversation away from the topic. "Your mother isn't the only one, either. My parents used to get so frustrated with me, the way I'd wander off." She laughs, shaking her head. "I could never keep a schedule."

"Oh, same here, totally!" I grin, happy for the distraction.

"What sorts of things were you doing? Because, like, most of the time I'm late or whatever because I found something cool and new to do in the city. There's not a lot of that here."

Grandma laughs, shaking her head. "Well, no. But that doesn't mean Fairbrooke is boring. At least not to me."

And that's what we talk about, through dinner and into the night. Grandma's childhood growing up in this tiny town, static and unchanging. How she learned to find adventure and peace in the changing seasons, in the magic of the kitchen, and in the relationships she formed with other people. How when Grandpa finally came along, it was the most rewarding relationship yet.

I don't get it, honestly. I still think that if I were stuck in the same place, with the same people, I'd lose my mind. But it's nice to listen to Grandma's old, weathered voice as she describes it to me.

The stories put me in a good mood, even after Grandma turns in for the night. My thoughts are cheerful as I shower and get ready for bed. But when I walk into the guest room with damp curls and clean pajamas, my feelings about Mom come rushing back. It's harder to forget about her here, where there are pieces of her everywhere.

They're subtle, but I know my mom better than anyone, and I pick up on all the little things. The end table has rings on it because she never uses coasters. There are scuff marks on the walls from shoes kicked off across the room. The quilt at the foot of the bed has frayed ends, just like all of the ones she fidgets with back home.

I walk over to the closet, where her old stuff is. I don't really know why. Maybe I'm hoping that if I get closer to her,

I can make sense of what I'm feeling.

There's not a lot there. A baseball bat from when she used to play, a few clothes she didn't bother taking with her. There's a stack of books in the corner, with a long thin one balanced on the top. I scoop it up.

Sycamore High School. That's the neighboring town, since Fairbrooke is too small to have its own high school. I flip through the pages, scanning names until I find Barnes. It's her junior yearbook. She probably had this picture taken just a few months before she got pregnant with me.

I recognize her as my mom, but she looks so different. Weirdly, she looks older at seventeen than she does now. It's the way she frowns at the camera, one glaring face among a sea of smiling ones. She always told me she wanted to fight the world at my age. But it's one thing to hear Mom talk about how she used to be and another to have her old self staring me down.

I flip through the pictures, trying to identify Mom in the group shots. She's not in any club pictures, which doesn't surprise me much. I do catch her at what looks like a pep rally. She's sitting in the stands with her arms and legs crossed, and it's a little grainy, but I think the camera might have caught her mid eye-roll.

The pages run out. On the back cover, which should be full of signatures, there's just a single note in Mom's familiar handwriting: *Since no one else wants to sign the damn thing, I guess I'll do it myself.*

A wave of fondness washes over me. Mom's a lot different now than she was as a kid, but some things never change. She's still got the same sense of humor, the same prickly determination. There's a reason she's moved up the ranks at her job, even without a college degree. She's the one who gets things done when everyone else is being an idiot.

I smile as I go to put the yearbook back. Looking at it helped, made me feel connected to her again. I stand on my toes to put the thin book on top of the stack, but I must've put too much force on it or something. The whole thing comes tumbling down with a crash.

"Oh, shit!" I hiss out several more swear words between my teeth, waiting to see if Grandma's going to come investigate the noise. But either she's a heavy sleeper or she's far too used to shenanigans going down in this room, because the house stays silent.

I start shoving books back into the closet, not really bothering to stack them up. I'll just get them to the point where I can close the door and pretend the whole thing never happened. I'm almost done when I see a folded-up piece of paper on the floor.

It looks old—yellowed, more like parchment than paper. I pick it up and turn it around, expecting to see Mom's messy scribbles again. But I don't. I think it's typed until I see the indents and the tiny spaces where the ink skipped. Someone wrote this in the neatest handwriting I've ever seen.

Dearest Charlotte,

I'm sure I don't need words to tell you how much I long for you. I've already done so, a thousand times over, in touch . . .

It's pretty obvious what sort of letter this is. And yeah, maybe it's kind of weird to be reading a letter from Mom's ex. I'm definitely playing with fire here, just asking to be grossed out by something TMI. To my credit, I do really think about putting it down. But in the time it takes me to think that, I read another sentence. And another. And another.

There's nothing too scandalous in here, anyway. The guy writing it sounds a little full of himself, but that's all. If I'm being honest, it's sort of cute that Mom kept the note at all. It probably made an impression. I don't think many of the guys she dated were the letter-writing type.

Mom's told me plenty of guy stories. Not gross ones or anything, just enough that I know she had a lot of boyfriends. Sometimes, I sort of figure that's why she's never told me about my dad—maybe she just isn't sure who he is. But from her stories, I sort of thought all the guys she saw were idiots and deadbeats. Not the sort of guys who waxed poetic about her hair. Which this guy does. For like a whole paragraph.

I try to imagine the sort of guy who would write sentences like this. *Every day we are together is a gift of the highest caliber from the universe itself. Do you feel it, the stars shining down upon us?* Honestly, I'd probably make fun of this if someone wrote it for me. It's just so ridiculously pretentious. He sounds like the sort of guy who only writes in coffee shops and public places. Or maybe the sort of guy who takes you to his slam poetry performance as a first date.

He signed the note with a flourish.

Meet me in the forest, my magnificent one. I'll be waiting for you when the moon is at its brightest.

Xavier

My stomach swoops. I stare at the word *forest* until it starts to wobble in my vision. Then I shove the note back into the closet, hiding it from sight. I close the doors.

I knew that someone had hurt Mom in the forest and

that's why she had baggage about it. But I sort of assumed it had been a stranger, someone she didn't know. But what if it was someone she trusted? What if it was someone she loved, someone who claimed to love her? Someone who called her *magnificent* and *beautiful*?

I try not to think about it. I try not to think about the way Mom always says she doesn't have time for dating, that she's had her fill of guys. I try not to put the pieces together. I don't want to see the picture it makes.

Snooping was a bad idea. I should've thought it through better.

I scoot back, curling up on the bed. But it's a long time before I get to sleep.

I slept through most of history class, but I'm pretty sure this is new.

The next morning, I try to forget the letter.

I'm on vacation. It's time to relax and have fun, not dwell on sad things I can't change. Getting all gloomy and mopey isn't going to make anything better.

If Grandma notices I'm a little quiet during breakfast, she doesn't say anything. She just invites me to play board games for a few hours, which does a good job of taking my mind off things. It turns out that my competitive streak comes from her. When I win, she teaches me a few new swear words to tuck away for a rainy day.

When she lies down for a nap in the afternoon, any trace of nighttime angst is forgotten. I head down to the bridge with a light heart.

Eden's waiting there, leaning against a tree and watching the stream. I wouldn't exactly call her expression calm. But it's definitely more peaceful than it was yesterday, the space between her eyebrows smooth instead of furrowed, her shoulders curving all casual instead of stiff.

She looks up when I step onto the bridge. "Hello."

"Hey! Are we heading back to the waterfall?"

"No. I thought it would be more fun to show you somewhere different." She looks at me sidelong, the faintest smile curling up her lips. "Somewhere safer so I don't have to worry about you scaring five years off my life again."

I grin. "You're underestimating my ability to get into shenanigans."

Eden groans. I laugh.

We start to walk. Eden leads, but I match her step for step. At first, we stay on the main path, but then we take a turn into the trees, onto a twisty dirt path I probably would've missed. A breeze whistles through the branches, filling my lungs with the sweet smell of the forest.

As we make our way through, Eden asks me about life back home. I lay it on a little thick, talking about the skyscrapers and tourist traps like they're as magical as the literally magic forest. But Eden smiles and asks follow-up questions, so I keep it up.

The conversation is light and easy and friendly. I can't stop smiling as we walk through the trees, the sunlight making spindly patterns through the branches across Eden's golden skin.

After about fifteen minutes of this, the path and the trees end. We arrive at a large, shallow pit. It's sort of shaped like a sports stadium, with wide, curving wooden bleachers surrounding a flat circle of dirt. The smell of damp earth and clay wafts up to us on the breeze.

"Is it a stage?" I ask.

Eden nods, hands folded behind her back. "The old amphitheater. I thought it would be a good place to look."

"What makes you think the treasure's here?" The stream's close enough to hear, but it's definitely not roaring like it was yesterday.

Eden smiles. "You'll see. Come on." She heads down the wooden bleachers, orange skirt fluttering behind her.

We walk across the stage. There's a narrow hallway off to the side, tilting into the earth beneath the bleachers. The damp smell gets even stronger as we walk to the door at the bottom. Eden opens it and ushers me through.

Inside feels small at first, but as my eyes adjust to the gloom, I realize it's actually pretty big—just packed full of stuff like old props, costumes, and sets. More importantly, I understand why Eden thought this would be a good place to look. Underground, the sound of the nearby stream is a hollow kind of roar. It sounds like being in a drum.

Eden moves fast, propping open the door and striking a match to light a lantern that sits on top of a small bookshelf so we aren't left in darkness. I lean against a dusty table and watch her. "You look like you know what you're doing."

"I used to come down here a lot when I was a kid." Eden smiles, soft and wistful in the darkness. "I liked the sound and all of the old props. I would find something new to play with every time. It's full of stuff."

"It'd be pretty easy for a treasure to hide in all of this, huh?"

"That's the idea."

I grin. There're a million things to catch my attention here. Probably more in this prop room than in the entire town of Fairbrooke.

Just like yesterday, Eden is methodical in her search. She takes her time with some things, either because she thinks they're a clue or she's just remembering the games she used to play down here as a kid. But she eventually sets them all aside in neat little piles.

In contrast, I'm a hot mess. I grab whatever catches my eye, examining things for ten minutes even after it's obvious they aren't a treasure. I find a feather boa I loop around my neck, a weird helmet I put on a mannequin, and a fake dagger I spend a good five minutes twirling around absentmindedly.

Eden doesn't seem too annoyed by me getting distracted. She compliments me on my boa and giggles at the mannequin's new look. When I find a dirty limerick scribbled in a prop book and read it dramatically, she actually laughs so hard she needs to sit down.

"Sorry to distract you from your important mission." I'm guessing she can tell by my grin that I'm not sorry at all. This reminds me of nights in Chicago with one group or another, all of us telling stupid jokes to one-up each other, laughter like friendship echoing across the streets.

"Don't be." She wipes at her eyes as her chest hitches with stray giggles. "Treasure-hunting has never been this *fun* before."

I sit on a rocking chair, rummaging through a large box. "Why do you keep doing it, then?"

Eden looks down at the small blanket in her hands. "I

want to finish it. I don't like leaving things unfinished."

There's a weight to her words, a maturity I can't really relate to. I've definitely left my fair share of shit unfinished. What's the point of sticking with something once it gets hard or boring? I almost say that, but then I remember the way Eden smiled when we found the treasure in the piano. The way her entire face lit up.

Even if I don't get it, it's clearly worth it to *her*.

I go back to searching, squeezing between a chest of drawers and a tall bookshelf. They cast shadows the light from the open door and the lantern can't quite reach. I must be moving closer to the stream, because that hollow drumming sound gets louder.

I close my eyes. It *is* a nice sound—it sort of reminds me of the streets back home. I can see why Eden liked to go here.

My eyes open and land on a stick.

"Oh, holy shit!"

Eden's voice floats over to me. "Lydia? Is everything alright?"

"Yeah. Yeah, it's fine." Already, the excitement is starting to fade from my voice. The stick is the right color, with carvings and everything, but it's not the actual treasure. For one thing, it's the whole staff—complete with a purple, teardrop-shaped crystal wrapped in thin, woven branches at the top.

Also, the carvings are wrong. I can't read them to know for sure, obviously, but looking at the real carvings just *felt* different. I chalk it up to fae nonsense.

I poke my head around the bookshelf, holding out the staff. "This thing got my hopes up. But I'm pretty sure it's not it."

Eden takes the staff and looks it over, pulling on it like she wants to make sure the real thing isn't hiding somewhere inside. Finally, she nods. "I think you're right." She holds it out, turning it back and forth in the lantern light. "It is pretty cool, though. It must be from plays they used to put on about the faerie war."

I squeeze my way out from behind the bookshelf, sitting down in the rocking chair again. "They used to put on plays about it?"

Eden nods. "Back when people still came into the forest."

"Huh." While I never really thought about it, I sort of assumed people stopped coming in here *because* of the war. "What happened? I mean, why don't they come here anymore?"

Eden shakes her head. "It's been like this for as long as I can remember."

"Oh." I take the fake staff, twirling it. The end hits the helmet off the mannequin, and Eden ducks as it goes flying across the room with a loud clang.

"Lydia! Be careful." She's laughing a little, though, as she takes the staff from me. Her hand brushes against mine.

"Sorry," I say, not really sorry at all. "Well, what about the faerie war then? Was it like a super-long time ago or . . .?"

She nods, looking at the staff. "Yeah. Yeah, it happened a long time ago. More than a hundred years ago, actually." She speaks slowly, like she's reciting an old story. "This forest didn't even exist yet—there was only Fairbrooke and, right next to it, the fae world. It disguised itself as a dark forest, and people would frequently get kidnapped or lured in."

"Why did they do it?" I curl a leg underneath me. "The faeries, I mean."

"To play." Eden's hands curl a little tighter around the staff. "Faeries—most of them—don't see humans as people. They see us as toys. And they don't play nicely. Back before the war, people would find the bodies of their loved ones months later, thrown out of the fae world like trash. Sometimes, they didn't find them at all."

Her voice is so low I have to lean forward to hear her. "So the humans fought back?"

Eden blinks rapidly and turns to face me. "Yes. Sorry. It's just . . . different talking to someone who hasn't heard the story before."

"You're good at telling it, though." And I'm glad she's telling me at all, considering how hesitant she was on that first day. She must trust me more now. The thought makes me smile.

She smiles back, ducking her head. "Thank you. To answer your question, yes, the humans fought, but not all at once. For a while, the people of Fairbrooke tried to survive as best they could. They warned each other away from the fae world, told them not to trust the faeries. But faeries had their tricks, and they never ran low on victims. So the humans decided to fight back. There were a few witches in Fairbrooke, and they called in as many reinforcements as they could."

The story is interesting, I admit. But I'm also sort of really into the firelight and the way it plays across Eden's grave, concentrated face. Her wispy voice sounds like it's made of the lantern light.

"For months, the humans fought and lost. But then something changed. One faerie, Florence, fell in love with a human man. She started to help the humans. And with her help, the tides of the war changed. Eventually, the humans found a magic that pushed all the evil faeries back into their world, where they were unable to reach our world ever again."

"What about the staff?"

Eden blinks, looking at the staff in her hands. "It belonged to the head faerie. I think I told you that? Florence stole it and used it to protect the humans while they handled sealing the bad faeries away."

"Oh, cool. It makes sense that people would do a play about it, then." But Eden never saw the plays. "How did you find out about it? Are there books or something?"

Eden shakes her head, her body language weirdly tense. "No. No, my parents told me."

And there it is again. Like before, when she talked about them finding the treasure. It's obvious her parents aren't like the others in town, or at least they weren't. Her eyes are so sad that I'm pretty sure "*weren't*" is more likely.

"Your parents . . ." I trail off. It's like with whatever happened to Mom in the forest. I don't want to know.

Except I do. I want to know more about Eden. Little things like her favorite color and what sort of food she likes to eat, but also, I kind of want to know the big things, too. Stuff I don't know about the people back home, like her dreams for the future and what she's scared of. It'll pass, probably, the same way my want to learn guitar or collect quarters passed. But now it's here, so I keep talking.

"Your parents," I say again, my voice quiet and strained. "Are they . . .?"

"Yeah. About a year ago. They . . . Well, they're gone now." The tenseness in Eden's voice twists my guts into pretzel shapes. I didn't want to make her upset. I shouldn't have said anything. I'm bad at this sort of stuff, these big emotional moments.

"Oh." I jiggle my foot nervously. "Well, thanks for sharing the story with me. It was a good one." I offer a smile and hope it doesn't come out too forced. "Do you have any others? Maybe a little less creepy?"

Eden cracks a smile, and the air between us feels a little lighter again. I hide a sigh of relief. I should know better than to try and talk about heavy stuff. I've only got a few days with Eden, so I might as well focus on what I'm actually good at: having fun.

What can I say? Sometimes you catch feelings.

It's hours later when Eden and I finally leave the prop room. Not like we have a treasure to show for it. We didn't even get another close call like when I found the staff.

But treasure or no treasure, I got to spend time with Eden. We swapped stories and messed around with props. I even got her to laugh a few more times.

The mood between us is bright and joking as we reach the stage. I skip right to the center of it, gesturing dramatically. "But, soft! What light through yonder window breaks?"

Eden giggles, hiding it behind her hand. "Well? Are you going to finish it?"

"I don't know the rest." I laugh. "Who has time to

memorize Shakespeare? Except, like, actors, I guess."

There's a pause, and then Eden throws her head back. The sunlight makes dramatic streaks across her face. "But, soft! What light through yonder window breaks? It is the east, and Juliet is the sun." She twirls, making a graceful little gesture with her hand to the sky. The shadow at her feet moves in a dreamy dance. "Arise, fair sun, and kill the envious moon, who is already sick and pale with grief, that thou her maid art far more fair than she."

At the bit about a fair maid, she turns and looks right at me. Her dark eyes are playful, a tiny grin clinging to the edges of her lips. Two thoughts hit me at once.

Thought one: *Holy shit, is Eden flirting?*

Thought two: *Holy shit, I have a big fat crush on Eden.*

I've always thought she's cute—*that's* no big revelation. But at some point I started remembering little things like how she hides her giggles behind a curled fist. I started feeling a little lighter every time I heard her voice. I started saying things just to make her happy, because I want to be the reason she smiles.

In other words, I've fallen in stupid, mushy *like* with Eden.

I know other people disagree, but I don't mind it, having a crush. It's like the carbonation inside of a soda making a home in my chest. Light and giddy and full of energy. It's fun, and it doesn't have to mean anything serious. I'm leaving in four days, and I don't intend on making visits to Fairbrooke a habit. Magic woods or no magic woods, it's bound to get stale after a while. I don't want that. I'd rather keep this in my heart as a super-cool magical week, not stick around long enough to get bored of it the way I get bored of everything else.

So in that spirit, I shoot Eden a grin. "Not bad. Do you want to be an actress?"

Eden's smile back is almost shy as she pushes her hair away from her face. "Maybe. But there's a lot of things I want to be. I sort of want to be everything."

"Wait, really?"

"What's *that* supposed to mean?"

"Sorry, sorry!" I flap my hands, like I can wave the words away if I try hard enough. "It's just . . . I don't know. You seem like the type to have a plan." Sure, I've got a different *when-I-grow-up* dream every week, but Eden? The same Eden who spent over a year searching for a treasure, even when it stopped being fun?

Eden laughs, relaxing now that she knows I'm not teasing her. "I don't know. I don't think about the far future too much. It's hard to plan for something when I'm not sure where I'll be." She looks up at the sky. "I don't want to be in Fairbrooke forever, you know."

"Well, yeah." I nudge her shoulder with mine. "I bet it gets old, seeing the same thing every day."

"You have no idea." Eden blinks, then turns to me and smiles. "Anyway, I'm sorry if I ruined your mental image of me having everything together."

I laugh. "Nah. I mean, you're, what, sixteen? Seventeen?"

"Sixteen," Eden supplies.

So she *is* the same age as me. I file that away while I keep talking. "Right. Well, my point is, you've got time to figure out what you want. And once you do, you'll stick with it. That's pretty awesome."

"That's a good way of looking at it," Eden says, all soft

and fond. "I'm glad you think of me that way."

There's a silence between us for a long moment, and for once, I don't want to break it. It sort of feels like if I'm quiet enough, the forest will wrap us up in a tiny little bubble away from the rest of the world.

Shit. I've got it *bad*.

Finally, Eden looks away. "It's getting late. Let me walk you to the bridge."

We set off.

The route back to Grandma's house is almost starting to feel familiar. Maybe it's the magic of the place, but the forest feels comfortable, as easy to navigate as my own home. I'd probably be able to find my way around even without Eden beside me. But she *is* beside me. Even when I'm not looking at her, I can feel her presence, solid and sure at my side.

Are my thoughts getting sappier because I recognized my crush, or have they always been this bad and I just never noticed?

It's weird. I'm usually a lot flirtier with crushes. But then again, I usually get crushes on people I know are interested in girls. I try to test the waters a little. "You know, I don't really have my future planned, either."

Eden glances over at me. "Oh?"

"Yeah. I mean, I guess I want what anyone wants. Like, enough money to live off of, a place of my own, a partner. But I don't even know what I'd want that partner to be like." I fidget with my pansexual pride bracelet, because I can't be *too* subtle. "I guess I'd want her or him or them or whatever to be adventurous? Funny. And not afraid to ignore authority."

Like a certain treasure-hunter in a certain forbidden

forest.

"I see." Eden's smiling a little, which means at least she's not disgusted by my specific use of pronouns.

"What about you?"

"What?"

"In a partner? What do you look for?"

For a second, I worry that Eden's going to call me out on how *painfully* obvious I'm being. But she just shakes her head. "I don't know. I guess I'd just want to be with someone who makes me happy? And I'd want to make her happy as well."

Her. That was a very, super-distinct *her*. I bite back the instinct to say something ridiculous, like, *You make me happy.* There's no need to get out of control here. We're talking about forever people right now, future people. That's not what this is.

I just wanted to know who a future person might hypothetically be. For scientific purposes.

"I see." I echo Eden's tone exactly.

We walk in comfortable silence. And maybe it's my more romantic frame of mind, but suddenly I'm noticing all these little things. Things like pretty pink flowers blooming up the side of a tree, or the way the wind through the leaves is almost like a love song. The stream twists and turns and I'm surprised it doesn't curl into a heart in my dumb, pining eyes.

I don't imagine that, but for a second I do think I'm imagining the shape. It's so out of place here; my eyes must be playing tricks on me. But it's no trick. There's *something* huddled at the base of a tree, so covered in vines and just far enough away that I can't figure out what it is.

I stop walking, tugging on Eden's shoulder. "Hey, what's

that?"

There's a long beat of silence while Eden peers into the trees. Finally, she shakes her head. "I don't see anything."

"Is that a person?" It's tough to tell, but it looks like features are poking out of the vines—a nose, a hand, a closed eye. But they're super dirty and weathered, more than a person could be. "Maybe it's a statue."

"Probably," Eden replies. "That makes sense. There are some in the forest. Mostly all old and overgrown like that one."

I take a step forward. I don't have a reason for it, but when has that ever stopped me from doing anything?

But then Eden's hand closes around my shoulder. "Don't!"

"Huh?" I look over at her, and for the first time I notice how tense she is. Only now do I realize it's been in her voice for a while. "Is everything okay?"

"Yeah, you just . . . You don't want to go over there. That's poison ivy."

"Oh, shit! Thanks." I put my hand on top of hers, which is *still* on my shoulder. Part of me wonders if I should be reading more into that. "You sure you're okay? You sound freaked."

I almost want to take back the question the second it leaves my mouth. If the answer is too serious, it could ruin the mood. Is there such thing as poison-ivy-related trauma?

Luckily, Eden smiles, and it's genuine and a little teasing and it does ridiculous things to my heart. "Yes. Just worried about you rushing off."

I put a hand to my chest in mock offense. "I would *never*."

Eden laughs and pulls back. I rub at the warm spot left on

95

my shoulder before realizing how *ridiculously* weird that looks. I drop my arms to my sides.

We walk away. I take one more glance over my shoulder and almost stop again. Because for just a second, I swear that statue opens its eye and stares at me.

But then I blink and it's back to normal. It must have been my imagination.

I turn my back on it so I can watch Eden's hair swinging in the sunlight instead.

11

You've never felt farther away. And not just, you know, geographically.

Grandma makes a delicious dinner, and we spend the evening chatting and joking. But as usual, she goes to sleep early. I'm left to shower and head to the guest room, alone with my thoughts.

Unsurprisingly, those thoughts keep turning to Eden.

It's a little weird. I get crushes all the time, but they're usually just physical. And it's not like I don't think Eden is super pretty. It's just that I spend as much time thinking about her laugh and her voice as I do her hair and her eyes. I think about the way she talks, the things she says. I want to know what she's thinking.

Even asking about her parents was a little weird for me. Olivia and I got into a huge fight once because she said I never asked about her. She thought that meant I didn't care about her as a person.

And maybe she was a little bit right. I missed being able to make out and stuff, but did I really miss Olivia personally when we broke up? I sort of feel like an asshole when I think about it like that. But just because I don't mope about someone doesn't mean I don't care. Hell, I probably won't mope about Eden once I leave on Friday. So what makes her so different?

Maybe it's this place. Fairbrooke is cooler than I thought it would be, but it still leaves me with large hunks of time with nothing to do but think. I don't get that back home.

I lean against the window, letting the cool night air of summer blow against my cheeks. The smell of grass and flowers from this side of the bridge feels duller somehow. Nice, but not captivating. Not the way it feels when I'm with Eden.

And there she is again. I wish I could talk to Mom about Eden. She's great for talking about crushes, never judges or anything. I love joking with her about cute people and telling her about my grand plans to get their attention. She rolls her eyes and never holds me to them.

I look down. The guest bedroom is on the second story, which is shorter than the first one. The roof of it juts out below the window. Mom used to tell me stories about sitting there with stolen bottles of wine, staring up at the stars.

Well, I don't really want to steal Grandma's alcohol, but a view is a view. I climb out onto the roof and find the highest point. I sit facing the forest under a blanket of stars.

It is a nice view. A little lonely, though. I wish I had someone to share it with. I'm definitely not thinking romantic thoughts about stargazing with Eden. I've just about met my quota of sappy thoughts for the day.

I take out my phone to get a picture, figuring I can at least share that with people, if nothing else. A single bar of spotty reception flickers in the corner of my screen.

I pull the phone closer to my face. My first thought is to text the group chat again, but they aren't really the people I want to talk to right now. Instead, I dial my mom. The phone gives a couple of tinny rings, a reluctant click. I sort of expect dead air, but that's not what I get.

"Doll? That you?"

At the sound of Mom's voice, any complicated feelings melt away, replaced by simple fondness. I missed hearing her. I press the cell phone hard against my cheek as I smile. "Yeah. Turns out the roof is good for more than teen rebellion."

Her laugh is perfectly familiar even with the crappy reception, and my smile widens. "You're on the roof?" I catch a note of wistfulness in her voice. "How are the stars?"

"Hmmm . . ." I look up, squinting dramatically even though I know she can't see it. "Like a million tiny helicopters in the sky."

Mom makes that fake snorting-laugh she does when she wants to poke fun at one of my jokes. I wish she could see me grinning at the phone, but a video call would probably be too much to ask.

"I miss you," Mom says, and that much is perfectly sincere. "Even your sass."

"I miss you, too." I stretch my legs out, rough tile tickling my calves. "How's work?"

Mom lets out a long, drawn-out groan, so familiar I have

to stifle a laugh. "Things would be going wonderfully if Evelyn and Tanya would just behave like adults."

"Oof. They're fighting again?" I lean back, and for a second it feels like I'm back in our apartment, watching her strip off her work apron, tugging her chestnut hair out of its frazzled bun. "I thought they were finally giving it a rest."

"They were, but I guess Tanya thinks Evelyn is making fun of her because yesterday she said something that I guess could be considered rude and now neither of them are backing down. And to top it off, Sandra is being a problem again. I think she might be . . ."

Mom goes off on her usual tirade, catching me up on all the work gossip. It's nice to just sit and listen. I occasionally add in the right noises so she knows I'm on her side. Sometimes I crack jokes that get us both laughing like it's 2:00 a.m. and we're trying to outdo each other's ridiculousness.

Except it's a little different from home, where I'd be interjecting with my own stories. It's not like I can tell her what I've been up to without admitting I know the truth about the forest, so I mostly keep quiet.

Mom must notice, because she eventually tries to coax more out of me. "Anyway. I'm more interested in you than my dumb job. Is everything going okay over there?"

"Yeah, totally! Grandma's really cool. We're having a great time." The forest looms in my vision, almost like it wants me to feel guilty for not speaking up about it. I'm upset at Mom for lying. Isn't it a little bit of a dick move to lie back?

Except I'm not lying. Just leaving out information. It's not the same, I tell myself, as Mom's lies over the years. I mean, she didn't just lie about the forest. She also told me magic didn't exist when she knew that wasn't true. That's sort of a big deal, isn't it?

Even omitting the truth makes me feel scummy, though, especially as worry starts to creep into her voice. "Is Mom keeping up okay?"

"Yeah, it's fine."

"Is she resting enough?"

I shrug, then make a noncommittal noise to match it. "She's got to nap in the afternoons usually. But it isn't so bad."

Mom hums sympathetically. "You must be so bored."

I jiggle my foot against the panes of the roof, looking out at the forest. I hate to hear her sound so guilty. And I want to tell her about Eden, the same way I'd tell her about any crush. Maybe I can, if I'm careful.

"I met someone to hang out with, actually."

"Oh?"

"Yeah." In spite of myself, I smile, thinking of Eden's dark eyes, her voice when she told me how she wanted to be everything.

Something in my voice must tip Mom off, because her tone turns teasing. "Okay. How cute are they?"

"*Mom!*" For one second, it really does feel like I'm talking to her about any other crush, giving up a token resistance like it's not painfully obvious. "It's not like that."

"Suuuure." I can practically hear her expression, the grin and raised eyebrows. "That's what you said about Devin. And Katherine. And Olivia."

"*Mooooom.*" I groan for dramatic effect. But I don't exactly try to hide my laughter, and I give in fast. "Okay, okay. You win. She's pretty cute."

"What's her name?" Mom's voice is obnoxiously smug. I roll my eyes.

"Eden."

"I'm surprised you met someone around your age to hang out with in Fairbrooke." A rare note of alarm creeps into her voice. "She *is* around your age, right?"

I nod rapidly before remembering she can't see it. "Yeah, Mom, Eden's my age."

"Good." I can practically hear her relief. "You know I'd never judge who you date, honey, but you have to be careful. When you get older, you realize what sorts of adults actually go after teenagers. They're not great."

"Yeah. I know." It's nothing Mom hasn't told me before. But now it makes my guts twist up. I never really thought about how she might be speaking from experience. The letter from the closet didn't really sound like a teenager wrote it.

"Doll? You listening?"

Too late, I realize Mom asked me a question. "Sorry! I zoned out. I guess I'm getting pretty tired. I'm gonna have to let you go." I am tired, but is that really the reason I want to get off the phone?

"Awww." Mom's voice is more teasing than disappointed. "You don't want to tell me all about your cute new friend?"

I do. But I know, deep down, that it would only lead to questions I don't want to answer. And I don't want to lie to her. "Maybe later."

I squeeze the phone close to my ear, a weird hollow ache in my chest. I want to hang up on her, and I want to keep talking to her. I'm frustrated with her, and I miss her. Mostly, I just want to hug her.

"I love you, Mom."

"Lydia." Mom's warm voice makes my eyes prickle a little, which is ridiculous. "I love you, too." Then, because we're incapable of being sincere for more than ten seconds, she makes overdramatic kissy noises into the phone. The distance crinkles them into static. Some of the pressure in my chest lightens and I hold the phone away from my ear, wincing and grinning at the same time.

"I feel it. I feel the love."

Mom laughs as I bring the phone back to my ear. "I'll see you on Friday, doll."

"See you."

I hang up. The silence in the wake of our conversation pushes against me. It almost makes me want to go into the forest. Maybe the sound of bugs and leaves and water rushing can quiet my brain the way the city streets do.

I really am starting to think of the forest as home. Good enough for this week, at least. But I don't think it would be the same in there without Eden by my side. It might be full of faerie magic or whatever, but she holds a magic all her own.

The thought makes me very, very glad that mind-readers don't exist. I sprawl backward on the roof, kicking my legs up to the starry sky. "Lydia Barnes, you're a goddamned sap."

But I'm smiling. Thoughts of Eden are much less complicated right now than the other ones that want to creep into my mind. I hold them close to my chest as I climb back down to the guest room window.

Hey, foot. Say hello to your old friend mouth.

I'm still thinking about Eden when I fall asleep, which is probably why she shows up in my dreams.

She's sitting next to me in this dream, her thigh pressing warm against mine on a checkered picnic blanket. It's night in the forest. The grass is a lush, dark green, and above us, the stars glow like snowflakes caught on neon signs.

"You know," Eden tells me in a soft, breathy voice, "if the conditions are just right, the stars come down from the sky."

I nod, drunk on dream-logic confidence. "Let's make some good conditions, then." I kiss her. She kisses me back. And the stars *do* come down from the sky, glittering around us like diamonds. They sing for us as we kiss, again and again, until the warmth of summer explodes out of my chest.

It still feels that way when I wake up. My mind immediately knows the kiss wasn't real, but it takes my body a bit longer to get with the program. I press my hands to my over-warm face and stifle a giggle while I wait for my heart to stop pounding.

I'm so distracted it takes me a minute to realize the house isn't silent like usual. Grandma's talking to someone downstairs. Curious, I get ready for the day as fast as I can, scrubbing my face and teeth and tugging on my T-shirt and overall shorts in record time.

The conversation stops the second I start walking down the stairs. I slide around the corner to see an older woman sitting at the kitchen table. She's the same woman who pulled Grandma away for a private conversation at the diner. Etta, I'm pretty sure her name is.

"Hello again," I say, and Etta gives a stiff nod. Grandma smiles at me.

"Good morning, sweetheart. Breakfast is on the stovetop if you want to make yourself a plate." She nods to several skillets on the stove.

Silence presses down against the back of my neck. I swear I can feel Etta shooting looks at me every time I turn my back on her. I grab a plate and load it full of fragrantly seasoned home fries and breakfast sausage, trying to ignore it.

But then Grandma grabs a bag. "You heading out?"

She nods, the crease between her eyebrows deepening. "There's a town meeting this morning. I wasn't expecting us to have one this week, or I would have warned you."

"Oh, cool. What about?"

I don't care, honestly. Even if it's a town of literal witches,

I'm pretty sure that meetings are boring no matter what. I'm just being polite by asking. But then Etta is shooting me an actual *glare*, to my *face*, and suddenly I care a whole lot more.

"That's none of your business."

"Etta." Grandma steps forward, putting a hand on Etta's shoulder. "There's no need—"

"No, no, it's fine." I set my plate down and walk around the counter to face them properly, crossing my arms over my chest. "If Etta has a problem with me, let's get it out in the open, huh? Tell me, are you an asshole to *everyone* who doesn't live here? Or is it *specifically* because my mom got knocked up in her teens and you just *can't* help being a dick to the result?"

Etta looks at me like I just summoned a demon, and even Grandma looks a little put out. "We should go," she says gently. But Etta doesn't look away from me, so I'm sure as hell not about to back down.

When I don't apologize, Etta narrows her eyes. "Your *mother* should have taught you better manners."

"Yeah, because you all have given me *so* many reasons to be polite! You've really fostered a welcoming, inclusive environment here." I coat my words in sarcasm so thick it could be dripping from my lips.

Etta grits her teeth and squeezes her eyes shut. "I don't have to explain the ways of our town to a *child*." She turns. "Dorothy. Let's go."

She starts to rush Grandma out the door, trying to get the final word. I want to rip that away from her. I don't want her to leave here thinking she's won. So I open my mouth, calling after her with all the venom I can manage. "Whatever. I'll tell the forest you say hi."

I want to get under her skin. What I *don't* want is for her to stop dead in her tracks. She turns to me with her eyes glittering, like I've just given her the ammunition she didn't know she needed. "You've been in the forest?"

Her voice is low and dangerous. My guts twist, alarm bells ringing at the base of my skull. "I . . ."

"Etta." Grandma's voice is firm enough to tear us both away from our staring match. "We're going to be late. Come on. We have too much to talk about at the meeting."

For one second, Etta seems on the fence. But then she turns. "Fine." She walks out the door. Grandma gives me a strained sort of not-smile and I give her a weird apologetic face, and then she's out the door, too.

The kitchen feels too quiet in the wake of them, the sound of the clock in the living room burrowing under my skin and buzzing there. I play music on my phone while I eat breakfast, but it only kind of helps.

Dwelling isn't my thing. So it's *weird* that I'm sitting here wondering if I could have been nicer. It wasn't my fault that Etta was a jerk. So why do I feel guilty about how it all went down?

I guess I did escalate things. And maybe Etta deserved it, but Grandma probably doesn't deserve to deal with the fallout.

"Bullshit," I hiss to myself. I need to get the hell out of this house and do something. That's the problem. Sitting around with my own brain is the actual worst. There's a reason I avoid it as much as possible back home. I finish my food and shove my feet into my boots, taking off as soon as I can.

The second I cross over the bridge to the forest, I know I've made the right choice. The sound of the stream and the wind in the leaves is enough to unsnarl the angry thoughts in my brain. The wind blows through my hair and scoops the bleached curls off my neck. I let out a sigh of relief, swinging my arms and letting the tension roll out of my body.

I'm early, so Eden isn't here yet. But surprisingly, I'm not impatient. It's honestly weirdly comfortable being alone in here. My favorite thing about home is the way I'm *never* alone, the way there's always something to occupy my brain. But this is nice in a different way.

Why are the people here so weird about the forest? Clearly they used to like it, or they wouldn't have built the theater or the room behind the waterfall. If it wasn't the war that pushed them away, then what was it?

Maybe it wasn't anything logical. Judgmental assholes are gonna be judgmental assholes, and they don't need much of a reason. It's the same as the people who give Mom shit when they find out how young she is or the ones who glare at me when they see me holding a girl's hand. Logic isn't the thing fueling them, that's for sure.

Etta probably wasn't being logical today, either. But thoughts of her and that whole situation are easier and easier to push away here. Good.

I take a few pictures for the hell of it as I walk, staying close enough to the bridge so I can see when Eden shows up. I am excited for her to come, even if I'm not impatient. As nice as the forest is, it's twenty times nicer with her next to me.

I find a mossy place to sit and watch the stream babble by. There's something very soothing about the water, almost hypnotic. My brain, usually so loud, clears out as my breathing shifts to match the current. I lean my elbows on my knees, and for once, I feel peaceful, like there's nowhere else I want to be.

That ends when *someone* snatches my phone out of my relaxed hand.

My head snaps up in time to see Florian retreating, his dark hair swinging. "Seriously?" I jump to my feet. "This isn't a running joke. It's just you being an asshole!" I'm laughing a little as I say it, though, so I can't really blame Florian for not taking me seriously.

He leads me on yet another chase. We stick close to the river as it twists and turns, until eventually we hit a tall tree. Its roots are large and thick, curling out of the ground and stretching all the way across the stream. My annoyance disappears.

Eden's sitting there with her back pressed to the tree trunk. Her legs are stretched out across one of the thick roots that reach across the stream, the skirt of her polka dot green dress hanging over the water. Her flats are set in the grass off to the side. A small paperback book is open in her hands, and she's too focused on it to notice Florian or me.

Florian climbs the tree, turning to me and winking. I roll my eyes, but I can't bring myself to call out to her and ruin the moment. Especially when he swings above Eden on a higher branch to drop my phone in her lap. Her startled expression is too cute to handle. I laugh, and her face softens when she sees me.

"You're here early." She looks up, but Florian's already disappeared.

"Yeah, Grandma had to leave for a thing so I figured I'd chill and wait for you." I hop on one of the roots, holding my arms out for balance. "Someone had other plans, apparently. Didn't turn into a kid this time, although I think he's still pretty goddamned childish."

I raise my voice a little, just in case Florian is still listening. It's hard to tell, but I think I might hear his laughter in the distance.

I pull myself up so I'm sitting next to Eden on her root, legs dangling over the stream with the soles of my boots just barely missing the water. She's looking at my phone with a smile. My lock screen is a picture of me and some of the people I hang out with. You can just see the top corner of my face in the bottom of the frame, with everyone else climbing a fence. The *no trespassing* sign is very clearly visible.

In our defense, it was an abandoned house and no one was using it anyway. We spent the night ghost-hunting, but nothing happened. Not quite as magical as the forest, I guess.

Eden hands the phone back to me. "You look like you have fun."

"Oh, yeah. Never a dull moment."

"You seem happy with those people."

"Sure. They're a good time." I squint at the picture. They are a good time, but I don't think I've talked to some of these people in months. We're not fighting or anything. We just don't talk when we're not planning something.

Eden smiles, but it's a bit wistful. "It's strange to think about. Hanging out in a big group with people my age."

I forget, sometimes, how sheltered Eden is. She's come out of her shell so much it's easy to forget how awkward she was when we first met.

"I bet they'd like you," I say. "You're pretty cool."

Eden giggles. The sound does funky things to my chest. "Thanks."

I kick my legs back and forth over the stream. "So what are you doing here? Reading up on faerie magic and treasures?"

Eden looks down at her book, smiling a little. "No, this is a fiction book. I read it a few years ago and loved it, so I decided to come here and reread it while I waited for our usual meeting time." She shakes her head. "If I'm being honest, it's been a while since I've done anything like this."

"Like what?"

"Like . . . relaxing." Eden shrugs. "I might have forgotten how for a while. For a long time, all my days looked the same and there was nothing to do but treasure-hunt. So I fixated on it, I guess. Now that you're here, I remember what it's like to do other things."

"Oh." My heart does something sappy and strange, fluttering against my ribs like butterfly wings. It's weird to think I could relax anyone. But she's smiling at me so soft and sweet I almost want to curl up here and watch her read for a few hours.

Before I can figure out what to do with that obnoxiously tender emotion, Eden stands. She makes her way carefully to the grass, stepping back into her flats and letting her skirt fall around her legs. "But that's enough of that for the day. Are you ready to keep hunting?"

The excited smile on her face is just as great as her peaceful expression. I grin back at her. "Yeah. Let's go."

If there's anyone I'd want to adventure with, it's you.

Eden leads me deeper into the forest than we've ever gone. At least it feels that way, with how different things start to look. The grass reaches all the way up to my knees at one point, and in another, we walk through fragrant wildflowers that brush against my legs with the softest petals I've ever felt.

Through it all, Eden and I chat. She talks a little about books she likes, and I talk about places I've been. The conversation flows naturally, even though we're so different and our lives couldn't be further from each other. I'm surprised by how fun it is—small talk like this usually bores the hell out of me. But with Eden, I don't mind.

Eventually, though, we reach a wooden bridge. It dangles

over a deep chasm, the stream rushing below. A waterfall babbles noisily over the edge of the other side, where a garden full of flowers and trees awaits.

Eden gestures at it, smiling. "Here we are."

"It's gorgeous!" I stomp over the bridge without a second thought. It rattles beneath my boots. Eden picks her way across more carefully while I wait on the other side. "So you picked it because of the waterfall?"

Eden nods, stepping onto firm ground. "It's not as loud or as large as the other one, but it doesn't hurt to check. Besides, there's a lot here. I thought you might like looking around."

The idea that Eden picked a garden to show me has all sorts of undertones, which I try really hard not to read into. But, hell, I like her and she likes girls. It's enough to turn me into a queer conspiracy theorist.

Doing my best to push down those thoughts, I grin. "Well, come on then!" I take off down a path of circular gray stones through the flowers, sort of vaguely following the sound of running water that comes from deeper in the garden. It's the sound of the stream we're looking for, after all.

Except it's not the stream. The noise comes from the center of a small pond, where a fountain arcs gracefully behind the statue of a beautiful woman. Vines climb up her ankles. "Who's that?" The second I ask, I notice a familiar-looking staff in her hands. "Wait, is it Florence?"

Eden sits down on a stone bench, legs crossed at her ankles. "Yeah, that's her."

I turn back to the statue. There's something familiar about her thick hair and the heart shape of her face, but I can't quite figure out what it is. My eyes drift down to the base of the statue. There's something small curled up there, too covered by vines to see what it is. "What's that at her feet?"

Eden comes to stand beside me, peering at the statue. "I'm not sure."

I stare for a long moment, trying to figure it out. And it's only because I'm staring so hard that I catch it moving. "Whoa! I think there's an animal or something in there."

I bend down to untie my boots, meaning to hop into the fountain to get a closer look. Eden stops me. "Lydia, that's impossible. There aren't any animals in the forest."

"Oh." I guess I did figure that out, back when I learned magic was real. I turn back to the pile of vines and moss. "I thought I saw it move."

Eden shakes her head. "Probably just the wind." She heads toward a path that winds through sunflowers taller than her, glancing over her shoulder with a smile. "Come on, there's a painting I want to show you."

I look back at the statue just once, but the movement doesn't repeat. I go ahead and follow Eden into the shade of the sunflowers.

The painting she leads me to is a whole mural on a stone wall depicting an old faerie legend. Eden explains it to me, pointing at the silver moon faerie and the twins who represent the sun. It's cool, and before I know it, I'm pointing out other statues and paintings. Eden has a story for each and every one.

Maybe it's a bit of a distraction—after all, we're supposed to be treasure-hunting. But Eden's eyes light up as she explains all of the old legends. She has all these theories about them, and she rambles adorably about which ones might be true and which ones probably aren't meant to be taken literally. If the price for Eden getting so passionate is ignoring treasures for a few minutes, it feels worth it.

The path twists until we're right on the edge of the little island, the stream rushing below. We keep walking and talking until we hit a tall gate.

I wrap my hands around the thin golden bars. "What's this?"

"A gate." Eden has a weird expression on her face. I can't quite place it, even though I like to think I've gotten pretty good at reading her.

"I see that." I tug on the door, but it's locked. "Where does it lead to?"

"The other half of the garden."

"What's in it?"

"Fruit trees."

"Oh. How do you get in?"

"With a key."

She's starting to remind me of when we first met, blunt answers without any follow-up. "Eden?"

To my surprise, Eden groans, pushing a hand to her face. "I know, I know. Sorry, I'm just embarrassed."

I laugh before I can help it. Eden shoots me a look, and I hold my hands up defensively. "Sorry! But why are you embarrassed?"

Eden gives a long-suffering sigh. "You need the key to get into it, but not out. A few months ago I was in there, and I forgot the key. The gate latched behind me and now I can't get back in." Frustration creeps into her voice. "I was having an off day."

No wonder she's frustrated. I know how annoying it is

when a tiny mistake has big consequences like that. But I don't think she should be so hard on herself. "That's not so bad, though! Like, I've definitely done way stupider things."

This coaxes a tiny smile out of her. "Well. I'm sorry you can't see it."

I squint up at the gate. It's tall, okay, taller than average. And straight vertical bars aren't exactly the best for climbing. But isn't it worth giving it a shot anyway? It would suck if the treasure was on the other side and we had no way to reach it.

Explaining my train of thought to Eden feels like it would take too long. So I just say, "We'll see about that." And I launch myself at the gate.

"Lydia!" Eden calls after me with the sort of tone usually directed toward overenthusiastic pets and bad puns. "Lydia, be careful."

I flap a hand at her, which almost sends me flailing off the gate. That probably wouldn't help my case. I cling to the bars and wedge my boots between the gaps until I have my balance again. Then I make my way up. It's clumsy and awkward and I've probably got more than a few bruises by the time I reach the top, but it doesn't take long enough for me to get bored and bail. With a triumphant shout, I fling myself over the side and drop.

"*Lydia!*" This time there's real fear in Eden's voice, and I realize the fence is a bit taller than I thought.

I brace myself as I land. Shock travels up my legs and I conk my forehead on the golden bars as my hands land in the dirt, but I'm pretty much okay.

"Are you alright? Lydia!"

I scramble to my feet and very consciously do not rub my

forehead, although it is a little sore. Instead, I flash Eden two thumbs up and a grin. "Fine! I'm fine."

She curls her fists around the bars like a prisoner. "You could've gotten really hurt!"

"Seriously? It wasn't even that high. What is your deal with heights?" I laugh a little. "Come on, tell me where the key thing is so I can get it for you."

"I don't . . . Lydia, you shouldn't have done that!" Shit, she's really upset. Guilt flutters in my temples. "I wouldn't forgive myself if you got hurt because of me."

Something dark and serious clings to the edges of her words. I lean against the bars. "Hey. Hey, it's fine. Even if I did get hurt, it wouldn't have been your fault." I stick a finger through the bars and tap a fingertip to her nose, because it's basically impossible to be serious after you've been booped. "You worry too much, Eden."

Eden startles back, mouth dropping open. But then she smiles and lets out a huff that's sort of a laugh, so I figure it's pretty much mission accomplished.

It takes a bit of shouted directions to get me to the key, but eventually I find it waiting for me on a small table. I wipe off the dust on the strap of my overalls as I hurry back over to the gate.

"I can't *believe* you did that." Eden shakes her head as I twist the key in the lock, but a grin spreads across her face. That smile is worth all the forehead bumps and bruises in the world. She slips through the gate quickly, like she's afraid it will slam shut if she doesn't act fast.

She looks at the trees. Then she spins around and hugs me. My first thought is, *Shit, she's so warm.* Her glossy hair brushes my arm and it's just as soft as it looks. I wrap my arms around her and tilt my head as non-creepily as possible, my cheek pressing against her shoulder. She smells earthy but in a nice way, almost like clay.

I laugh a little. "Hey, you're welcome."

Eden steps away, smiling all soft and shy. "I used to come here a lot with my parents. Dad called it the Garden of Eden. Said he named it after me, although Mom would cut in and tell me he named me after it. It was this whole bit they would do." A fond smile creeps across her face.

"That's really cute." I try my best to ignore the soft, mushy feeling in my chest. "Makes sense, too. With all the fruit trees." I stand on my toes and pluck an apple from a branch, knowing just enough pop culture to see the irony in that. But I've never been religious, and while this forest is pretty extraordinary, I'm pretty sure it doesn't have the *literal* Garden of Eden in it. I go ahead and take a bite.

"You know, they say that if you eat food from the fae world, you can never leave it."

Shit.

I stand there with a mouthful of apple as Eden stares at me. Finally, a grin splits across her face. "It's okay, Lydia. This place has fae magic but it's not the actual fae world. There's food all over and it's perfectly safe."

I grin and swallow, shaking my head. "Thank God. No offense to your hometown or whatever, but spending forever trapped here sort of sounds awful."

Eden looks off, quiet for a moment. She breaks the silence just before I decide to. "Do you see that?"

That turns out to be a giant pile of sticks. None of them

look like they have carvings, but they're in such a jumble that I can't tell for sure. And they're all the exact same size, shade, and shape as the one from the piano.

"I think the forest might be trolling us."

Eden laughs. "Come on." She kneels by the pile, beginning to sort through the sticks one by one. The sunlight through the trees plays across her patient face.

I kneel on the other side, doing the same. "I thought treasure-hunting would be more action-packed."

"Sometimes it is. But a lot of the time it's like this. I'm sorry to disappoint you."

"You don't disappoint me." The words tumble out of my mouth, and I hurry on before Eden can read into it. "Besides, we can make our own fun! Let's play a game."

"A game?"

"Sure. Like Two Truths and a Lie or something."

"What?"

"Oh!" I thought everyone knew how to play that game. Maybe there's no point in a small town where everyone knows each other. "It's pretty easy. You say three things about yourself, two that're true and one that's fake. The other person has to guess the fake thing. It's super easy. I'll go first."

Eden smiles a little. "Alright."

"Uhhh . . ." I twirl a stick between my fingers. "My favorite color is red, I'm a Gemini, and I've never left the United States. Now you have to guess the thing that isn't true."

I try to keep a straight face, but I'm not a very good liar, and I'm sure a flush creeps onto my cheeks during that second one. Luckily, Eden is too focused on sorting through the sticks to notice.

"Is your favorite color not red?"

"Nope! Aries all the way. One point for me."

"There are *points* in this game?" Eden finally pauses to look up at me, smiling.

"There are if we want there to be." And what's life without a little friendly competition, anyway? "Come on, it's your turn."

Eden looks back to the sticks, arranging her rejects into a neat pile that puts my tinier heap to shame. "My favorite color is green, I'm a Virgo, and I've never left Fairbrooke."

"You've left Fairbrooke before." She probably goes to the same high school Mom did, although I guess she could be homeschooled. But she's had to have visited family outside of this tiny town or something, right?

But to my shock, Eden shakes her head. "My favorite color is blue."

"Seriously. You've never left once?"

Eden shrugs, looking down at the stick in her hands. "I want to. But that's not really something I can control yet."

She must have really strict . . . guardians or whatever. I guess it sort of tracks with how sheltered she is. She's obviously not happy about it, so I decide to focus on a cheerier topic. "Where will you go?"

"Huh?"

"When you can leave. Where are you gonna go?"

Eden blinks up at the trees. When she finally speaks, it's in a hushed voice. "Everywhere. I'll start in China, visit the cities where my parents were born and raised. Then I'll keep going, see all the places I've read about—Paris, Agra, Peru,

Cairo. I want to cross every ocean. I want to see the world."

The hunger in her voice surprises me. I never really considered exploring the world. Chicago has always been entertaining enough for me. But then again, this forest is more fun than I ever thought it would be. Maybe there are all sorts of exciting things to experience around the world, just like this.

I'm not *serious* when I respond, but I am sincere. "That sounds really cool. I'm in."

"You're *in?*" Eden laughs, giving me a sidelong look. "Who said I was inviting you?"

I gasp, although my grin makes it clear I'm not offended. I'm honestly a little thrilled that she's teasing me. It's such a far cry from the blunt, annoyed girl at the cliffside. "How could you not? I am a *delight.*"

"Hmm." Eden taps her chin in mock thought. "Convince me."

"*Convince* you?"

"Yes. Convince me to take you on my worldwide adventure."

I fling my arms out. "Well, look at this week! Are you telling me that searching for treasure isn't way more fun when you've got a friend around?"

Eden's teasing face goes soft all at once. "Yeah. It is."

If I were better at the whole emotion thing, I'd probably come up with something with the right amount of sap. Instead, I scoff, doing my best to hide the fact that I'm maybe a *little* flustered by the gentleness in her voice. "Well, there you go. Treasure-hunting is more fun with a friend, and so are worldwide adventures."

Eden laughs, complete with an adorable little snort. "Okay. I can't argue that." She looks me right in the eye, and I do my best not to put the *pan* in *panic*. "You can travel the world with me."

I know we're just goofing around. No one can say *we're going to travel the world* and mean it for real. But when Eden meets my eyes, I sort of believe it.

And in that moment, in the sunlight with her, I want it.

14

Good to know a lack of heterosexuality runs in the family.

By the time Eden and I sort through all the sticks, we've gone through too many rounds of Two Truths and a Lie to count. In a weird way, it makes the whole day worth it, even though we didn't find a treasure. I replay the little facts I learned about Eden in my head as we go back to the bridge. Her favorite color is blue. She prefers skirts to pants. She's never worn her hair shorter than her shoulders. She hates the cold.

It's also nice to know she has the same little facts in her head about me. I wouldn't have guessed it, but there's something thrilling about being *known*. And I'm glad it's Eden—honest, determined Eden—who knows me.

Before I can mentally call myself out on the ridiculously

sappy tone of my thoughts, Eden's hand clamps around my wrist. She drags me behind a tree, pressing her body up against mine with her free hand clutching my shoulder. The images that flash through my mind are definitely not G-rated, but once she's got me pinned, she just stands there.

"Eden?"

"Shhhh."

Voices break through the layers of gay panic clouding my brain. Someone is in the forest. Or at least on Grandma's bridge. Eden peers around the tree trunk, dark eyes wary. Then her entire body untenses. "It's just your grandmother and Florian. I wasn't sure . . ."

"Oh. Yeah." Of *course* Eden doesn't want to get caught in the forest. Thank God I didn't mention her to Etta this morning. The memory comes up sour.

Eden steps away from me. My heart does a pathetic little twist as she goes, never mind the fact that my Grandma is literally right around the corner. My stupid traitor brain doesn't let that stop it from replaying the memory of her pressed against me in vivid detail, imagining her doing it again for less urgent reasons.

She doesn't. She takes another step back, glancing toward the bridge. "I'll see you tomorrow." With an abrupt turn, she walks away. It's a little weird for her to not come say hi, but it's not exactly hard to guess that she isn't comfortable around people.

People who aren't me, anyway. Trying not to read too much into that, I smile.

"See you tomorrow, Eden."

I watch her go, then face the bridge.

Grandma stands on it, talking in a low and urgent voice to Florian, but she stops when I walk up. "Hello, dear." She offers a strained smile.

Florian's smile is almost weirdly genuine in contrast with hers. "Young Lydia! Have you been enjoying your adventures?"

"Yeah, sure." Most of my attention is still on Grandma's expression. Does it have anything to do with what happened this morning?

Part of me wants to ignore it. I don't want things to get serious. But maybe if I was more serious about all this, I never would've said anything to Etta in the first place. I came so close to messing things up for Eden. I didn't, but that was just luck. It would have been easy to. My gut twists.

I do my best to look Grandma in the eye. "So how bad did I mess up this morning?" I offer her a lopsided grin, like maybe this won't be so uncomfortable that way.

Grandma shakes her head. "You didn't mess up, dear. I told Etta you've just been sitting near the bridge, that you haven't been causing trouble."

Family full of trouble. The phrase echoes around my head. "Does this have to do with what happened to Mom?"

Grandma doesn't answer. But the look on her face when she and Florian exchange a glance is easy to read.

"*Bastards!*" I don't even know the full story, but I know enough for my temper to flare. "I can't believe these backward assholes think they can blame her for . . . for what happened." I can't even say what I think. There are several options and they're all awful. But however Mom got hurt in here, I know it wasn't her fault.

"I know, dear. It isn't right." Grandma puts a hand on my shoulder. I shrug it off, pacing up and down the bank of the stream.

"I should go over there. I wish I would've gone to your stupid meeting. I would've told them what they can do with their shitty opinions. Hell, give me a chance and I *will*—"

"No." It's probably the firmest I've ever heard Grandma speak. "Lydia, I know your heart is in the right place, but that won't be helpful."

Florian leans against a tree, grave except for his always-sparkling eyes. "It could put your friend at risk."

That makes me stop right in my tracks. Grandma swoops in. "He's right. People might find out she's been in here, and then she could get in trouble. We can't have that, can we?"

"That's a lot of logic I didn't ask for." I grab a handful of rocks and toss them into the stream. Logic or no logic, part of me wants to lash out anyway. I'm angry.

But I don't want that anger to hurt Eden. I wouldn't have thought about that on my own, but now that Grandma and Florian brought it up, I can't ignore it.

I throw another rock at the stream. "Do they blame Mom for their weird hatred of the forest, too?"

Grandma sighs, eyes on the ripples in the water. "It's . . . complicated."

I fight the urge to roll my eyes. I know she promised Mom she wouldn't tell me stuff, but does it really matter anymore? I already know so much. "Does it have anything to do with the war?"

This makes Grandma look at me. "How did you find out about the war?"

"Eden told me. About how faeries used to kill humans but witches were able to push them back. They created a barrier that kept them from getting into our world or something? Oh, there was a good faerie, too. So I guess they weren't all assholes."

My eyes flicker to Florian. I'm not sure where he fits into all this. Maybe only the really evil faeries got pushed back? I don't want to offend him or anything.

He just laughs. "*Most* of them were."

"The war is part of the reason people are so frightened of the forest." Grandma's voice is slow and grudging, but at least she's talking. "There are so many awful stories about what happened here. They're afraid bad things might happen again."

"But the bad faeries are gone? That's dumb."

Grandma just shakes her head. "Fear is rarely rational. Like prejudice and judgment."

It makes sense, but it still sort of bothers me. Sure, prejudice doesn't need a logical trigger. But that sort of thing has *always* existed. People used to come into the forest. What changed?

Florian's voice pulls me out of my thoughts. "Did your friend tell you the name of the faerie who helped turn the tide of the war?"

Grandma makes a noise somewhere between a groan and a laugh. When I look at her, she's facing away, silver hair hiding her expression. I turn back to Florian. "Yeah, her name was Florence."

"I'm glad it's remembered." A pleased smile spreads across Florian's face.

Grandma raises her eyebrows at him, all fond amusement. "Such an *ego*."

"I've been thinking about going as Florence again. I've been going as Florian for years now. It's time for a change."

"Is that so?"

"I know you're partial to Florence, as well."

"I like you no matter what."

Are they talking in a secret code? Because that's how much I'm following this conversation right now. "Okay, back up." They both look at me. I have so many questions it takes me a second to figure out what to ask first. "Right, yeah, okay. First off, Florian, I've been mentally referring to you as *he* this whole time. Sort of wondering if I'm off the mark. Are there other pronouns you like better?"

Florian cocks his head to the side, a bemused little smile on his face. "I do not mind, young Lydia. Generally people refer to me as *he* when I go by Florian and *she* when I go by Florence."

"I've known Florian to go by both over the years," Grandma explains. "He switches when it suits him. I know it can be a bit hard to understand—"

"Nah, it's totally cool." I wave a hand with all the confidence of a certified GSA member. "So you're like genderfluid or whatever?"

Florian's smile widens. "So there's a *word* for it now. You humans and your labels. It's very charming."

"Right, cool, glad that's settled." I press my palms together. "Now that we've got that squared away, *are you the one who helped stop a literal actual magic war?*"

I'm not shouting. Just speaking very loudly. I know he's

older than he looks, but *that* old? Eden said the war happened over a century ago.

He shrugs a little, more amused than modest. "I suppose I am. I never had much taste for my brethren's games."

"Yeah, those were pretty messed up." It's a bit of an understatement, but how else am I supposed to respond?

"I find that humans are just as amusing when they aren't suffering." Florian winks at Grandma. She actually giggles, which is so weird I sort of wonder if I've fallen into a parallel dimension or something. "And on that note, I believe I must bid you adieu."

There are about a million other questions I want to ask, but Florian sinks into the trees and disappears.

Grandma laughs, rolling her eyes. "A flair for the dramatic, that one."

"Okay, I've gotta ask: do you guys have, like, a thing?"

"Goodness, not in years." Grandma walks over the bridge, like that's a satisfying end to the conversation. I hurry after her.

"But you did have a thing?"

"If that's what you'd like to call it, yes." Grandma laughs, shaking her head as we make our way back to the house. "It was never anything serious, though. We always knew it couldn't last."

"Why not?"

Grandma turns around, her face wistful in the late-afternoon sunlight. "Human lives are very short to him. We always knew our time together would be limited." She turns to me and smiles. "But that doesn't mean our time together was any less special. In fact, it was more special. Does that make sense?"

My chest does something fluttery and disgustingly warm. I can't help comparing it to what Eden and I have now—the way she makes me feel, the way she looks at me. Both of us know I'm leaving in a few days. That's why Eden's been showing me all these cool places, because she knows she won't get a chance to later.

Like Grandma said, knowing it's short makes it special.

Since I'd rather die than say something so silly and sentimental out loud, I just shake my head with a grin. "Sure, sure. So about you being 'partial to Florence . . .'"

Grandma gives me a knowing smile, raising her eyebrows with enough smug energy to power a Mack truck. Without a word, she turns and heads onto the porch. I follow after her, boots thudding against the steps.

"Grandma! Is *that* why you were so chill with me coming out? I've joked about queerness running through my veins, but I didn't think it was *literal*."

We enter the house on a warm wave of laughter.

Cue the cheesy romantic
soundtrack!

The next morning, disaster strikes. Because instead of sunlight streaming through my window, I wake up to rain.

I do my best not to sulk through the morning with Grandma. I'm here to see *her*, after all. She tries her best to keep me entertained, staying up even longer than she normally would when she sees I can't go out. I *do* have fun with her, playing games and swapping stories and all that stuff. But my heart sinks every time I look outside. The skies are dreary and dull, fat raindrops turning even the forest all muted and gross.

It's *Wednesday*, is the thing. Mom's picking me up on Friday. Even if I manage to sneak out that morning, that's still only three days left with Eden. Having one stolen because Mother Nature is an asshole stings.

Plus, rain is certifiably the worst. I can't go anywhere when it rains. Even in a two-story house like Grandma's, I'm ready to climb the walls after about an hour.

Hope comes late in the afternoon. Sunlight starts to break through the gray skies, and the large drops turn fine and light. When Grandma falls asleep with a book tented on her chest, I take up watch by the window, jiggling my foot so hard it starts to cramp.

Finally, the rain stops. I lace up my boots and shoot out the front door in record time.

It's quiet as I cross over the bridge. The silence, thick with the smell of wet dirt and grass, presses against my skin. It's cooler than usual beneath the leaves, and I wrap my arms around myself.

Eden's not here, which makes sense. This is after our usual meeting time, and she probably wouldn't have come to the forest in the rain anyway. But the skies are clearing up, so maybe she's on her way.

I pace the riverbank, mud squelching beneath my boots. I don't know how far away Eden lives, so I'm not sure how long to wait before assuming she isn't coming. I want her to be coming. I want her to be as psyched to see me as I am to see her.

I'm sure she is. She seems like she is. She'd let me know if she wasn't, right? If she didn't want me around? At the very least, she's a lot nicer to me than when we first met. But what if she's just tolerating me? Maybe she's counting the days until I go home. Maybe—

"Lydia!"

Eden's there, walking toward me with damp hair and sprinkles of water across the shoulders of her lavender blouse. It's enough to stop my thoughts right in their tracks.

Anyway, I was being dumb. Of *course* Eden would tell me if she didn't want me around.

"Hey, Eden!" I hurry over to her, kicking up droplets from little puddles in the dirt. "You're wet."

Eden smiles a little, touching her damp hair. "Well, I saw the rain was stopping. I decided to come see if you'd be here. I'm glad you are."

"Yeah. I'm glad to see you, too." I sort of mock punch her shoulder and immediately regret it. *Accept the nice words from your crush like a normal person, you freaking weirdo.* I hurry on, like maybe she'll forget it happened if I talk fast enough. "So where are we treasure-hunting today?"

"Well—"

That's all she gets out before the sky cracks open.

I guess the rain was just taking a break, because all at once it's falling faster and thicker than ever. The droplets are large and cold and almost painful. I holler, covering my head with my arms, but it does absolutely nothing.

"Shit!"

It feels like I've walked into a television playing white noise. The trees are vague looming shapes, and Eden is blurry even though she's hardly a foot away from me. For a long moment, she just stands there. I'm not sure, but I think she might look between me and the path a few times. Then she shouts something. I can't make it out above the rain's hiss.

"What?"

133

Eden's by my side in an instant. Her hands, gripping my shoulder and arm, are shockingly warm. But not as warm as her breath at my ear. It travels all the way to my gut and shivers there.

"Follow me!"

The hand on my arm slides down, fingers lacing together with mine. I try not to read too much into it. She's being practical; we'd get separated for sure if she didn't. But dammit, this is maybe the most romantic thing that has ever happened to me in the history of ever. I'm not sure if the cold of the rain is making my heart pound or something else.

Eden breaks into a run. I don't think she can see the trees around us any better than I can, but she never wavers. Thank God one of us knows where she's going. Our locked hands are the only thing keeping me from careening off another cliff.

The ground beneath our feet changes. Instead of dragging me across the grass, Eden's brought me to . . . stairs? I look down to confirm that, yes, we are walking up a set of rustic wooden stairs in the middle of the forest. Honestly, considering all I've seen this week, I don't question it.

Eden leads me up them carefully, her hands in both of mine for balance. I'm too distracted by that to realize where we're going until Eden hip-checks a door and leads me through it. The rain stops falling on us as soon as we step inside.

I blink, trying to figure out where Eden's taken me. But it's too dim. The single window on the far wall might as well be painted on, because none of the gray light from outside reaches in. I can sense walls around us and smell damp wood, but that's about it.

"Hold on." Eden's wispy voice travels across the space, half obscured by the rain drumming the roof over our heads. I can barely make out the sound of shuffling, then careful movements as she walks across the room. There's some rummaging before warm yellow light pours from a lantern in her hands, illuminating the space.

A thick rug takes up most of the floor. There's a bed in the corner with a lot of blankets, a desk near the window, a chest covered in more blankets, a mirror, and some drawers. Eden's left her sandals by the door, and she walks comfortably across the room in bare feet.

It sort of looks like a cabin, complete with wooden planks. Except one of the walls curves, made of bark instead.

"You have a treehouse? Eden, this is so cool!"

Eden's smile fades as she gets closer. She puts a hand on my arm. "You're shivering."

Oh. Yeah, I guess I am. But Eden's shoulders tremble, too. "So are you." I laugh a little. "Rain's cold."

"Hold on." Eden hangs the lantern on a hook over my head. Then she kneels by the chest, setting the blankets aside so she can open it. She pulls out a towel and hands one to me. "Here."

"Thanks." I swipe it across my arms and legs, then scrub it against my thick curls. It helps, but my damp clothes still cling to my body. I follow Eden's example and take off my boots and socks, but it's still not really enough. I shiver.

"Here." Eden holds out a dark yellow dress with a sheepish smile. "It might be a little big on you, but . . ."

"At least it'll be dry." I take it and do my best not to think anything too sappy. "Thanks."

135

"You're welcome." She leans over the opened chest and pulls out another dress—this one's brown with white frills at the collar. She turns her back on me and starts unbuttoning her blouse.

I bite the inside of my cheek and spin around so fast I almost fall over, my heart pounding. I fumble my way out of my T-shirt, then let my jean shorts slide to the floor with a wet *plop*. My numb fingertips wrestle with the buttons on my borrowed dress.

Meanwhile, most of my attention is focused on Eden. I can hear every goddamned shift of fabric, even with the rain drumming above us. I'm not going to turn around to watch her change—that would be totally creepy. But I'm hyperaware of her, of every movement she makes behind me. It tingles against my spine, tickles against my lungs.

I'm mostly buttoned up when she asks in a soft voice, "Are you done?"

"Yeah. Practically." I finish the last few buttons as I turn around.

Eden's all put together in her fresh clothing, damp hair smooth against her back. I can't help but compare her to how I must look. I know how my hair gets when it's wet, all matted and weird. I'm a mess in an oversized dress.

Still, Eden smiles when she sees me. "Better?"

"Way better, thanks."

Eden nods and crosses the room, hanging our wet clothes to dry, making sure everything is orderly. She seems really comfortable here. How long has she had this place? Did she find it, or did her parents make it? Hell, maybe Eden made it. She's full of surprises.

My gaze drifts to one shadowy corner. A walking staff sits propped against the tree trunk wall. The shade of the wood is familiar, and once I get close enough, I recognize the carvings spiraling around its surface. These are the first five treasures.

It's weird to see it all together like this. I think about the amount of time and effort that went into getting these. How did Eden feel, fitting that fifth treasure into its place after so many months?

I can't imagine it. I've never done anything to compare to it.

"It's sort of amazing, isn't it?" Eden's voice is soft next to me.

"Yeah." It is, but that's not why the shiver runs up my spine. Eden's shoulder brushes against mine, and it's sort of doing things to my pulse.

Eden notices my shiver. A crease appears between her eyebrows. "Are you still cold?"

I grasp eagerly at the excuse. "A little. But it's no big deal."

Eden hums and takes my hand. I'm aware at once of how alone we are here, together, just the two of us. It's always been like that, but it's different under the open air and a clear sky. With the rain obscuring everything, it feels like the world's shrunk down to just the two of us.

Eden tugs me by the hand in the direction of her bed, which does *not* help me chill.

She wraps a blanket around my shoulders and another one around her own. Part of me sort of wishes she'd wrap the same one over both of our shoulders so we could sit closer, but honestly? Even this sort of drives me crazy. I keep thinking about how easy it would be to close the distance between us.

How it would feel to have my fingers tangled in Eden's hair. How it would feel to have her breath against my skin.

Does she want that? Is she hoping for that? Or would trying that royally screw everything up?

"I'm sorry it rained," I blurt, mostly to distract myself from how kissable Eden looks. "I guess we've lost a day of treasure-hunting."

"That's alright. I'm just glad you're here. I'll be able to look for the treasure anytime, but . . ."

The unspoken reminder of our limited time hangs between us. It reminds me of what Grandma said yesterday about limited time being special. It's easy to believe right now.

"I'm glad I'm here, too." I laugh, quiet. It feels right to be quiet, with the rain pattering outside. "I wasn't expecting this week to be so much fun. But you've made it really great. Thank you, Eden."

"I should be thanking you." Eden's eyes lock with mine for a moment, but then they skate away. "To be honest, I've never really had a friend like you before."

Does she mean that in a gay way? I do my best to shove the thought down. "Yeah? I get that. I'm pretty awesome." My lame joke does little to ruin the mood. It's like something is sucking away at the space between us, pulling her closer with every breath.

Eden lets out a soft laugh. "You are." She shifts. The sides of our hands slide against each other on the mattress. She doesn't pull away, and I'm sure as hell not about to.

"You are, too." I don't think I've ever been more sincere in my life. "I mean, it's not every day someone saves me from falling off a cliff and tells me this amazing story about magic treasure."

Eden laughs again, looking out the gray window. "I thought you'd meet interesting people every day where you're from."

"I do," I tell her. "But none of them are like you."

She turns to me. Lantern light flickers warm in her dark eyes. She doesn't say anything.

"Back home, it's so easy to get distracted. I've never met anyone like you." I talk quickly, like maybe I won't get embarrassed if my words come out fast enough. "You're so determined. You decide what you want and stick to it, and that's something I've never been able to do. So I think it's really amazing that you're like that. *You're* amazing."

The silence stretches between us for so long I worry I've said something wrong. Eden just stares at me, and her face is full of emotion, but in the dim light, it's unreadable. My gut twists and my heart wages war against my ribs.

Finally, she speaks. "You're amazing, too."

For maybe the first time in my life, I'm speechless.

"Maybe I am dedicated," she continues. "But I hesitate—a lot. And I worry too much about consequences. You don't. You're fearless. You do what you want and make it work. You find the fun in everything. You make everything feel so exciting. That's . . . I really like that about you."

Our hands are still touching. I scoot mine so my pinky overlaps with hers. "I really like you, too."

I practically hold my breath, looking for any signs of discomfort, waiting for her to pull her hand away. But she doesn't. She smiles softly, the lamplight shining against her hair like a magic glow. Not to be dramatic, but I think she's maybe the prettiest person I've ever seen.

"I'm glad," she says.

And for a while, that's all there is other than the rain. I've never felt this comfortable sitting in silence with someone. I've been attracted to people, I've wanted to be with people, but never in the same way I want to be with Eden right here and now.

Finally, I say, "You should come visit me."

Eden blinks rapidly, like I've pulled her out of a trance. "Huh?"

I didn't even really think about why I said that. I make sense of it as I talk. "I mean, you've gotten to show me all the cool stuff in your hometown. It only feels fair that I return the favor."

Eden smiles so gently my guts turn to Jell-O. "That sounds fun." She cocks her head to the side. "Where would you take me?"

I pause, trying to think of something that matches this back home. But there isn't. The forest is special and private and almost secret. There are no secret places in Chicago.

But maybe Eden would like that. Maybe she'd want something she's never experienced before. After all, she's the one who wants to travel the world. I blurt the first thing that pops into my head. "I'd take you to Navy Pier."

"What's that?" Is Eden inching closer to me? I'm not sure, but I also know she hasn't moved her hand out from under mine. I keep talking.

"Navy Pier is on the water. It's got a bunch of shops and restaurants and stuff. An indoor garden you can walk through without worrying about getting rained out."

Eden giggles a little at this. I'm very aware of her arm pressed against mine now, her weight shifting to rest against me. I keep talking, like I can lure her in with my words.

"We could walk up and down the boardwalk, take in the sights. It's beautiful and a great place to people-watch. And then, right before it gets too dark, I'd take you on the Ferris wheel."

"The Ferris wheel?"

"It's there year-round. From the top, you can see the whole city."

Eden leans her head against my shoulder. And for a moment, I allow myself to get swept up in the idea. I'm basically pulling it out of my ass, and I suck at sticking to plans. But I imagine us in that Ferris wheel, watching the sun set over the city skyline, the lake sparkling below us. I imagine her putting her head on my shoulder, just like this.

It's pure sap. But it still fills me with a warmth the sun couldn't hope to compete with, no matter how bright it shines whenever the rain decides to clear.

As far as I'm concerned, it can take its time.

What's the opposite of a calm before a storm? This.

When the rain stops, it breaks a spell.

We do stay in the treehouse for a bit longer, just to make sure it won't start up again. But it's no longer comfortable to sit still. I start to jiggle my foot, and when Eden stands up, I follow her example and go to my clothes. They're a little damp, but they'll be comfortable enough to wear.

"I'm gonna get dressed," I warn Eden.

"Okay." She turns her back.

I consider making a joke about inviting her to watch and have to bite the inside of my cheek to keep myself from blurting it out. It's weird, because I'm not exactly the type to be cautious with my words. But Eden's different. I don't want to embarrass myself in front of her.

I turn my back and slip out of my borrowed dress, changing back into my own T-shirt and shorts. They're cold against my skin but warm up quickly from my body heat. I go ahead and stow the dress back in the chest Eden got it from.

She has a lot of clothes in here. A lot of stuff in general, actually. Things like the books and even the lantern make sense. But there's enough food to last for days, a bed, an entire wardrobe. It's a little much for just a treehouse.

It's almost like she lives here.

Part of me wants to stop the thought in its tracks, but I can't turn off my stupid brain. Eden never invites me back to her place. She was in the forest, by herself, even though there was rain.

I look around. There's only one bed, although there is a cot tucked up high in a dusty storage space. The clothes are all Eden's size. This place is hers and hers alone.

I know her parents aren't around. But someone has to take care of her, right? She's only sixteen, like me. Sixteen-year-olds don't fend for themselves in treehouses, not even in a town as weird as Fairbrooke.

"Lydia?" Eden's voice tugs me out of my thoughts.

"Do you—" I stop, redirecting at the last second. "Do you spend a lot of time in here?"

Eden hesitates. Her shoulders stiffen, and she presses her lips into a tight line before answering. "Well. It's good for treasure-hunting."

I don't think she'd lie if I asked her outright. But I don't want to. I'm afraid the answer might be too real. This afternoon has been so incredible, the way we sat in the quiet, our hands slowly finding each other. I don't want to ruin it.

So I laugh. It's easier to lighten things, to crack jokes. That's what I'm good at. That's what I'll stick to. "So this is like Treasure-Hunting HQ?"

Eden laughs, too. The line of her shoulders relaxes. "Something like that." She heads toward the door, dark hair swinging. "Come on."

She leads me down the stairs, walking slow so she doesn't slip on the wet wood. The forest is thick with that after-rain smell, and the grass squelches beneath our feet. It does feel, a little, like we're coming back to Earth.

"So where to?" I ask.

Eden looks up at the sky. "I don't think we have much time for treasure-hunting. But I'll walk you back to the bridge, at least."

I surprise myself with how disappointed I am. I definitely don't regret the way today turned out—sitting in the treehouse with Eden was special, almost more than my stupid pining heart could take. But I'm more invested in this whole treasure-hunt thing than I thought.

Still, I do my best to shrug it off. "Ah, well." I start toward the sound of the stream. "Better luck tomorrow, I guess."

Eden laughs, and fondness flutters all up my ribcage. "Lydia, your Grandma's house is *this* way." She points in the opposite direction.

I frown. "Really? Because I hear the stream over here."

"No, the stream is definitely this way." She cocks her head, a puzzled frown spreading across her face. "I'm not sure *what* that is."

"Wait. Eden." My chest tightens, and I work out why as

144

I talk. "The riddle—"

"—talked about the sound of the stream," Eden finishes for me, her eyes wide. "Not the stream itself. Just the sound of it."

I don't even think. I break into a run.

"Lydia!" Eden's voice cracks, nearly a shout. Then her footfalls pound behind me. I grin, and I really hope this is actually going to lead to something. I'd hate to get Eden's hopes all up only to bring them crashing down. Also, I'd be pretty bummed. My pulse is thrumming. I *want* this to lead to something.

The sound of rushing water grows louder. I swear it almost echoes as I run, turning the sound booming and hollow. I skid to a stop in front of a slick wall, dark green moss and vines with only a few patches of damp gray rock peering through. I pace along its edge, trying to figure out where the sound is coming from.

"Lydia. Look at this."

I spin around. Eden's standing maybe five feet back, eyes wide. At first, it looks like she's got her hand on the wall, but when I get closer, I realize it's actually gone right through it, disappeared up to the wrist. It's not a wall at all. It's a cave, its entrance so overgrown with vines and moss I walked right past it. The echoing water sound comes from inside.

I turn to her, grinning. "Do you really think the treasure is in there?"

Even as I ask, I know the answer. It hammers against my ribs like a second pulse, too fast to keep up with, a physical version of the way my brain sometimes gets.

The treasure is in there.

I can tell Eden thinks so, too. There are high spots of color on her cheeks, a glimmer in her dark eyes. "Let's look." She steps carefully past the vines, like she doesn't want to show how excited she is. I grab her hand and tug her forward. She stumbles with me, laughing.

It's like we've walked onto the set of a sci-fi movie. There's plenty of light from large holes in the damp gray ceiling, but it's all filtered through moss, turning everything green and alive and breathing. Rain collects in the plant life and runs down the jagged, craggily walls like a small but very loud waterfall.

I gawk. This space is about the size of a ballroom, but there's more to the cave—it twists off in countless directions, narrow paths like spider legs.

"Have you ever been in here?" My voice echoes against the tall walls and high ceiling.

"No." Eden stares, awestruck. "I didn't even know this place *existed*."

With every step we take, the certainty that the treasure is close grows. It makes me want to run laps, climb walls, do *something*. I can't remember the last time I've been this hyped. Maybe I've never been.

Eden walks over to a wall, running her fingertips over the damp stone. She's reading, I realize—etchings like the ones on the treasures. I know they're probably important, but honestly, they don't hold my interest for more than a second. I want to keep moving. That want prickles in my lungs like the time I tried a cigarette just to see what the fuss was about.

Maybe Eden notices my restlessness, because she looks over her shoulder with an amused smile. Maybe a little annoyance, although I just might be imagining it because I'm so keyed up. "I know it's not very exciting. But this is part of the treasure hunt."

"I'm not bored." I'm not. I know boredom, and this is something else, something bigger. "Aren't you getting—I don't know—a vibe from this place?"

Eden's furrowed brow answers the question before she does. "No? What are you talking about?"

I flap a hand at her, which probably looks a little rude. But trying to find words for this feels about as possible as turning my ribs inside out and showing her the heavy pound of my heart.

"Never mind. Divide and conquer or whatever?"

We've never split up before. But nowhere has felt like this. For the past few days, at least to me, this has just been about hanging out with Eden. Now it isn't. It's about *doing* this. No wonder Eden's so focused on finding the treasure. If this humming in my chest is magic, I want more of it. It's a better high than any adventure back home.

Eden opens her mouth, closes it. Then she shrugs. "Okay. Just be careful?"

I shoot her a sloppy okay sign before turning and going deeper into the cave, picking one of the narrow pathways at random.

But it doesn't feel random. I take every turn with confidence, as sure as I would be when following a GPS. The path inclines up for a while, getting steeper with every turn. It stops with a wall that comes up to my waist, and I have to haul myself up on top of it to keep going.

I step out onto a narrow ledge. I'm back in the main space—and I'm up high. Either the path had more of an incline than I realized or there's fae nonsense afoot. I scoot forward until I'm right over Eden. The top of her head is the size of a baseball. "Hey!" I holler down at her.

She looks up at me, and even from this height, I can see the worry in her face. "How did you get *up* there?"

"I walked," I respond, a giggle caught somewhere in my chest. I feel like I could float right up to the ceiling. Whatever's causing this, I'm close. I can *hear* it coming from a ledge that sits right over my head.

I grip it with my fingertips and jump. It takes some fumbling, but eventually I get one elbow over the edge, then another, grunting with effort. From a million miles away, I think I hear Eden call something, but I don't know what. I'm too busy trying to make sense of what I'm seeing.

It's a door. Except it isn't a door. It's a smooth sheet of rock, but I see the door anyway, a perfect square that is and isn't there. It is and isn't glowing with a thousand tiny pinpricks of light. It's silent, but I can hear it singing.

It's beautiful.

I try to pull myself up to get a closer look, and that's where I screw up. My foot hits the stone too hard, throwing me off balance, and suddenly I'm staring at the too-quick retreating ceiling of the cave. Eden shouts my name.

I think, *Well, shit. This is gonna hurt.*

Then I hit the ground hard, and I might black out for like half a second. But by the time Eden reaches me, I'm able to sit up. I'm probably not going to die or whatever. My side hurts like fire and it's sorta hard to suck in a breath, but I've done way stupider shit and gotten hurt way worse before.

I'm talking before Eden even drops to her knees beside

me. "I'm fine. I'm totally fine." Maybe the fact that I'm wincing and rubbing my head hurts my case a little, but whatever.

Eden's head whips around to look up at the ledge I fell from, then back to me. "Lydia. How are you okay right now?"

I shrug. Eden and her weird height fixation. "It's cool. My spine took most of the impact." Judging by Eden's face, I guess the joke doesn't land. "Hey. Really, I'm fine. And I saw something kinda weird up there!"

"Weird?" Eden doesn't seem all that interested in potential treasure leads. Ordinarily I'd be flattered, but mostly I just feel bad that I worried her so much.

"Yeah, it was like . . . a door? Except it didn't actually look like a door. I just knew it was one . . ."

I worry that Eden's going to think I'm concussed or something. But she nods. "I know what you're talking about. It's an entrance to the faerie world. They're all sealed, of course, but sometimes you can see them if the conditions are right."

"Oh. Shit. I thought it might be a treasure lead." I stand, wincing as my bones grind against each other a little. It's fine. They're getting back to where they belong. It's not the first time this has happened to me.

"You shouldn't . . . Lydia, you could've gotten really hurt!" Eden actually looks close to tears.

"Oh, shit, don't cry. It's fine." I pat the top of her head, which feels stupid as soon as I do it. But I don't know what else to do. Panic spikes way harder at her shiny eyes than it did while I was falling. "I'm not hurt. Don't even worry about it! And, like, now we know. That's one place you won't have to look."

Eden's quiet. I don't really know what to say, so I don't say anything. That silence seems to fill up the entire cave.

Finally, Eden stands and sighs. "That's enough treasure-hunting for today. Let's go."

And because I don't want her to freak out on me any more, I agree.

Seriously, what is it? Are you trying to sell me essential oils?

All through the walk back to Grandma's, Eden keeps stealing looks at me like she expects me to collapse. It's ridiculous, because I'm fine. It reminds me of this one time when I jumped out a window to avoid getting caught when a bunch of us broke into Riley's ex's apartment to get something back. Riley swore I'd broken my ankle and they wouldn't let it go until I caved and went to the hospital. Sure enough, I didn't even have a sprain. At least Eden isn't trying to make me deal with unnecessary medical bills.

Thinking of home doesn't make me feel that restless ache like it used to. Maybe because I know I'll be there soon. Tomorrow is my last full day here.

I kind of wish we would've stuck around the cave. We

were so close to the treasure—I'm sure of it. How cool would it be to find two treasures in a week? I can't stop imagining how excited it would make Eden. Hell, I'd be excited, too.

Eventually, we reach familiar territory again. Things are still quiet and weird. I turn.

"Hey, Eden."

"Hm?"

And what am I gonna say, here at Grandma's bridge with the water trickling beneath our feet? Everything I can think of is a downer ("Hey, soon I'll be back home and you'll be on your own!") or sort of embarrassing ("I want to impress you so bad it's pathetic!"). Instead, I shoot her a couple of finger guns. "See you tomorrow."

Eden blinks, staring blankly. "Right." She shoots the finger guns back. "See you tomorrow."

I hug her. I'm not sure why I do it, honestly. Maybe it's because she still seems worried about me. Maybe I'm still harboring big gay feelings about the afternoon in the treehouse. Maybe it's just because she's fun and cool and I've thought she was cute since the moment I met her. Whatever the reason, it startles a smile out of Eden, and she actually laughs a little as she wraps her arms around my shoulders.

"Goodnight, Lydia."

"Goodnight."

Grandma's in the kitchen when I walk inside, fussing over the stovetop. She smiles over her shoulder when she hears me come in. "You were out late. Did you get caught in the rain?"

"Yeah, but it was cool. Eden and I were able to stay out of it." I find myself not mentioning the treehouse. It's not like I don't trust Grandma with the information. It just feels special, something I don't want to share with anyone but Eden.

Maybe secrets aren't all bad.

I set the table while Grandma finishes up dinner. I still ache, but it's concentrated in my back and my side, where I landed first. I pull up my T-shirt to examine the frankly impressive bruise across my ribs. I let out a low whistle, poking at it.

"Goodness! What happened to you?" Grandma's eyes widen in worry as she scoops a mountain of creamy pasta onto my plate.

"Don't *you* start." I take a bite and immediately regret it as I try to talk through a mouthful of hot noodles. "It's fine. We were in a cave and I heard singing from one of the closed-off faerie portals or whatever? I tried to get a closer look, and I fell. No big deal."

Grandma frowns. "You're *sure* you heard singing?"

"Yeah, why? Is that weird?"

"Not so strange." Her voice stays calm, but she doesn't stop frowning, either. "I never heard anything coming from the other side, is all."

"I don't even think I mentioned the singing to Eden, so I don't know if she would've thought it was weird." I shake my head. "She was just so worried. She's super weird about heights. I'm pretty sure she thought I was gonna die or something. Maybe I'm just tough, though." I grin. "Maybe I'm a witch after all! Do witches have like super-awesome healing or something?"

Grandma laughs, shaking her head. "Not to my knowledge, dear."

153

I shrug, still grinning. I didn't really think I had magic powers or anything. It's just sort of fun to think about. It would be badass to be able to jump off buildings without getting hurt. Or skydive without a parachute.

Somewhere, I imagine Eden shuddering and not knowing why.

"Lucky I don't need magic. I'm just that awesome without it."

Grandma shoots me an amused look. "And so modest, too."

"I learn from the best." Mom doesn't have a modest bone in her body, and I'm pretty sure Grandma doesn't, either.

Grandma laughs again, and we chat through dinner, the conversation light and easy. It's comfortable here, with nothing but quiet outside. I don't like it more than Chicago, obviously. But just because it's different doesn't mean it's bad.

After dinner, I help Grandma with the dishes. Her shoulder bumps companionably against mine as I stare out the open window over the sink. The grass looks different at night, like it sucks up the coolness of the dark sky. I can't see the forest, but I can hear the trickling of the stream and the soft, secret sound of the wind through the branches.

I glance over at Grandma. "It really is pretty here."

A soft, fond smile creeps across her lips. "I'm glad you think so. I was a little afraid you'd hate it here." She laughs. "I guess I have Eden to thank for making your visit so much more entertaining."

I flick water at her with my fingertips. "Hey, don't sell yourself short! I've really liked spending time with you, too."

I surprise myself with how much I mean that. The time

spent with Grandma hasn't been quite as exciting as exploring with Eden. We've shared more quiet moments, stories over dinner, board games. They're not my usual thing, but they're not bad, either. I can even sort of imagine myself doing it again.

Fondness softens Grandma's whole face. I wonder if she can see what I'm thinking. "I've enjoyed it, too."

I open my mouth, as careless as the phone call that got me here, to say something like, *Maybe I can do it again*. Except this time, I'm not sure if it would be such a chore. Quiet mornings in Grandma's kitchen, afternoons with Eden, and evenings spent just like this. I can almost hear our future conversations mixed in with the sounds of the forest.

Wait.

Someone *is* talking. Voices come from outside.

"Do you hear that?"

I'm moving before Grandma can answer. That isn't Florian's deep rumble, and I don't even think I'd hear Eden's wispy voice.

"Lydia!" Grandma's shout follows me out the door.

I leap off the porch, bolting around to the forest with fists clenched. There's no logic to the fire in my chest. It just feels, in that moment, like someone is threatening the forest. And part of me hates that.

Two people around Mom's age stand in front of the bridge. One of them looks ready to run the second he sees me, his sunburnt shoulders around his ears and his blue eyes wide. But the woman next to him just stares at me, arms crossed over her plaid shirt and blonde hair tied in a low ponytail.

"What the hell are you doing in my grandma's yard?" I

snap.

"Jesus, you really are Charlotte's kid, aren't you?" The man shakes his head. "She didn't teach you any damn respect."

The woman doesn't take her gaze off me. Her voice is clipped and even. "We're walking through her yard to get home. Is that a crime?"

"Uh? Yes, literally. Trespassing. Look it up."

I'm being more aggressive than either of them, but I can't help it. They sure didn't look like they were walking when I came up. And besides, I know they're lying. I can see it in their eyes.

Grandma reaches us, her bright skirt billowing around her legs in the slight summer evening breeze. "Tim, Gina, I see you've met my granddaughter, Lydia."

"These people were doing some shady shit." I can't prove it, but that doesn't keep the grumble out of my voice.

The woman—Gina—gives Grandma a level look. "We were just crossing through your yard on our way home. Dorothy, do you mind?"

"Of course not."

Tim grins with all the maturity of a middle schooler. "Well, there you go. We're not trespassing then."

"Let's go, Tim. Now's not a time to be *awake*." Gina looks at me intensely, and I get the sense she's searching my face for something. More sass, probably. I'm all too happy to provide.

"It's literally 7:00 p.m. I get that your lives are boring, but seriously? That boring?"

"No manners." Tim shakes his head, lacing his fingers through Gina's.

Her gaze doesn't stray from me, though. "You should

156

learn to think before you speak."

Mom said something similar, which should piss me off enough. But there's an unease under that, twisting my guts into balloon animals. Does she know I've been in the forest? Does this have something to do with what I told Etta?

It's too late to ask. Tim and Gina are already heading back toward the main road, hand in hand. I turn to Grandma, who watches them go. "What the hell is their deal?"

Grandma turns to me and smiles. "Nothing, I'm sure. Their farm is just down the street, and it really is a faster walk for them to cut across my lawn."

"Uh-huh." I cross my arms. "I don't buy it."

"What else do you think they were doing?"

I peer into the forest, like the answers might appear in there. But it's the same old trees and path, just with shadows that are a little longer in the setting sun. I'm sure they weren't trying to get in there. People here avoid the forest like it's radioactive.

But then what were they doing?

I don't have an answer, but it bugs me on and off through the rest of the night. I forget about it for a little bit, but then it comes back, like a song I can't get out of my head.

It's the worst in the shower. Underneath the spray, I can't find anything to distract me. By the time I'm dried off and in my pajamas, it's all I can think about. I head across the hall to Grandma's room.

"Hey, Grandma, about those people—"

But Grandma isn't in her room.

I head downstairs, calling out. She's not there, either, which is when I start to get worried. Did those assholes come back and kidnap her?

It isn't until I look out the living room window that I see her. She's standing on the bridge in her nightgown, her white hair tied back from her face. Florian stands just beyond. Even in the shadow of the trees, I can see his beaming smile when he takes her hand, pressing his lips to her weathered knuckles. She shakes her head, and although her back is to me, I can imagine her amused smile.

An answering smile tugs at my lips, distracting me from my earlier questions. And anyway, it didn't really mean anything. Grandma isn't bothered. I made a big deal out of nothing.

I step away from the window to give Grandma her privacy, putting the town assholes out of my head for good.

18

Maybe I want you to remember me a little.

Grandma's too tired to do much the next morning, so I munch on cereal and we spend some calm time chatting. Even though she's taking it easy, I can tell she wants to nap pretty early on. Weird, she wasn't out talking to Florian all that long. Maybe a week of company's tired her out. Next time I'll shorten the trip to a long weekend or something.

There it is again. The idea of coming back. I always sort of assumed this would be a one-time thing. Maybe I'll feel that way again when I get back home.

But here, this morning, it feels weird to think I've only got one more night of cool summer breezes and cicadas. One more morning of waking up to clear sunlight and birdsong.

One more day of Grandma's cooking, her company, and treasure-hunting with Eden.

Eden. Of course, she's on my mind. How can she not be? I've gotten crushes on tourists before, so maybe I shouldn't be making such a big deal about things. But it's never been like this. Maybe it's because I'm the one doing the leaving this time. Then again, maybe it's just because it's Eden. I meant it, back at the treehouse, when I told her I've never met anyone like her before.

I'm going to miss her.

If I'm going to leave, though, I want to leave our time together on a good note. I want it to be something amazing, something Eden will never forget. Something like, for example, finding two treasures in one week.

So when Grandma finally goes down for a nap and I meet Eden at the bridge, my first words to her are, "Let's go back to the cave."

Eden blinks at me, all startled like a cute owl. "Huh?"

"I mean—" Trying to explain my thought process feels too hard, especially when some of those thoughts are honestly too embarrassing to say out loud. "I had a good feeling about it. I want to check there again." I grin. "I've enjoyed the grand tour and all, but I think the cave is the way to go."

"I don't know . . . Why don't we go back to the amphitheater instead?"

I give her my sassiest look. "Is that the one where I'm least likely to fall to my death?"

Eden scowls. Shit, she's serious. "Don't joke about that! I would've felt so bad if . . . if something happened."

"Whoa, hey." I put a hand on her shoulder. She's wearing

a checked dress with thin cloth straps tied at her neck, and her bare shoulders are warm from the sun. "I'm sorry I scared you."

I want to crack a joke or something. But she's taking this seriously, so I guess I have to, too. She looks tired. Hell, did she lose sleep over all that? A pang of guilt curls in my gut.

"Look. Let's go back to the cave." She opens her mouth to argue, and I hold up my hands defensively. "I *promise*, I'll be so careful you won't have to worry about a thing." I still think she's overreacting. But I'll play along if it makes that scared look on her face go away.

"Well . . ."

"I'll stay by your side every second, even if you just wanna stand around and read carvings I can't make sense of." I clap my hands, inspiration striking. "We can even come up with a super-secret hand signal."

"A what?" Eden's lips press together in a tight, trying-not-to-smile line. *Progress.*

"You know, if you do this"—I tap a finger to my nose and shake my head, trying for a stern expression—"I'll know it means, 'Holy shit, Lydia, just sit and chill for a sec.'" Eden hides a little laugh behind her hand, and something like victory flutters in my chest. "Come on. Eden. Eeeeeeden." I shake her shoulder gently.

Eden groans through a smile. "You don't give up, do you?"

"Only when it's boring. And you're anything but boring."

There's a long silence. I consciously fight my urge to fill it. Finally, Eden sighs. "Fine."

I pump a fist in the air in victory. "Hell yeah! Come on!"

Raw anticipation courses through my veins as we make

161

our way to the cave. Have I ever been this excited in my life? Maybe once, when a bunch of us tried to stay in the Art Institute after closing, just to see if we could. Of course, someone chickened out eventually and we all went running, but my heart might have pounded like this while I waited to see if we'd get caught.

This is different, though—better. Because this time we're working toward an actual goal.

The cave entrance is smaller than I remember. It's even easier to miss when it's dry and silent. But it's bigger on the inside, teeming with magic.

I walk to the carvings Eden examined yesterday. "What do they mean?"

"I'm not sure." Eden walks up behind me. "I can make out a few words, but they don't make sense. Either they're in code or a dialect I don't know."

That makes sense, but I can't help but think it's more than that. Now that I'm actually slowing down enough to look at them, they feel like they mean something, like they point in a certain direction.

I drift toward the back. It reminds me of how the forest grabbed my attention when I first got here, only I'm not zoning out this time. There's no singing, no calling, nothing like that. Just understanding. As easy as breathing.

"Lydia?"

Shit. I should've said something to Eden first, before following . . . whatever this is. I promised her. I turn around. "Sorry, sorry."

Eden jogs over to me. "A hand signal doesn't do much if you're not *looking* at me."

"I'm looking at you now, if you wanna do it." I tap a finger to her nose. She swats at it half-heartedly, then breaks, giggling just a little. I bounce on the balls of my feet. "Anyway, now that you're here, I have an idea! Follow me."

Eden looks up at the ledge from yesterday. "The door doesn't have anything to do with the treasure."

"No, I know that. This is something else. I'm following the carvings? I think?"

"Following them?"

"They're like a map. Or arrows. Or something. I can't explain it, but I feel like they're leading me. Don't you?"

Eden shakes her head slowly. "I don't know what you're talking about."

"Well, come with me anyway." I grab her hand. "What do you have to lose? It's not like we have any other leads."

Eden looks at our hands, still clasped together. She hasn't pulled away. At any other time, I'd be reading more into that, but right now I just want to get moving. I know what restless feels like, and this is so much more than that.

Still, I don't want to rush off without Eden. She's been doing this for way longer than me, and she's the one who has to finish it after I leave. She's got more skin in the game than I do.

Finally, she nods. "Okay."

I smile, and she answers it with her own. I pull her along.

The gut feeling leads me back to the twisty pathways. Whenever it forks, I pick the direction immediately, moving on pure gut instinct. And Eden follows. She only stops me once at the first turn, scooping up a rock to mark the wall with a scratch so we can find our way to the exit.

163

I nudge her shoulder. "We make a good team."

"Oh?"

"Yeah. I get us moving. You idiot-proof us."

Eden laughs, shaking her head. "If you say so." But there's something fond in her smile. And the fact that she's laughing at all says a lot. She wouldn't have laughed at that on the day I met her. She might not have even laughed at it before sitting in the treehouse with me.

We're close, and not just because the pathway we're walking through is narrow. Her shoulder keeps brushing mine, and sometimes she reaches up to touch my arm, like she wants to make sure we won't get separated. It's almost as dizzying as whatever is leading me on.

We turn. And I almost run into the stone wall blocking our path.

No. This is wrong. This is supposed to be the right path. I'm so sure of it that I actually press on the wall, like I expect it to move. But it doesn't. This is a dead end, no matter how strong my gut instinct is. I spin on my heel and move back down the paths. Maybe there's a way around this stupid-ass thing.

"Lydia?"

Eden stays at the dead end, palm pressed flat against the cool stone.

"Let's just go. We're not getting through that thing."

"Hold on a second."

She bends to examine the ground. I dance from foot to foot, impatient and annoyed. This isn't what I wanted it to be, and I don't want to sit here and waste time with it. But Eden squints at the ground, frowning.

"Come look at this."

I walk over, not sure what she expects me to see. It's just rock and more rock, the smooth gray of the wall hitting the dusty gray of the ground. "What?"

"It's not all one. See? There's a seam." She brushes her fingertips against the floor, right where it meets the wall.

I blink. She's right. This wall isn't all one piece, naturally grown together like the rest of the path. It's a separate thing, a barrier. Or—

"It's like a door, you think?"

"It could be."

"Then how do we open it?"

Eden frowns, looking around. "That's what we have to figure out."

I look around with her. When it doesn't come to me within the first five seconds, I kind of want to call it off, try something else. But my *something else* is usually gut instinct, which isn't so helpful when said instinct is trying to convince me to walk through solid rock.

Besides, Eden's not moving. And, well, she's the treasure-hunting expert. If she's not ready to give up, I guess I can't, either. I pace around in little circles more than I actually help, though.

Finally, I can't take it anymore. "Eden—"

"Lydia, come look."

Her tone stops my complaining cold. I walk over to where she's standing.

There are carvings in the stone. They're so light they'd been basically filled in by dust, but as Eden wipes her hand across the stone, they become more legible. My heart shoots up into my throat as I rush to help her, using the bottom of my T-shirt to reveal more carvings.

"Eden, they're like the ones at the entrance!"

"You can feel what they're saying?"

"I think so? It's like . . ." I tap the carvings with my fingertips, as easy as pressing buttons on a video game. The stones rumble. The door slides up.

It reveals a wide chamber with only a single rock table sitting in the middle. The treasure floats above it.

Eden lets out a strangled gasp and darts forward. Part of me sort of expects a giant boulder to come out or something, but I guess fae treasures aren't into booby traps. Eden grabs the stick from the air with no trouble.

I rush in after her, peering over her shoulder. "Holy shit, Eden!"

She turns to me. I don't think I've ever seen her smile so wide. "You did it!"

"Uh, no, *you* definitely did it. I was ready to give up way before you found those carvings." I acted on instinct. Eden was the one who stuck around even when the answers stopped being obvious.

Eden smiles at me, and it sets off something soft and fluttery in the base of my spine. "Well. We *do* make a good team."

And because I don't know what to do with these soft, fond feelings, I fling my arms around Eden's neck in what is probably more tackle than hug.

"Lydia!" She snorts out a laugh, nearly falling over. But then she's spinning, and soon we're both stumbling around in what aren't quite dancing circles, like a weird clingy version of when dogs get so excited they can't stand still. We *did* it. We found the treasure. Now, there's only one more to go.

Which reminds me: the treasure has carvings like the last one. I tug us to a stop, swatting tiny little hummingbird pats at Eden's arm. "Well? What's it say?"

Eden scans the treasure, twirling it in her hands to read it. Her grin fades as her brow furrows in concentration. "It says . . . It says the journey—the search?—ends. The final treasure can be captured . . . No, can be *won* . . ." She squints, lips pressing together in a thin line for a long moment before she finishes. "The final treasure can be won in Fierborne."

"Fierborne? What the hell is that?"

Eden frowns. "Give me time to think about it."

We're mostly quiet as we walk back through the twisting path, following Eden's scratched-out directions. I keep trying to figure out what Fierborne could mean, but I'm not the one who is familiar with this stuff.

Finally, when we get outside again, Eden turns to me and smiles. "Listen, Lydia. Let's not worry about this right now."

"Huh?" It's probably the last response I'm expecting. "What do you mean?"

"You're leaving tomorrow, right?" She looks off into the trees. "I don't want us to spend our last day just . . . sitting around researching. You wouldn't like that, would you?"

"Well . . ." No, that sounds like hell, actually. I try for the most honest answer I can. "I want to help!"

"You have. You've helped me find two treasures this week. That's huge. So I'd rather show you something special." She leans toward me, her eyes sparkling. "Can you come back to the forest tonight?"

"What?"

"After dark. I'll be waiting for you by the bridge. I have something really cool to show you." She takes my hands, and my heart goes ahead and does a backflip under my stomach. "Will you come?"

I'd probably agree to commit arson for her. "Yeah. Yeah! Okay."

Eden looks down at our hands. Her hair covers her face, but I'm pretty sure she's smiling. "Good. I'm glad."

19

IS THIS A DATE???

Eden and I head back to the bridge. I don't want to stay later and get Grandma worried, and Eden says she wants to get stuff set up for tonight. Which, of course, makes it so I can't think about anything else. All through dinner, I wonder just what the hell Eden is planning.

Finally, once Grandma goes to bed, I head up to my bedroom and sit in front of my suitcase. I guess I could wear the same overalls and T-shirt I'm wearing now. But she saw me in this outfit earlier today. And it sort of feels like this requires a change?

I'm overthinking the clothes. Probably because I'm overthinking what this is.

Eden didn't say it was a date. But, well, she didn't say it wasn't. And when a girl who explicitly likes girls holds my hand and asks me to meet her for a literal moonlit rendezvous, I think I'm at least a little entitled to wonder.

There's more to it than that, anyway. Like the way she looks at me sometimes. And now that I think about it, maybe sometimes her touches last a little longer than they need to. Plus, there's the afternoon in the treehouse to think about. None of that felt like an average *just-gals-being-pals* hangout session.

But I'm not an idiot. Maybe I'm reading into things too much, Eden doesn't see me as anything more than a friend, and this is just her way of platonically sending me off. Even if it isn't, does it matter? I get attached fast, but I get unattached just as fast. Shouldn't I focus on the moment and not get so caught up in what it means?

The answer is yes. But I still change into black shorts and a white top that ties at the back of my neck, which is probably the nicest outfit I packed. Also, I make an actual attempt at makeup, using the eyeliner that makes my blue eyes pop.

I stick with my combat boots, since they go with the outfit and I'm capable of being practical every once in a while. But because I can't be too practical, I climb down the trellis instead of going out the front door. Yeah, okay, I don't think Grandma really cares if I go out past dark, but pretending to sneak out like my mom used to do is fun. Sue me.

Silver stars are just starting to blink to life against the purple sky. The trees beyond the bridge seem to actually be breathing, swaying in the moonlight. I bet they'll look even prettier once I get over the bridge.

They do, but I don't really give a shit. Because Eden waits right on the other side for me, and she's prettier than anything

170

else the forest can offer.

The moonlight frames her in a soft glow, landing silver on her dark hair. Her shoulders are bare in a pale blue dress with cream lace scalloping the hem and forming a thick band around her waist. She has a few small white flowers tucked behind one ear. Her dark eyes reflect the rippling water at her feet as she looks up and smiles at me.

My heart doesn't quite skip a beat, but it does stutter, and I'm pretty sure my brain crashes for half a second. I scoop my metaphorical jaw off the floor and cross the bridge to meet her.

"You look really pretty," is the first thing out of my mouth, because I have absolutely no filter.

Thankfully, Eden keeps smiling. "Thank you. So do you." Before I can go down the spiraling rabbit hole of trying to analyze that, she offers me her hand. "Are you ready?"

This time, there's no rain to use as an excuse. It's dark, but not so dark that we can't see each other. She's reaching out because she wants to. I might die right here on the spot. What a way to go.

Instead, I lace our fingers together, trying my absolute best to play it cool. "Born ready."

Eden laughs. "Come on." And she tugs me deeper into the forest.

The trees greet me like an old friend. The sense of the forest as a living, breathing thing is stronger than ever. It's almost like a chorus. Or a band. The trees, stream, and cicada noises harmonize to the drumbeat of our footsteps. I even imagine I can hear singing, barely carried on the wind.

"It's really beautiful here," I say.

"It is. Sometimes I forget, since I see it so often. Having you here is a good reminder." Eden shakes her head, smiling. "Like tonight, for example. This time of year is special."

"Really? How?"

"Well, it's almost the summer solstice." Eden leads me off the forest path and through the trees, her footsteps confident and sure. "The actual night is a good time to stay in, because it's one of a few times every year where the spell that separates the fae world and ours is weak. The faeries can't get out, but humans can go in, and it's possible to get tricked if you don't know better."

"Oh, shit." Honestly, that feels like the understatement of the century, but I don't know what else to say.

Eden looks at me and smiles, soft in a way that's so cute I want to scream. "But that's not until Saturday. In the days leading up to it, there's no danger of seeing anything tricky or scary. Instead . . . Well, you'll see."

I might detonate on the spot if she keeps looking at me like that. Part of me wants to make a move, because she's throwing out more signals than a cell tower. But I'm a little terrified I'm reading into it too much. This is our last adventure together, and I don't want to screw it up.

I just say, "I'm excited to see." But I don't let go of her hand.

She smiles, gentle in the moonlight. "Good. Because here we are."

At first I don't get it. All I can see are skinny trees barely far enough apart to walk through, their branches high above our heads. But wedged between two of them is a red blanket smoothed across the grass, making a cozy little nook. Eden sits down, curling her long legs under her, and pats the empty space at her side.

She doesn't have to tell me twice. I plop down next to her. It's a small space—ridiculously small. We basically have no choice but to sit with our thighs smooshed together. Every time she breathes, her bare shoulder brushes mine.

It feels like someone ripped out my spine and replaced it with a live wire. All I can think about is how close she is, how easy it would be to grab her hand or her face or—

I take a deep breath. "What—"

"Shhhh." Eden tilts her head up to the sky, leaning her weight back on her palms. Moonlight filters through the trees, pools in the hollow of her throat and curls around her collarbone, and suddenly I sort of understand what all those poets and musicians write about. "Listen."

I do.

The forest is singing.

It's way more than an echo now. There's a high, clear sound like a bell coming from about five feet in front of us, where a door like the one I saw in the cave sits. The singing comes from the other side. I can't see through it, but I get a sense of light. Light and *waiting*. Something is going to happen.

In my dream, stars fell from the sky. In real life, they flow from the door.

They teem around us like fireflies, only silver and *singing*. They don't sound human, and they aren't singing words. Instead, they chime in a language I don't understand but feel my heart respond to anyway.

Am I still dreaming? That's how perfect this is, but I could never make all of this up. Not the fresh earth smell, not the summer air in my lungs. And definitely not the warmth of Eden beside me.

I turn to face her. The light plays across her face in patterns. "What is this?"

"It happens the few nights before solstices, equinoxes, and similar dates. I call them starflies." She pushes her hair out of her face. "Do you like them?"

Our thighs are still pressed together. At some point, we started holding hands. And Eden's face is maybe an inch from mine.

"Eden," I say carefully, more carefully than anything I've ever said in my life. "This is amazing. Probably the most romantic thing anyone's ever done for me."

I say it light and joking, leaving her an out if she wants it. But she doesn't pull away. She just cocks her head to the side, smiling. "Oh?"

"Yeah." That's it. Enough hesitation. Why keep dropping hints when I can lob a tactical nuke? "I could kiss you right now."

Silence stretches between us for so long I might crawl out of my skin. With the shifting light from the starflies, I can't read Eden's expression. When she finally speaks, it's almost too quiet to hear.

"Then why don't you?"

I feel as breathless as I did the moment I met her, but this time there's no accidental cliff dive to blame it on. I know if I take too long to think about it, I'll screw it up somehow. So I don't. I do what I always do, and I *act*.

Which, in this case, means closing the distance between

us and pressing my lips to hers.

It takes a second for her to respond. But then, all at once, she's leaning into me, pressing a palm to my cheek, gripping the arm I wrap around her waist. Her hair gets in the way for a second, and when I push it back, she lets out a breathless little giggle right into my mouth and it's maybe the best thing that's ever happened to me in my life.

I've kissed a few people before, and every kiss is special. But kissing Eden is *special*. Part of it might be the starflies and part of it might be how incredible this week has been, but most of it is just Eden. I can't get over how warm she is. Or how soft. I want to run my fingers through her hair forever. My head spins and I might pass out because I don't want to break apart from her for even a second, not even to breathe.

It is, without a doubt, the perfect memory to leave with. I couldn't ask for a better one. There's only one problem: I don't want things to end like this.

I want more.

"Eden," I blurt when we break apart. "Let's be pen pals."

This is, maybe, not the most romantic thing to say. Eden laughs, half confused and half amused. "What?"

"I mean—" I laugh, too, still giddy and high from the kiss. "I'm going home tomorrow. And I know you don't have a phone, but I can write letters! I can get your address—"

"That's . . . complicated." Eden looks off, frowning. Like something is wrong, like she's closing off again.

My gut twists. This isn't the reaction I expected. This isn't the reaction I *wanted*. I hurry on, like if I say enough words I can make her smile at me again. "Well, fine. Maybe I can send letters to Grandma and she can leave them on the bridge for you? And then when I come to visit again—"

"What?"

The raw panic in Eden's voice hits me like a lightning bolt. I jerk away, my back bumping up against a tree. This isn't right. Things were going so well a second ago and I don't get why they're suddenly not. "Well, yeah. I can come back and help with the treasure hunt and—"

"No."

"What?"

"I don't *want* you to come back and help!"

"*What?*" My emotions swirl, a vortex of bad. I catch a thread of anger and cling to it because I'm pretty sure the alternative is bursting into tears. "What the hell, Eden? Why'd you kiss me, then?"

"I . . . I was having fun." Her voice is quiet. "I just wanted one more night of fun with you. I just . . . wanted to try."

"What's that supposed to mean?" Eden starts to answer, but I cut her off. My chest burns and my heart pounds, and whatever she's going to say, I don't actually want to hear it. "What was all this, huh? Am I just some sort of game to you? Something to get out of your system?"

Eden opens her mouth, then closes it into a tight line. She looks away. She doesn't say I'm wrong.

Slapping me would've hurt less. My voice wavers, caught somewhere between anger and hurt. "What about Chicago? Navy Pier?"

Eden sighs. She doesn't even have the decency to look me in the eyes. "You and I both know you weren't serious about that, Lydia."

And she's right. I wasn't. But I wanted to be. And I

wanted Eden to be serious about us, too, the way she's serious about other things.

Maybe I'm just not the kind of person anyone can be serious about.

It's too much. It's all too much. It went so bad so *fast*, and staying here any longer can only make it worse. So I scramble to my feet. Eden doesn't try to stop me or call me back. I run off, aching with the rejection I don't get close enough to people to feel.

20

That's it. I'm done. I'm exiting stage goddamn left.

Part of me expects to get lost in the forest—it would be the cherry on top of the shit sundae this evening turned into. But I get to the bridge quicker than I expected. Maybe even the magic forest recognizes how pathetically I got rejected and gave me a pity win.

I walk through the front door. It's still dark, but I don't have the energy to care about being sneaky. It doesn't matter anyway. The house is quiet, and upstairs, the sound of Grandma's even breathing drifts from her room. I scrub the makeup off my face and throw my nice clothes on the floor in a messy pile.

Even once I settle into bed, I'm too angry to sleep. I spend most of the night scrolling through pictures of home.

It'll be better there. I'll be able to forget all about Eden, and this ache in my chest won't be so bad once I'm surrounded by distractions. I close my eyes sometime around when the sky starts to lighten, imagining skyscrapers and constant noise and endless possibilities.

When I wake up, the sunlight streaming through the window is way too bright. I check the time and swear. Mom's going to be here in an hour, maybe less. It's probably shitty that I didn't spend my last morning with Grandma. She's the one I came here to see, after all. I let Eden complicate everything.

As if summoned, Grandma passes by my room, smiling when she sees I'm awake. "I was just about to come wake you if you weren't already up."

"Yeah. Sorry." I scrub gunk from my eyes and try not to scowl too hard.

Grandma shakes her head. "Oh, don't worry about it, dear. You must have had a late night." She realized, then, that I snuck out. Her tone is light and teasing. If Eden and I had just ended it on that kiss, if I hadn't gotten so dumbly attached, I'd be rolling my eyes and joking back.

Instead, I'm horrified to find myself near tears. I never cry. I'm not about to start now. Not over Eden. Where does she get off, anyway, making me care this much? I don't care. I've known her for a week. She shouldn't be this important to me.

"Yeah. It was bullshit." I pretend the roughness in my voice is anger.

Grandma frowns. "Oh?" She pauses, maybe giving me a chance to fill the silence. But before I can even figure out what to say, she just shakes her head. "Well. I'll make you some tea."

She walks away, and I start shoving stuff into my suitcase.

I try not to think of Eden. It should be easy. I'm usually good at forgetting people who piss me off. If they're not fun anymore, they don't matter. That's how it always is. That's how it was with Olivia, who I actually literally dated. Why is Eden so different?

I never expected that Eden wouldn't want me around. I wanted her to miss me, at least a little. But she didn't. The idea of seeing me again disgusted her, if the panic in her eyes was any sort of indication. Just thinking about it makes my gut twist.

Once I'm packed and dressed in my most comfortable pair of travel shorts, I head downstairs. As promised, a mug of tea waits for me on the counter, and Grandma is putting cookies in the oven. She smiles. "I thought you might want some treats for the road."

"Thanks."

I sip at my tea. The kitchen is too quiet. This is the point where I should be telling Grandma how glad I am that I came to visit. If Eden hadn't been so awful, I could even tell her I hoped to come back. But none of that is true now.

There's one thing that is, though. "I had a lot of fun with you this week, Grandma."

Grandma pats my head, tucking a curl behind my ear. Mom likes to do the same thing. The reminder aches a little. "Oh, sweetheart. I'm so glad you came to visit."

This is what I'm going to hang onto, I decide. Family's the most important thing, and if I focus on that, all the rest of this shit will fade away. I congratulate myself on this very mature decision, which has nothing to do with petty heartbreak–related reasons.

I wonder how much Grandma's buying it, because she keeps looking at me sidelong as she moves around the kitchen. "About your friend . . ."

"That's over." I don't mean to snap, but the anger comes out anyway. "It was never going to last longer than this week, anyway."

"Well." There's a long pause. Finally, Grandma sighs. "I'll keep an ear out for you. I'm sure Florian will let me know if she wants to see you again. He has a way."

I wrap my hands around the mug. "That's *not* going to happen." Eden made that crystal clear.

Grandma doesn't say anything more, which I appreciate. Maybe she's just not into talking about heavy things. I can relate. Mom and I can talk about shit, but it's because we don't take it seriously. Hell, maybe that's why she lied about magic.

Remembering that gets my guts twisting for a whole other reason. "Grandma, I don't know if I can keep lying to Mom about what I know."

Grandma puts a hand on my shoulder. The weight is comforting. "She might not like to hear what you have to say . . . but she had to know the risk, letting you come here." Fondness crinkles the corners of her eyes. "We Barnes women have a way of getting into trouble."

And in spite of the dark thundercloud of rejection hanging over my head, I smile. It's not an answer to my problems or anything, but I can't expect Grandma to give me that. She just wanted a fun week with her granddaughter, not all this.

The window's open, so I hear the engine as Mom pulls up

the long, winding driveway. It's weird. Once I get back to Chicago, I'll be hearing cars all the time, and one driving up the dirt won't make any difference.

I'll put all this behind me there, find someone hot to kiss who won't give me mixed signals. Maybe I'll just forget that magic ever existed. I'll convince myself it was all some weird hoax or dream or something. That sounds simpler.

Mom walks in, and she looks so *familiar*—casual in dark jeans and a beige blouse, her chestnut hair a little messy from the way she plays with it while she drives. I launch myself into her arms, not caring about magic and lies. I just don't want it to matter anymore.

Mom laughs, stumbling backward as she wraps her arms around me. "Whoa! Hey there, doll." Her voice is scratchy and fond, so much warmer than over the phone. "Miss me much?"

I smile, some of the thorns around my chest loosening. I'm pleased when my voice comes out matching hers, like nothing is wrong. "Yeah, yeah. Don't let it go to your head."

Mom ruffles my curls, grinning as she nods to my suitcase by the door. "You're set to go already? I'm surprised you're not dragging your feet a bit more. Did you get to say goodbye to Eden?"

The name prickles in my chest, but I grit my teeth, rolling my eyes like I would over any petty fight. "Don't even get me started." It comes out just how I want it, annoyed but careless, angry but not upset. But I don't feel any of the emotions I'm supposed to feel.

Anger is easy and uncomplicated and unimportant. It's what I want, but my actual emotions feel too big for my chest. My voice hits all the right notes, but inside, I'm a yawning pit.

I wonder if I'll ever stop falling.

Mom might notice that something's wrong. Her eyebrows do that scrunchy thing they do sometimes. But luckily, she doesn't call me out on it. "Looks like I'll be getting a story on the ride home, huh?" She grabs my suitcase. "I'll get this packed up while you say goodbye." Her eyes dart to Grandma. "Mom. Sorry I can't stay. You know how it is."

Grandma nods. "Of course."

They had almost the same conversation at the beginning of the week. I didn't understand it then.

Mom heads out, and Grandma and I are alone in the bright kitchen. Before, it felt homey, but now it just feels too unfamiliar, like a movie set.

"I hope . . ." Grandma sighs, then smiles. "It was lovely to have you, dear."

"Yeah." There's a beat of silence. I'm supposed to say, *I'll be seeing you*, promising to visit her again. But I don't have that in me. "Love you, Grandma."

I hug her. She's solid and warm and I try not to think about the fact that this might be the last time I do this. Grandma can't visit Chicago and I'm not sure I can come back and stare down at that forest night after night.

It's too much. I break the hug and leave the house as quick as I can.

Mom raises an eyebrow when she sees me. Maybe she expected me to take longer. "Ready to go?"

"God, yeah." I roll my eyes. "Grandma is really nice and I love her, but I'm, like, so over this place. I'm pretty sure if I've gotta hang around here for one more second I'm gonna lose it." It's true. It's so true, but I don't know if I'll ever be able to tell Mom why.

She laughs, opening the driver's side door. "Poor kiddo. You did a good thing, though."

"Yeah." I should say something more as I get into the passenger seat, something about how I have no regrets, how coming here was worth it to make Grandma happy. But I don't say anything. Mom either catches my mood or is waiting for me to start the conversation, because she's quiet, too. She doesn't even turn on the radio. It's silent as we roll down the driveway, dirt crunching under the wheels of the car as we make our way out of Fairbrooke.

Out of Fairbrooke. I'm not sure what it makes me feel. You know how when you mix too many colors together, it turns into a mushy brown? That's what my emotions are doing.

I squeeze my eyes shut, like this will be easier if I can't see the trees rolling past my window. *I don't care, it doesn't matter, I don't care.* I repeat it like a mantra, but that doesn't make it true.

My brain feels like buzzing static, but my body is on overdrive. My heart races and my head pounds and I want to *scream*, to blurt the entire story out to Mom. The words pulse against my throat like they're going to rip through my skin.

"Doll?" Mom asks.

Inside me, something jolts.

Except it's not inside at all. The car is shaking. Mom lets out a string of swear words as she pulls off to the side of the road, slowing to a boneless stop. The brakes aren't working. The gas isn't working. When I open my eyes, it's to a dead dashboard and smoke curling up the windshield.

I should be feeling something, but there's still that yawning emptiness of too much emotion. I get out of the car, feeling like I'm in a dream as Mom pops the hood, waving smoke away from her face, still swearing up a storm. Slowly, I turn around.

We're right on the edge of the woods. Tree branches reach in our direction like beckoning fingers. It's like the rustling leaves are telling me they aren't done with me yet.

I have just one question: what the hell?

"Jesus, what'd you *do* to this thing?"

The mechanic gawks at our engine, stained trucker cap tucked under one arm. Mom grimaces before smoothing out her expression. "I didn't do anything." The distress in her voice is so quiet only I could notice it.

I hear all this, see all this, but part of me feels a million miles away. Or, more accurately, ten feet away, where the forest sits. The mechanic towed Mom's car back to Grandma's driveway, and now the trees loom in my peripheral vision. I pace up and down the driveway, past the car and Mom and Grandma hovering in her doorway. It doesn't matter where I turn. The forest is always there.

"*This* doesn't happen for no reason." The mechanic jerks a thumb toward the engine. "Jesus H. Christ, the whole thing is—"

"Forget why it happened." I stop pacing, whirling on him. "Focus on how to fix it."

The mechanic glares at me, but I'm so beyond giving a single shit. *Let* him argue with me—let him try. I'm almost disappointed when he turns back to the car. "I'm gonna need to call in some parts. I got a guy. He'll get 'em to me as quick as possible. But they won't be here until tomorrow."

Mom groans. "You can't do it any sooner?"

He shoots her a dark look. "You think we want you sticking around?"

I get right up in his face, pettily satisfied when he stumbles back against the car. "Watch it, asshole!"

Mom puts a hand on my shoulder. "Easy, doll. It's fine." But her voice is tense, and her hand shakes a little. She's never exactly been great about putting on a brave face for my sake. We don't lie to each other; we're too close for that.

At least I thought we were.

The mechanic scoffs. "Fine? You think this is fine? Everything's gone to hell in a handbasket, and we both know who's to blame."

"I don't know what you're—"

"They're *waking up*, Charlotte."

The words make no sense. So why does the blood rush from Mom's face like that? She actually sways on her feet, and she doesn't react when I grab her arm.

"What?" Her voice is as quiet as the wind.

"Eric, don't," Grandma pleads, but Mom shoots her a look

that stops her cold. Then she turns back to the mechanic, putting on her professional *take-no-shit* face.

"Tell me."

Eric crosses his arms over his chest. "Tim and Gina scanned the forest on Wednesday. The magic has shifted. They're starting to move. And the only thing different is your kid running around in there."

Shit.

Shit.

Shit.

I step away from Mom just in time for her to whirl on me. "You've *been* in the *forest*?"

The betrayal in her voice makes guilt twist in my gut. But the anger in my chest burns more. "Yeah, but you didn't tell me magic is real, so I think we're even."

Now it's Grandma who Mom spins to face. "What did you tell her?"

"Nothing." Grandma holds out her hands, palms up. "She walked into the forest on her own, and whatever she found out, she didn't find out from me. I kept my promise, dear."

Eric, apparently sensing epic family drama, inches back toward his truck. "It's all them," he murmurs. "You didn't even—" He cuts himself off and turns to Grandma. "Don't bother coming to the next meeting. We've got decisions to make without you." He jumps in his truck and starts down the driveway, clouds of dust under his wheels.

Grandma presses a hand to her mouth, eyes glassy and upset. Mom's even worse. "I can't believe you!" I'm not actually sure which one of us she's talking to. I'm the one who speaks.

"What did he mean about . . . waking up?"

Mom stares me down, more pissed than I've ever seen her. "Forget it. Forget everything about that place, Lydia. I don't know what you saw in there, what lies you heard, but the forest is bad. It's dangerous."

"That's not true, dear." Grandma's weak protests stop when Mom glares at her.

"You *can't* just pretend nothing happened and everything's fine! You always want to—to—*ugh*!" She stomps a foot, looking for a moment like the angry teen this place turned her into. Then she storms into the house.

I turn to Grandma. "You're not going to tell me a single goddamned thing about what this is all about, are you?"

"I made a promise." Grandma looks down. "I'm sorry."

"Fine." That's all I have in me—no argument, no fire. Just determination, the same sort Eden uses in her treasure hunt.

I run to the forest.

"Lydia!" Grandma's voice echoes after me, but I don't care. If I'm going to find answers anywhere, it's here. And maybe I shouldn't care. Maybe Mom is right and the forest is dangerous. Maybe whatever's waking up wants to hurt me.

But everything's been weird since the starfly disaster. It keeps getting weirder, and part of me worries it won't just go back to normal when I get home. I need answers.

When I cross the bridge, I don't have a plan. I don't know anything about anyone awakening. Or do I? I remember the figure covered in vines, the one Eden said was a statue. But she lied about a lot of things. And I swore I saw its eyes open.

It's oddly easy to retrace my steps, even without Eden guiding me. The figure is still there, still covered in vines. I

189

step off the path and crash through the trees, loud enough to wake the dead. The figure doesn't stir.

But it's *not* a statue. It's a person. They're so grown over with moss and vines they're practically fused to the tree. The parts of their face that do stick out are weather-beaten, but that's definitely skin. And their chest rises and falls beneath the vines, their lips barely moving with even breaths.

My stomach and heart swap places, the trees wavering in my vision. I grab a branch to keep from keeling over. "What the *hell*?"

The person's eyes flutter, and their face twists. "Too soon." Their voice is barely there. "Why . . ." They sigh and go still again.

I stare. And stare. And keep staring. I want to scream in their face, want to rip the vines and the moss away with my bare hands, want to get my answers even if I have to claw them from this sleeping person's throat myself.

"Causing mischief, young Lydia?"

A scream builds in my chest, but the breath gets snarled in my ribs before I can voice it. I spin around. Florian stands among the trees, his lanky shadow stretching across the ground.

"Hi, hello, what the *hell* is this shit?" I gesture at the sleeping figure wildly.

Florian smiles. The light of the setting sun is bright orange, reflecting amber in his dark eyes. "Oh, I don't know if I should say. Your grandmother wanted—"

"Screw what she wants. Screw what *everyone* wants. *I* want answers." I stalk right up to him, jabbing a finger in his chest. "The only thing I know is that everyone's been lying to me. There's more going on here than just a treasure hunt and I want to know what it is!"

Florian leans against a tree. "Ah, yes. The treasure hunt. Did you ever wonder, young Lydia, what the staff does?"

"Fae magic?"

"Fae magic indeed."

I wait, but he doesn't say anything else. "Florian, if you don't tell me everything, so help me, I'll—"

Florian cuts me off with his booming laugh. "I like you, young Lydia! Such fire. Nothing's been the same since you arrived. I've been around long enough to know how rare that is." He pats a tree stump. "Sit down, young one. Let me tell you a story."

Part of me wants to snap, but if this is how he's going to give me answers, I don't have a choice. I plop down, foot jiggling impatiently before I even settle into the seat.

Florian smiles. "This forest is special. Surely you know that. You've seen towering stones and endless caves, places that seem impossible from the outside. You've heard birdsong and insects, although neither inhabit this space. But do you understand why? This isn't the fae world, after all, so why is it like this?"

"How the hell am I supposed to know?"

"A fair question, young Lydia!" Florian laughs. "It all began during the war. The humans devised a spell that was more powerful than even fae magic, you see, one that would trap the faeries in their own world forever. My kin learned of this early, and when they discovered there was nothing they could do to stop it, they *raged*. If they were to be trapped forever, they decided not to go quietly. No, they would take as many humans into the fae world with them as possible, turning them immortal to trap them there for an eternity of torment far worse than what any had experienced before."

I shiver. Florian continues.

"Of course, I didn't much like the idea of that. My lover's brother would have been one of the ones captured, and he would have been *so* distressed. But the spell to trap them was already set in motion. There was nothing I could do to stop it."

"What did you do?" I'm almost afraid of the answer, for some reason.

Florian leans forward, a conspiratorial air about him. "I stole the staff, imbibed with fae magic, that would trap the humans."

"That's what the staff is used for? Trapping people?" What the hell would Eden want with something like that?

But Florian shakes his head. "Trapping humans *or* freeing them. But I couldn't free them when the spell to trap them was already started. What I could do, however, was redirect the magic to trap them here instead—in a forest of my own making, safe from the rest of my kind. But creating that forest was too complex for the staff. It shattered once I finished the spell." He shakes his head. "It was an imperfect solution. The humans were still trapped here. They were still immortal. But at least they were out of reach of the other faeries and within reach of their loved ones in Fairbrooke."

"You're telling me . . . Wait—" A thousand thoughts clog my brain. "That's an immortal person." I point to the person sleeping on the ground. "And Eden . . ." My gut drops to somewhere around my ankles. If Eden is hundreds of years old, that puts several things in perspective.

"Ah, Eden. She is a special case."

"Special *how*?"

Florian smiles. "Relationships between immortals were nothing new. They were always careful, but careful only goes so far. A couple became pregnant, and for a while, it was the talk of the town. Would the child be immortal like them? Would they be able to leave the forest? Even I couldn't have told them for sure."

I don't say a word. I can guess where this is going, but I want—need—to hear Florian say it. Finally, he does.

"As it so happens, it wound up being no to both. The child aged at the rate of a normal babe—but she couldn't leave the forest."

"Eden's *trapped* in here?" Even after everything I learned from Florian's story, this knocks the wind out of me.

"Oh, yes. And her parents, well . . . they'd made peace with their lot in life. But the idea of their daughter living and dying without ever once leaving the forest? They made it their mission to discover a way to free her—and after months of searching, they discovered the first piece of the staff." Awe seeps into his tone. "Amazing. I'd assumed we'd lost the staff forever. But somehow they managed it—complete with instructions to find the next piece! Fae magic can surprise even those of us who wield it."

If I'm being honest, I couldn't give two shits about how mysterious the magic is. "What happened to Eden's parents?" Even in the summer warmth, a chill creeps up my spine.

Florian shakes his head sadly, but his eyes still glitter with joking light. "It's tragic, truly. They were doing so well. They found treasure after treasure. But one gave them trouble. They couldn't figure it out." He leans forward. "Eden's mother became convinced the treasure was in the fae world. She slipped in while the veil was thin. And a year later, motivated by grief or belief that his wife was right, her father followed. They're both certainly dead—faeries don't play kindly with their toys."

I knew Eden's parents were dead. But *killed*? Like *that*? It's too much. "No."

"Oh, yes. And then, the most tragic part? A month later, dear young Eden found that treasure all on her own. Her parents sacrificed themselves for nothing."

I'm reeling. Everything I know about Eden changes with this new information. How much of her determination was desperation? How much of her carefulness was fear?

How much of her liking me was just plain loneliness?

"It's a shame." Florian sighs. "Once I knew to look for it, I felt that the treasure was still in my forest, although I couldn't sense where. But they were so *sure*."

My head snaps up. I'm still processing everything, but these words stick in a way the rest of them didn't. "Then why didn't you tell them?"

Florian shrugs. "Watching them search is the most fun I've had in years, young Lydia! I was on the edge of my seat, seeing what they'd do, what Eden would do. She's held up admirably. And then there's you, of course." He taps a fingertip to my nose, laughing when I jerk away from him. "Two treasures in one week! What a marvel you are."

"But those were Eden's parents! You could have saved them and you didn't!" The way he talks, he doesn't sound all that different from the faeries in stories, the ones who saw humans as toys.

"Look at it from my point of view, young Lydia." He smiles, weirdly gentle. "I have no hope of ever leaving this forest, even if the humans manage it. And I've been here for over a hundred years. If you were the one trapped here with the same people, what would you do?"

And the worst part is, I understand. What he's describing sounds like my own personal version of hell. But that doesn't mean I'd make his choices. I refuse to believe that.

I open my mouth to tell him as much, but then Mom's voice echoes across the forest. "Lydia!"

I look away for just a moment. When I turn back, Florian is gone. I'm alone with the sleeping figure and a chest full of rage.

Can we stop the ride? I want to get off.

I don't know how to talk to Mom about this.

I want to try the second I head back to the bridge. But she's shaking and her eyes are glassy and she just looks so vulnerable in a way I've never seen before, so I hold off. And then I keep holding off. What am I supposed to say?

I love her. And I'm angry at her. And I feel guilty for scaring her. And I'm nervous, because we don't talk about stuff like this, stuff this deep. I know how to joke with her, how to hang out with her, how to get her to go along with my stupid plans. But I don't know how to talk about something like this.

Mostly, I'm scared.

I'm scared about what all this means. I'm scared that we're still in Fairbrooke when we should be home. I'm scared that if

I let it, this place is going to ruin Mom and me forever, that I'm never going to be able to joke with her again.

I lie on the couch that night, desperately trying to sleep, because the sooner I go to sleep, the sooner I can leave all this behind. I thought getting answers would help, but I only feel worse, knowing what I know now.

Eden's trapped in that forest. Her parents died trying to free her. And there are other people, sleeping just like the figure fused to the tree. Why are those people sleeping? Why were Eden and her parents awake? And what does any of this have to do with Mom—with me?

I want to forget it. But I can't. I roll around on the couch until I fall off, thumping to the floor in a tangle of blankets and swear words. Sleeping is a lost cause. Now that I've opened this up, now that I started, I need to keep going. It doesn't matter that I'm scared.

I walk up the stairs as quietly as I can. Grandma's asleep in her room, but the guest room—Mom's old room—is silent. I push open the door.

From the looks of it, Mom couldn't sleep, either. The closet is open, books and clothes strewn about the floor. Shreds of paper add to the mess. They're a distinct yellow color—she tore up Xavier's letter.

The bed is empty, but the window is open. It doesn't exactly take a genius to figure out where she's gone. I take a deep breath and clamber onto the roof.

Mom sits there, her face bathed in moonlight as she stares at the stars. She doesn't turn when the tiles rattle beneath my weight. I sit next to her with my knees curled to my chest and try not to choke on the silence.

When she breaks it, her voice is soft. "I never knew how to tell you. I wanted to. I wanted to be able to tell you in a way you'd understand. But I could never find the words. I couldn't . . ." A quiet noise escapes her lips, and she swipes at her dry eyes. "I thought it would be better if you never knew—so you'd never ask questions I couldn't answer." She finally looks at me. "You must think I'm awful."

"I . . ." I shake my head. Cicadas buzz while I gather my thoughts. "I'm just so confused, Mom. I've spent the past week looking for treasure with Eden, and now I'm finding out that the stakes are so much higher and I don't understand why she lied to me about it. I don't understand why *you* lied to me about it."

I try not to sound bitter. I love Mom more than anything, and I don't want to be unfair to her. But finding out that she lied stings. I've always trusted her so much. I thought she trusted me, too.

Mom goes back to staring at the sky. "What do you know? About the forest."

"Well, it's got a bunch of people trapped in it." I jiggle my foot, hands curling into fists against the rough tile. "They're asleep. And immortal. All except for Eden, I guess." I glance at her, gut twisting unhappily. "She *is* trapped in the forest, though."

Mom nods slowly. "That makes sense. I didn't know her name, but I remember when she was born. That was only a little bit before . . ." She sighs. "Lydia. I don't think you want to hear this."

"I don't, either." I don't want to know what makes her eyes look like that. I want her to be the same Mom she's always

198

been. "But I don't think that matters. I need to know."

Mom sighs, then nods. She stares at the forest, her gaze distant and sad. "I always hated this place. That much is true. I was one of the only ones without magic, and everyone else looked down at me for it. Everyone but him."

"Xavier," I guess, then clap my hand over my mouth. Mom gives me a startled look. "I found the letter in your closet. I didn't mean to snoop. I just missed you."

Mom stares down at her lap, running her palms across her jeans. "I was your age when we met. He was trapped in that forest, and I knew he was much older than he looked. He was . . . Well, okay, he had an ego the size of Texas and an even bigger dramatic streak. His favorite thing to do was outsmart me." She shakes her head. "But he was fun. I had fun with him. He made me laugh and held me close and called me his magnificent creature. I felt *mature,* knowing that I interested someone as old and smart as him. For the first time, I felt like someone was seeing me."

I have ideas about where this is going, and I like none of them. But I stay quiet as Mom continues.

"I didn't love him. Not like that. But eventually things . . . happened. I wanted them to happen, but . . ." Mom turns to me. The love in her eyes is almost painful. "I'm sorry, sweetheart. I never wanted you to think . . . I never regretted having you, not for a day, not even for a second. You're the best thing in my life."

She just looks so fragile. I want to climb into her lap like I used to when I was little, want to wrap my arms around her. Here on the roof, all I can do is take her hand. "What happened?"

"When I found out I was pregnant . . . I *knew* you wouldn't have magic, and I knew this town would treat you like it treated me. I always wanted to leave, but you were the one who gave me the strength to actually decide to do it."

There's silence for a long moment. Even if I wanted to, I'd have no idea how to fill it. Finally, Mom takes a deep breath.

"I decided that Xavier deserved to at least know. I didn't expect . . . He never acted like he wanted to be a father. He definitely didn't take us seriously. But he said it would be unfair to take his child away from him." Her breath hitches. "I told him we could compromise. I'd bring you to visit him. We could share custody if he wanted to be in your life. But that wasn't enough for him. He said he'd have all of you and nothing less."

A shiver claws up my spine. I picture this Xavier as a looming, dark figure, Mom trembling in his shadow.

"He . . . He kidnapped me. Kept me locked up in a shed, I think. I don't know. It was far from everyone. Forget treating me like a friend. He hardly treated me like a person. He fed me and gave me water, did the bare minimum to keep my body healthy, but other than that, he completely ignored me, no matter how much I begged and pleaded and promised I'd never leave him."

Her voice wavers, lungs taking in too much air. I squeeze her hand. She shuts her eyes tight and a tear spills out, rolling down her cheek.

"I was around eight months pregnant, or close to it, when a couple found us. A couple with a baby."

"Eden's parents," I breathe.

Mom nods. "They found me on an equinox, when the barrier between worlds was at its thinnest. That meant—"

"Faeries couldn't get out, but people could get in." My lips feel numb, and my voice sounds like it comes from miles away. "Eden told me that much."

"Eden's mom saved me. She pushed Xavier through to the fae world."

I sit in silence, trying to digest this. My dad got killed by faeries. More than that, he *deserved* to get killed by faeries. No wonder Mom never told me about him. Part of me wishes I didn't know it.

"So." I swallow. It takes me a minute to gather my thoughts. "So . . . okay. It makes sense—why you lied about it." I don't like it, but I understand it. "There's still one thing that doesn't track, though."

Mom turns to face me. "What?"

"Why is everyone here so weird about the forest? Grandma made it sound like it had something to do with what happened to you, but I don't get how all that led to things being like this."

"Oh. That." Mom's face pinches up with stress. "Well, people were disturbed by the way Xavier kidnapped me. It was too much like how faeries acted for comfort. Things spiraled from there. They started saying that because the people in the forest were immortal, they'd forgotten what it meant to be human."

"But Eden's parents saved you!"

"I know, but people were scared. Scared that they'd be next. Or their children. And scared people aren't rational. There was talk about going to war, but the trapped humans didn't want that. In the end, they cast a mass spell that would make them sleep for a hundred years instead. To prove that they meant no harm, that all they wanted was peace."

"And Eden? Her parents?"

"They must have dodged it somehow." Mom looks out at the forest, her voice soft and sad. "It makes sense. They'd live through the hundred years, but Eden wouldn't."

The thought hits like a sucker punch to the gut. "That's *really* messed up, Mom."

"I know." She gives a low noise that only sort of sounds like a laugh. "You'd think at least people here would be kinder to me after all that. But they blamed me almost as much as they did the humans in the forest."

"That literally makes no sense!" I'm starting to get a headache.

"They were hurting and lashing out. I couldn't deal with it. I left for Chicago, and I promised myself I'd put Fairbrooke behind me." She sighs. "But I guess I never really did that. I've just been ignoring it, pretending the hurt isn't there, like that will make it go away." She presses her hands to her face. "Oh, God, I'm turning into my mother."

This is . . . It's too much. It's weird to see Mom so unguarded. "So why did you let me come here?"

"Because Mom missed you so much. And she promised she wouldn't tell you anything. I knew there was a chance you'd find your way into the forest, even knowing how much I hated it, but I knew it wasn't *actually* dangerous, really. And I didn't think anything in there would hold your interest. I didn't expect any of this."

I curl my knees to my chest. "Me either."

"Lydia . . ." Mom puts a hand on my arm. "I know it's all too much. That's why I left in the first place. So let's just go home tomorrow and put all of this behind us. For *real* this time."

I swallow, and something clicks in the back of my throat. It seems too easy, almost. Anticlimactic. But this is what I should want, right? I've never wanted anything hard. Adventure, yes, but teen-shenanigan adventure, the kind that ends with breathless giggles or a slap on the wrist. This is way more than that.

I press against Mom's side, breathing out slow. "Okay." I really, really try to mean it. "Just . . . no more lies, alright?"

"Alright." Mom wraps an arm around me, leaning her head on top of mine. It should make me feel better.

Maybe if I pretend long enough, it will.

What sort of Children of the Corn
bullshit is this?

"Doll?"

I wake up to the sound of Mom's voice and the knowledge that I slept like shit. Catching a few hours between racing thoughts and dramatic rooftop conversations did not cut it. My back aches, my head throbs, and my mouth tastes like stale spit.

"Hey." My voice crackles.

Mom gives a sympathetic hum as I rub my eyes. "The car is ready." She kneels in front of me, putting a palm on my knee. "We can go home. Okay?"

Home. I felt conflicted about it last night, but now the word is music to my ears. Please, God, let me go home, where things make sense and people are who they say they are. Back in my room with my bed and Internet. Back with people I can talk to without having to think about bigger issues like whether they've had their goddamned parents murdered by goddamned faeries.

I'm not proud of these thoughts. Even if Eden was an asshole to me, she doesn't deserve that bullshit. But I'm tired and I'm crabby and I just don't want to care.

"Okay." I peel myself off the couch. "Give me a few."

Mom smiles. Relief lights up her face like the windows of a skyscraper. "I'll be waiting outside."

I slept in my shorts and T-shirt yesterday, so there's no need to change. I head to the downstairs bathroom, brushing my teeth and giving my face a quick scrub. Just the bare minimum to get out as quick as I can.

Grandma's waiting by the front door, looking out the window at Mom's car idling in the driveway. She turns to me and offers a too-thin smile. "Well. This is it."

"Yeah." I realize, all at once, that I don't want to hug her. I don't know what to think of her, the woman who kept Mom's secrets but still encouraged me to go into the forest, in her own way. Combined with the lack of sleep, it makes me feel prickly.

I know I'm not being fair, though, so I force myself into her arms. I don't get any of the good feelings I usually get from a hug—it's actually a little uncomfortable—but it's more for her than me.

"Bye, Grandma."

"Take care, love."

Her voice wobbles with more than just age and I'm pretty sure I'll see tears in her eyes if I look. So I don't. I walk right out the door to where Mom's car waits.

Mom is already sitting in the driver's seat. The mechanic stands in the driveway, thumbs hooked into his belt loops. He eyes me. "Time to head out."

"Yeah, thanks for the goddamned hospitality." The words come out on instinct, but I'm not looking for a fight. I feel off. Part of it is lack of sleep, but this isn't my first time running on two hours and I know what that feels like. This is different.

I shrug it off as I get into the car. As Mom backs up, I stare at the forest and try to imagine Eden in there, poring over books and trying to figure out what Fierborne is. The thought fills me with a sour kind of fondness.

I hope she figures it out. Really, I do.

Grandma comes out to watch us go once we reach the edge of the driveway. The mechanic lights a cigarette, still standing there, and all at once I realize what's bugging me.

"Mom, how's he getting home?"

Mom pulls onto the dirt road. "That's not our problem."

She's right. I *guess* she's right. But my gut still feels wrong, full of the sort of paranoia I usually only get from staying up too late and watching horror movies. A truck passes us in the opposite direction, and Mom has to slow to a crawl to let it go by. I make eye contact with one of maybe eight guys sitting in the back of the pickup.

"Where do you think they're going?"

Mom doesn't say anything. Maybe she steps on the gas a little harder when she's able. Her silence is enough of an answer—she doesn't care, and she doesn't want to know. I don't either, really.

But I can't stop myself from looking in the rearview

mirror. So I see it when that truck turns into Grandma's driveway.

And I see it when a car follows behind from the other side of the road.

And I see it when people approach on foot.

"Mom."

"Lydia, no."

"Mom, they're all going to Grandma's. They might—"

"They're not going to hurt her, doll." She sighs, eyes pinching up in the corners. "I'm not sure what they're doing. But they're not monsters."

"They're doing *something*, though!"

"And that isn't our problem." She grips the wheel tighter. "Trust me. We'll only make it worse if we stay."

"But we can't just—" I stop. A thousand words clog my brain, but only a few matter. "Mom, please, stop the car."

"No."

"Come on."

"No."

"*Stop* it!"

The dashboard lights flicker. Mom slams on the brakes so hard I have to brace myself to keep from headbutting the dashboard. She turns to me, eyes wide and face too pale.

"Lydia, what are you *doing*?"

And it's crazy, the idea that I'm somehow messing with her car, but it doesn't matter if it's true or not. What matters is the look in Mom's eyes, like something between us is changing, and I'm not sure if either of us can take it back.

I don't have time to think about it. I fling open the passenger door and I run.

When I get back to Grandma's, my gut sinks. People stand scattered across her lawn or bunched up in her driveway. It's still a small crowd by my standards, but it's more people than the trade in the diner.

Grandma stands at the head of the driveway. Etta has a comforting hand on her back, but she doesn't seem to notice. Her long gray hair billows in the wind, and her voice is desperate. "You *can't* do this!"

"What the hell is going on?" Heads swivel to face me, but I don't get an answer. The crowd is utterly, creepily silent. I recognize Tim and Gina, Clyde, Dale. The only sound is the wind in the trees and Mom's engine as she pulls into the driveway behind me.

Clyde is the one who finally speaks. "You should've gone home."

"I didn't ask for your opinion, asshole."

"What's going on here?" Mom's voice drifts over my shoulder. She's still sitting in the car, engine idling. "Lydia? Mom?"

"Get your kid out of here." Dale narrows his eyes against the sunlight reflecting off Mom's car. "We're handling the mess she made."

Mom sits there for a long moment, tightening her grip on the steering wheel. Then she flings open the car door and stalks out. For a second, I think she's actually listening to him, but then I realize that the fire in her eyes, so like my own, isn't directed at me. "Don't you dare. It's bad enough you all acted like what happened to *me* was my fault. Don't you *dare* do the same to my daughter." She jabs a finger into Dale's chest.

My eyes actually start to sting. As much as things are

weird between us now, she's still on my side. It means more than I can say. I walk beside her and grab her hand.

Gina joins Dale, glaring at Mom. "What are we supposed to think?"

"The ones in the forest aren't even supposed to be close to waking up," Tim agrees, walking up on Dale's other side. "The only thing that's changed here is your kid running around in there, doing God knows what."

"We can't trust them." Etta doesn't move from beside Grandma, but her voice carries. "We're human because of our mortality. They've forgotten what that is like."

Grandma steps forward, her voice loud enough to echo. "The people in that forest aren't your enemy! You've all forgotten where the real enemies are—in Fierborne."

The crowd gasps like a goddamned hivemind. Some of them do this weird shuffle, and even Etta jerks back. A voice hisses from a cluster in the grass. "You know better than to speak the name of the fae world out loud."

My ears ring like someone replaced the breeze with television static, and I have to remind myself to breathe. Fierborne is where the final treasure is. Fierborne is where Eden's parents went, never to return.

I bolt toward the forest. Dale tries to stop me, grabbing my arm tight enough to bruise it. I punch him in the stomach as hard as I can. He lets go, staggering back with a pained noise. I don't care. I keep running even after I tear across the bridge and into the shade.

"Eden!" My voice bounces off the trees. Being in here has never felt more natural, and I swear the branches are guiding me. "Eden!"

"Lydia?" Eden's voice, alarmed, sounds from close by. I run toward it. And all at once, there she is.

She's dressed more casual than usual in a simple blue dress over gray leggings, running shoes replacing her usual sandals or flats. She stares at me, and I stare back. My breath scorches my lungs, and I'm sure I look like a crazy person, wild-eyed and chest heaving.

Finally, she folds her arms over her chest. "What are you doing here?"

"Eden. I understand everything now." I'm winded, but I force the words out. "Mom told me about your parents saving her and I know you're trapped and I know you're planning on going to the fae world, right? That's where the final treasure is. And that's why you were so awful that night. Right?"

Eden bows her head, long hair covering her face before I can read it. "Does it matter?"

"Of course it matters!" I'm shouting, but I can't help it. "It matters to *me* that you didn't just want to throw me away!"

Eden looks up, her expression carefully blank. She opens her mouth to speak, but Mom beats her to it, voice echoing through the forest.

"Lydia!"

"Mom?" For a moment, my only answer is crunching twigs and thundering footsteps. Then Mom turns the corner. She's pale-faced and shaking, and she sort of looks like she might barf. She's terrified.

And she's here. Here for me.

I rush over and wrap her in a hug. "I'm sorry. It's just . . . Eden's going to the fae world. The last treasure is in Fierborne and I didn't know what it meant and she got all weird when I told her I wanted to stay in touch and I thought it was because she hated me but it wasn't. It was because she wouldn't be here."

The words come out in a nonsensical rush, like I'm trying to explain the plot of a dream. Mom looks up and locks eyes with Eden.

Eden pulls herself up, squaring her shoulders. "It's the summer solstice. Tonight, the barrier will be thin enough for me to slip through. I *know* it's risky. But I have to try."

"You won't have time." Grandma's voice makes us all jump. She plucks her way through the forest, obviously exhausted.

Mom rushes to her. "You shouldn't be in here."

Grandma ignores her. Instead, she looks right at Eden. "You have to find a place to hide. Somewhere damp or high up, preferably both."

"What are you talking about?" I ask. "What does she need to hide from?"

Before she can answer, there's a roar like an engine starting. Flames consume the trees around us.

It's too bright, too fast, too much. I may not be a forest expert, but even *I* know that trees don't just spontaneously combust. "What the fuck?"

"They're *burning* the forest?" Mom sounds as shocked as I feel. Does she think the townspeople are doing this? She said they weren't evil, and this seems like overkill, even for them. Then again, the flames have to be magic—there's no way normal fire spreads this fast.

Grandma looks impossibly old in the firelight. "The trapped humans can't age, but they can still be killed. The

211

others must see us as acceptable casualties." Her eyes are full of tears, either from smoke or betrayal.

"No." The flames drive Eden closer to us, playing across her face like a horror show. There's a moment, as Mom wraps an arm around my shoulders and pulls me close, when I want to take her hand. This is terrifying, and she shouldn't have to face it alone.

I look around, heart pounding rabid and terrified in my throat. There *needs* to be a way out of this. But the flames are everywhere I turn. Heat sears across my face and I bury it in Mom's shoulder, like I can hide from the danger there.

"I don't want to die in here," Mom says with barely a breath as the fire closes in. My heart splinters.

"You don't have to."

My head whips up. Florian stumbles out from the flames, a far cry from his usual grace. Dark char lines rip through his skin, matching the whirls of fire that consume the tree trunks. His face is contorted in pain, and that teasing light in his eyes is finally gone.

"Florian?" Grandma's voice wavers. He gives her a look that's almost heart-meltingly tender and tears his hand through the air. A streak of golden light appears, like he's ripped a hole in time and space.

Eden stares. "Is that . . ."

"Fierborne," Florian confirms. "The barriers are so thin already that I can weaken them enough for you to get through. But I can't hold it indefinitely. Go. It's your only chance. You cannot walk through the fire as I can."

Grandma rushes to him, and he catches her in trembling arms. "Come with us."

Florian offers her a soft smile. A dark line creeps up his face and cuts through his eye. He cries out, bowing his head. When he lifts it, the eye is closed tight. "I wish I could, my dear. As long as I'm connected to this forest, I feel its pain." Smoke rises from his nostrils as he exhales, and he coughs. "But I need to stay here and hold the portal. And there are the sleeping humans to think about. If enough of my forest survives, so will I, but they don't have that luxury. I can at least attempt to get them somewhere safe."

I step forward. "You'd do that? You'd risk your life to help them?" I can't believe it, after what he said.

Florian offers me a pained smile. "I cared for humans once. I think I'd like to again. It hurts to inevitably lose them . . . but I believe it hurts more to never hold them in my heart in the first place."

Grandma lets out a choked almost-sob and throws her arms around Florian's neck. It should look silly when she presses her lips to his, with him so much taller and younger-looking. But he holds her so tenderly, so gently, that it just looks sweet. At least until his arms start to tremble and glowing, fire-red lines join the black ones on his skin. He sets her on her feet and pushes her toward the portal. When he speaks, it's in a pained rasp.

"Go."

She does, her white hair streaming behind her. Mom lets out a distressed noise and follows her.

I turn to Eden. "Let's go."

Eden shakes her head, eyes wide and frightened. "I can't. I'm not ready."

Sure, I get it. She lost both her parents to the place on the

213

other side of that portal. But the flames are creeping closer. It's getting hard to breathe. "We have to." I try to keep my voice gentle, even as Florian makes a pained noise behind us. The portal warps a little around the edges, like he's struggling to hold it open.

"You don't understand!" Eden shouts. "I have to—"

There's no time to let her finish. No matter how scared she is, no matter how much she doesn't want to do this, I can't leave her here to die.

I grab her by the waist and tackle her through the portal.

24

I've been told to "go to hell" before.
Never thought I actually would.

You know how when something explodes in a
movie, the screen goes white and the sound cuts to
loud ringing? Passing through the portal is a little
like that.

On some level, I'm still hearing and seeing things. But it's
like my mind can't process them or my body parts don't know
how to work in this new world. My lungs get with the
program first—they pull in a breath that burns my throat like
I swallowed sandpaper.

Everything snaps into focus.

I've got Eden pinned, lying in shockingly green grass. She
stares up at me, mouth hanging open and eyes full of horror
and shock. I open my mouth to say something—apologize,

maybe—but I start coughing instead and have to roll away because I'm afraid I'm going to barf in her face.

I *don't* puke, but only barely. Once I settle down, I hear something like bells or wind or the most distant, strange voices. I look up.

The first thing I see is Grandma and Mom, which is a relief. Grandma looks a little rocky, with Mom rubbing her back with one hand and wiping tears from her own eyes with the other. Eden is still lying on the ground. Grass stretches into the distance, and while there are some trees to our left, we're pretty out in the open here. Luckily, no one else is around.

Everything is so *weird* here. I blink rapidly, trying to figure out what's different. But there's no one thing. The grass is too bright, swaying in wind I hear but don't feel. The trees are too tall, branches stretching too far, leaves shaped too strange.

I look up. Two suns hang in the sky, neither of them bright or warm enough. I shiver, and the feeling rolls all the way down my spine.

Then Eden is not quite *shoving* me, but the prod to my shoulder sure as hell isn't a tap. "How *could* you?"

The fury in her voice brings my own frustration bubbling to the surface. I just saved her ass, and *she's* angry at *me*? "How could I? Shit, Eden, did you miss the magic inferno?" She glares at me. It stings, but I don't back down. "What's your deal? You were coming here anyway."

Eden laughs, but there's no humor in it. "Yes, Lydia, I was. Tonight. When I was prepared, with my supplies. Thanks to you, I don't have those." She speaks slow, like she's trying to explain something to a five-year-old.

I scowl. "Your supplies were probably already burnt! We'll make it work—"

"How are we supposed to make it work without the staff?"

That catches me off guard. I sort of thought *supplies* meant food and water. "What?"

"The staff." She's back to that annoying, condescending tone. "The magic staff. As in the only way for humans to *leave* Fierborne after coming into it."

Oh. That can't be right. Florian wouldn't have pushed us through without giving us a way back. Right? Everything happened so fast. Maybe he didn't have time to think about it. Or maybe he assumed Eden would find a way. Or maybe it was a trick. I want to believe in him after he seemed to sacrifice himself for us, but can I?

Saying any of that out loud would feel like admitting defeat, though. I cross my arms over my chest instead. "Well, excuse me for not thinking about that when our lives were at stake."

Eden actually rolls her eyes at me. "Of *course* you didn't think about it. You just—" She cuts herself off, and somehow that hurts more than any insult she could fling at me.

"Well, maybe I would've thought of it if you had just told me the truth instead of letting me think you hated me!" Blaming all this on me is bullshit. Maybe I did act without thinking, but I didn't have a choice. There's no *time* for thinking in the middle of a fire. And she can't act like she hasn't done anything wrong.

She sure as hell seems to be trying, though. "We've got bigger problems than hurt feelings, Lydia! Dying of thirst is a best-case scenario. If the faeries catch us, they're going to do a lot worse."

Behind us, Mom bursts into tears.

I want to scream a million cutting words at Eden—that she's missing the point, that her not trusting me is the cause of a lot more than hurt feelings. But Mom's sobbing rips through the charged air between us until I have no choice but to turn.

"Hey . . . Hey. It's gonna be okay, Mom." I put a hand on her shoulder, kneeling in the grass. It's too soft underneath me. "We'll figure this out."

Mom just shakes her head, burying her face in her knees. I know she's young—younger than most of my friends' moms. But she's never really looked young to me before now.

"I never wanted this for you," she cries.

Guilt finally breaks through the anger, as chilling as getting caught out in the rain. Mom just faced down one of her biggest fears to keep me safe. She's still more worried about me than herself.

"We're going to be okay." The words feel hollow. She deserves more than this. Maybe things would've gone better with a plan. Or at least with the staff. Maybe Eden would have been able to get it. Maybe Florian would've been able to summon it, if I'd given her enough time to ask. Maybe, if I'd heard her out . . .

But maybe she would've died. So it's pretty goddamned worthless to wonder, in my opinion.

I can't sit still anymore, or I'm going to scream. I stand up and start to pace. The air shifts against my skin, and even that feels different. It pulls too easy into my lungs.

Silence presses in on me. Except it's not silent, not really. There are so many sounds, but they're just too far away for me to figure out what they are. It drives me a little crazy. I want to run in their direction until I find their source, put the mystery to rest. I have to force myself to spin around, pacing back and forth instead.

"Okay. Okay!" I'm talking before I even know what I want to say—anything to drown out the strange sounds of this place. "We'll be okay. We can come up with something."

"Like what?" Eden folds her arms over her chest. I want to scream at her for how awful she's being, but also for the hopelessness in her eyes, the exhaustion in her face that says she's already given up.

I open my mouth to do just that, but Grandma steps between us before I can. "Take a deep breath." Her face is wan and tired, but her hands are steady as she spreads them. "We can't control what's happened, so let's focus on what we can control. Which is getting out of this open field, staying out of sight. We'll work on coming up with a plan in the interim." She turns to Eden, her gaze soft. "Maybe Florian will be able to get the staff through."

"For now, you should stay with us." Mom's voice wavers. "Your parents saved me once. I'll do my best to keep you safe. It's the least I can do."

Eden's shoulders slump, the fight draining out of her in a rush. "Fine." Her tone is curt and harsh, every bit as tense as when we first met.

I turn to Mom. She's wiping at her eyes, but at least she's stopped crying. Some of the tension's faded from my chest, too. Grandma is good at calming people down, I guess. Or maybe it's just easier to be calm when I'm not looking at Eden.

I offer a hand to Mom and pull her up. She stands, then

crushes me in a hug. I hug her back, and I swear I feel Eden's gaze on the back of my neck. I try not to wonder if she's thinking about her own mom or if she's still back there just hating me.

No.

The thin trees in the forest aren't much, but at least their branches provide more cover than we had in the field. We walk through them for the better part of an hour, following a silver river that winds through the grass like a snake, with an ominous hissing noise to match.

That's all the time it takes for the suns to set, even though it was morning when we left. There's only one moon, but it's too big and seems to cast shadow instead of light. The trees turn so dark they look like charcoal drawings.

It's just as well that night came too quick, because we're all exhausted. Grandma can hardly stay on her feet. We find a place where the stream cuts into the ground, turning into a ditch that's a few feet deep. There's a round alcove beneath a tree, mostly hidden by roots and vines. Grandma points at it.

"You and Eden should hide in there."

Eden goes to it immediately, but I hesitate. "What about you and Mom?"

"Mom can rest out here while I keep watch," Mom says. Grandma nods. "I'll wake you in a few hours for the next one."

Maybe I should argue more, but I *am* tired. I haven't really slept since before the starfly disaster, and so much has happened since then. I need at least a few hours of rest if I'm going to think about this in any rational kind of way.

I climb into the alcove after Eden.

It's a tight fit. Eden's curled up as small as possible, and we're still too close. Our spines press together as we lie back-to-back.

Before, my chest would've fluttered at this close contact. My mind would've been racing. I probably would've tried to wrap an arm around her waist or something. But now, she might as well be a million miles away. She doesn't even acknowledge me, doesn't react to my body pressed against hers.

There's already so much competing to make me miserable. This is just one more thing.

Maybe I should stay awake for longer than I do. I'm in a strange place, with too much to process. But I'm exhausted, and while this world is unfamiliar, I wouldn't call it uncomfortable. I fall asleep quickly.

I wake up to screaming.

My first instinct is to jump out of the alcove, but there's something blocking my path. Eden's got her arm wedged in front of me, and before I can even fully get my head around that, she presses her palm against my mouth.

I turn to face her, and she shakes her head once. Her dark eyes glitter in the strange moonlight.

I look out. From our angle, I can only see four pairs of feet in the grass—two familiar and two not. Mom and Grandma struggle in the grasp of the two strangers.

"Well, well, what have we here?"

The voice sends shivers down my spine. It's high and nearly a screech, drawing out the words like my mom does when she has a little too much to drink. But there's something awful and knowing about it, too. Like it already knows exactly where we are, even before it asked its question. Like it's toying with us.

"Too long," a second voice echoes, and if the first one was a shiver of fear, this one is a gut punch. It's a nondescript rumble that shakes the little alcove we're hiding in. Dust sifts down, and I instinctively bury my face in Eden's shoulder to muffle my sneeze.

Definitely because of that, not the terror that rips through my bones.

She stiffens for a moment, but then she lowers her restraining arm to wrap it around me instead. In spite of everything, it loosens a little something in my gut.

"You're right," trills the first voice. "It has been too long since we've had fresh humans to play with." Grandma gasps and flinches, but I can't see what they're doing to her. "These don't look as resilient as the last ones were, but we'll make do."

Eden goes still beside me. They're talking about her *parents*. In the past tense. I wrap an arm around her in return, hoping to comfort her the same way she comforted me.

"Please." Mom's whimper breaks my heart. I should want

to run out there. I should want to fling myself into any danger to make sure she and Grandma stay safe.

But I don't want to, is the thing. I'd punch any asshole human who tried this shit, and I wouldn't fear a thing. But even the faeries' voices make me feel like throwing up. If their voices are that bad, what do their faces look like? What would they do to me if they found me?

Eden thought dying of thirst was our best-case scenario. For the first time, I get it.

There's a strange sound, a half-wind and half-popping noise, like a suction cup being removed. All four of them vanish.

"No." I'm not even sure what I'm feeling—horror, grief, guilt, some awful combination of the three. I rush out of the alcove, and Eden doesn't stop me. "No, no, no. *Shit*."

They're gone.

What was I thinking? *Why* was I thinking? I shouldn't have even stopped for that. I should have done more. I should have—

"I'm sorry, for what it's worth."

Eden's voice is a blank slate. I turn to see her sitting in the alcove and looking down at her lap. She can't meet my eyes.

And all at once, I'm furious at her. "You. You held me back!" I was going to jump out before she stopped me. I wouldn't have had time to get scared if I did. I would have done something.

Eden's head snaps up. "What should I have done? You would've given us both away!"

"But I could've—"

"*What?*" Eden's voice cuts across mine, quiet but sharp

and impossible to ignore. "What could *you* have done?"

"*Something!*" I fling my arms out wide, like I can throw away the burning that's in my chest. "Something instead of hiding away like a *coward*—"

"Keep your voice down." Eden glares, which just makes me angrier. "It's not cowardly to be careful. It's smart."

"So, what? You think I'm stupid?"

"Who cares what I think of you?"

I let out a frustrated noise. She's trying to change the subject, wants me to forget why I'm pissed at her. "It's always better to act. You didn't let me do that."

"You didn't seem all that willing to rush out once you heard their voices." Eden gets to her feet, arms tight at her sides. "You've got *some* self-preservation, even if it's hidden under a layer of . . . of . . ."

"What?"

"Recklessness!" It comes out in an angry hiss. "Lydia, this is not the time to be reckless!"

"But my family is gone!" I'm practically shouting again, but I don't care. If I'm so reckless, then let me shout, let the stupid faeries find me. Let me face them down and prove that the fear was a momentary weakness brought on by Eden holding me back. Let me prove I'm not a coward who would let my mom and grandma down.

"I know that, and I'm sorry." She doesn't sound it. Her voice is clipped and measured, like she's trying not to shout. I hate it. I hate that she's acting like she has the moral high ground right now, like I have no right to be as angry as I am. "You have to understand that—"

"Let's go find them."

"*What?*"

"They want humans to play with?" I clench my fists. "Fine. I'll play whatever stupid goddamned games they want, and I'll win."

"No, you won't."

"Watch me!"

"Lydia!" Eden grabs my arm, her dark eyes locking furiously with mine. "If you go after them, you will die. It will be slow and painful and awful. That fear you felt, hearing their voices? You will feel a thousand times worse. They will break you. Do you understand me? First they'll try to break your body, and if they can't do that, they'll break your spirit. They don't play fair."

I tear my arm away. "So that's what's happening to Mom? To Grandma?" Eden at least has the decency to look away at this, down at her feet. "You can't ask me to just give up on them!"

"You don't have a choice." Eden's voice is horribly quiet. "They're already gone."

"But there's a chance!"

"To die with them!"

"Or to save them!"

"You can't do that!"

"I can try!"

"This is *exactly* what I'm talking about!" Eden practically growls. "Lydia, this isn't something you can just throw yourself into without thinking. It doesn't work like that. That's what got us *into* this mess in the first place!"

I can't believe how awful she's being. This isn't about being reckless just for recklessness's sake. I *can't* stand by and do nothing. I'd never forgive myself if I just let Mom and Grandma suffer without even trying to help them. They're my family. Can't Eden understand that?

"If it were *your* family," I shout, "you'd do it!"

Eden's eyes widen, air rushing out of her like I punched her in the stomach. Only then do I realize the weight of my words. Eden's family. Her parents. The people who went into Fierborne to save her. She *just* heard the faeries talk about them, got reminded of their deaths all over again.

You don't have a choice. They're already gone. Those words weren't just about me.

I step forward. I want to take the words back. I want to do *anything* to wash that primal, wounded look off her face. "Eden. Eden, I'm *so*—"

Her expression crumples in on itself as tears spill over her cheeks. She presses both hands over her mouth, but that doesn't do much to muffle her sobs. Her shoulders heave and her whole body trembles, and for a second, I think she might collapse, fall into a jumble of torn-up pieces at my feet.

She turns and runs away instead, leaving me alone in the silver moonlight.

It's not going to end like this.

I walk through the forest, calling out as loud as I dare.

The sky starts to lighten to a weird purple shade, although I don't see the sun. *Suns.* I shiver. At least there's enough light to help me look. Without it, I might have missed Eden sitting up in a tree, knees curled to her chest.

"Eden," I call. She flinches but doesn't look down. "Eden, I'm sorry."

She stays silent. But she doesn't go running when I climb up to meet her, so that's probably a good sign.

It takes me a while to get settled in a place where I'm sitting next to her on the branch but not too close. And then, once I do, I have no idea what to say. I don't think Eden does, either. Her face is raw and pained and exhausted. My heart feels about the same way.

"I really am sorry about your mom and grandma." Her voice is hoarse from tears. "I do care."

"Shit. I know." I scrub at the bridge of my nose. "It was never you I was mad at."

It's true. I see that now. She was a convenient person to direct my anger at because she was there, a target on my level, one I could fight. One that didn't fill me with impossible, bone-deep fear.

"Everything's been awful," I say. "I was just so *scared*. And angry. I took it all out on you and you didn't deserve it. Me dragging your parents into it—you *really* didn't deserve that. I was totally out of line, and I'm sorry."

Eden sniffles, looking down to the ground below. "I'm sorry, too. Everything you said, about being scared and angry and taking it out on me, I've been doing the same to you." She sighs. "I shouldn't have gotten mad at you for pushing me through the portal. Of course, you didn't have time to think— there was a *fire*. It's unfair to hold how you reacted against you."

"Being angry with each other—it's not doing any good, is it?" It felt right in the moment. It felt good to let out that anger. It always does. But maybe it's not worth it if it feels this awful after.

"No. It isn't." Eden breathes in, then lets it out slow. "Thank you for apologizing for what you said. I forgive you."

A knot in my chest loosens. "Thanks. I forgive you for getting mad at me, too."

Eden closes her eyes. It's not perfect. It's nowhere near where we were before. There's still so much we're not saying. But the silence between us sits just a little bit easier, which is at least a step in the right direction.

"So what do we do now?"

It feels weird to ask. Part of me still wants to *go*, to throw myself into the first fight I can find. But I've cooled down enough to admit it's a bad idea. Besides, it wouldn't feel right to leave Eden alone.

"I don't know." Eden shakes her head. "You know, I *planned* on challenging the faeries to a game. It would've been different with the staff."

"Different? How?"

Eden frowns, her forehead creasing in thought. "Well . . . it has to do with the carvings on the treasure, the clues. Those are a special magic—sort of like a contract that's impossible to break. And the phrasing of the last clue was very particular. It said the final treasure could be won in Fierborne."

"Okay?" My confusion leaks into my voice. Eden continues.

"Faerie games aren't *supposed* to be winnable. But because the staff said we *could* win the final treasure, that would have made it possible. Not easy, but possible. That was enough for me. But since I don't have it . . ."

Guilt crawls up my spine. "Oh."

I guess what I'm thinking must be obvious, because Eden sighs. "I probably would've burnt to death before getting to the treehouse. You can't blame yourself for that. The fire . . ."

She trails off. Is she putting it together? Is she wondering if I had anything to do with the townspeople getting angry? What would I tell her if she asked? It isn't my fault. I would've been more discreet if I'd known the whole story. Right?

In the end, Eden just sighs again. "There was nothing else

we could've done in that moment. Anyway, even with the staff, it would've been a long shot. But I would've *tried*. I wouldn't have had a choice. I wanted—needed—to see the hunt through to the end." Pain pinches her face. "It's pointless now, though."

"Yeah." I hate the heaviness in her voice. I wish there was some easy way to make it all better, like I could crack a joke and instantly fix the mood. But this isn't Fairbrooke, and it isn't the light-hearted treasure hunt I thought it was. I can't be the same person I've always been. Not here.

I look down. Below our dangling feet, starflies swirl in a lazy pattern. Except it's not lazy, not really. They're all going in the same direction—one by one, they slip behind a too-thin tree trunk and disappear.

I jump off the branch, landing on the ground. From my angle, it really does look like the starflies are vanishing in the time it takes them to cross behind the tree. But when I peer around the corner, I see what's actually going on.

There's a portal to Fairbrooke. Everything looks desaturated through it, like I'm looking through a weird filter. Part of it's probably that everything is so vivid here; my eyes got used to the strange, too-vibrant colors of Fierborne, so home looks dull in comparison. But part of it is also that everything on this side is healthy and alive. Fairbrooke is the opposite.

Most of the trees are charred husks. But there are still patches of alive grass, tree trunks here and there that aren't a total loss. It gives me hope that maybe if the fire didn't consume the forest totally, it didn't consume Florian totally, either. He could be safe, and he could've helped the trapped humans, too.

The starflies swirl around my waist, tickling like sunlight. I press both palms against the barrier and lean my weight into it. It's less solid than I thought—the texture sort of reminds me of plastic wrap. But no matter how hard I push, it doesn't break.

There's something on the ground on Fairbrooke's side, something that isn't a tree or a plant. When I realize what it is, I laugh. It's not funny, but I can't help it. "The universe is a *bastard*."

From close behind me, Eden says, "What? Oh."

Part of me wishes I could've warned her first. I'm sure it's hard to see her treehouse, her home, crashed on the ground, half-burnt and rubble. It could be worse—it could be totally destroyed—but it could be a hell of a lot better.

How many memories burned? Did she have things belonging to her parents in there, things she wanted to keep?

Worst of all, the staff has to be right there. There's no way that thing got burned up in the flames. It's sitting in the rubble, barely ten feet away, but it might as well be in Antarctica for all the good it does us.

We'd have a chance with the staff. Eden admitted it. But we can't get to it, not here, not like this.

I press harder against the barrier, wishing it was as flimsy as it feels. I want it to rip apart beneath my palms. I want to give us a fighting chance.

"Let it go, Lydia." Eden's voice is gentle. And it would make sense to listen to her. But I can't. I can't believe this is hopeless. I punch the barrier, letting loose a growl of rage. Taking out my anger on Eden wasn't fair, but taking it out on this stupid thing feels like it's fair game.

I kick. I claw.

I push through.

It's barely for a second, but the difference is obvious. The air scorches my lungs, but it also sits calm and familiar against my skin, so unlike Fierborne. It's the difference between slipping into an old hoodie and trying to break in a new pair of shoes.

I'm *home*.

And then I'm not.

I'm thrown backward like a ragdoll. I hit the ground hard and roll. The air feels all the more charged here now that I've remembered what the human world is like. My heart pounds like I just ran a marathon.

"Lydia!" Eden drops to her knees next to me. "Are you alright?"

"I'm fine. *Look*." I hold up the sole of my boot for her to see. It's covered in a fine gray film, impossible to mistake for the black earth here.

Eden's brow furrows as she turns to look at the barrier. Her eyes glide down to the ash that coats the ground on Fairbrooke's side. Her mouth drops open.

"That's *impossible*."

"It happened." I scramble to my knees, then my feet. "Eden, I was there."

I push against the barrier again. It's still the same as it was, but the texture makes more sense now. It's less like plastic wrap and more like a rubber band, ready to snap me back if I push it too hard.

Eden stares at it. "There's . . . I've never heard of anything like this happening. The closest thing I can think of is a fae blessing."

"What's that?"

"Back before the war, faeries would sometimes bless humans, allowing them to enter Fierborne for just a short period of time." Eden shakes her head. "It happened so rarely, though, and was usually used as a trick."

"Could it happen the other way around?" I follow Eden's train of thought easily enough. "Like, could a human trapped in Fierborne go back into the human world for a minute?"

"If it happened, no one ever wrote about it." Eden pushes against the barrier. "Do you think . . . Did Florian bless us?"

"I don't know. What does the barrier feel like to you?"

"Solid."

"It doesn't feel stretchy? Sort of?"

"No, not at all. It's as solid as stone."

I frown. "Maybe he only had time to bless one of us."

Eden's brow furrows. "*Maybe.*" She pauses, then sighs. "I can't think of a better explanation."

To be honest, I don't care about the reason. "Do you know what this means, Eden? If I can stretch the barrier far enough, if I can get to the staff—"

"There's . . . It's not . . ." Eden shakes her head. "What if you get thrown back again?"

"You said yourself that our best-case scenario is dying of thirst in here before the faeries get us. I'm pretty sure smacking into a tree is the least of my worries." I bounce on the balls of my feet, so full of energy I could explode. "This is a chance! It could change everything!"

Eden bites the inside of her cheek. She doesn't say

anything.

I don't need her to, though. I hurl myself at the barrier. It pushes back against me, but the more I dig my heels in, the harder it has to work.

And then I'm there again, back in Fairbrooke. I can feel the barrier trying to push me out, but I struggle against it. I take one step toward the fallen treehouse. Two, three. It looks weird, like I'm staring at it through cloudy glass, but it's there. It's getting closer.

I grit my teeth. My heart thunders like a freight train and everything in me is screaming to give up. This is too hard. I've flaked on things that were way easier than this. But the stakes were never this high.

Just one more step, I tell myself. *Just one more step. Just one more step.*

Just one more.

And then there really *is* one more step. I can hardly breathe from the effort of pushing against the barrier, and it sort of feels like I'm on one of those spinning amusement park rides that go so fast they stick you to the wall.

I grab the edge of the doorway to pull myself forward. For a second it's solid beneath my hands, but then it dissolves like sand. I slide back.

"No, no, no—shit!" I fall to my stomach and try to claw my way forward on my hands and knees, but it's no use. I grab *something* but it's not the staff. I see it for one endless moment among the rubble, just out of reach.

Then I fly backward and I really *do* slam into a tree. Whatever I managed to grab clangs to the forest floor.

"Lydia!"

Eden's hand is on my arm. Her voice sounds tinny for a moment, but I think that's less from the impact and more from the lack of air. I heave in giant breaths, trying to get my head to stop spinning.

"Goddammit! I was so *close*!" I punch the tree, which in retrospect was not the smartest decision. I shake out my now-aching hand, grumbling under my breath.

Eden scoops up what I did manage to grab—a metal container with a matching metal bottle strapped to it. "Well, some of the food survived, at least. So did my canteen." She opens it up and takes a swallow before offering it to me.

I take a drink, then stand up. "I'm trying again."

"Lydia . . ." Eden sighs. "It's fine. You've done enough. We'll figure something else out."

The disappointment in her voice is obvious. She got her hopes up, even if she didn't want to. Still, here she is, offering me an out.

If she had done this back at the cave, I would've taken her up on it. I wanted to give up then. And a part of me wants to give up now. But I can't let myself. Not this time.

I get a running start and throw myself at the barrier again.

It pushes even harder against me, but I don't stop. I scream, for once using my rage for a constructive purpose. I let it fuel me, push me forward. I will not let this stupid barrier deny me. I am not going to go down without a fight. I'm not giving up on my family, on Eden.

I pass through the doorway of the treehouse again. Debris crunches beneath my boots. The staff is there on the ground. I reach for it with one shaking hand, my entire body aching with effort.

My fingertips brush against the wooden surface. They fumble.

I grab hold.

I'm flung backward even harder this time. I try to turn it into a barrel roll, which is less graceful but also less painful than slamming into a tree. I'm covered in dirt and ash and I feel like death warmed over.

But I'm also hugging the staff to my chest.

"Lydia! Lydia, are you . . ." Eden trails off as I sit up. And even though I feel like utter shit, I have to smile when I see the expression on her face. She doesn't say a word, but she doesn't need to.

I know this changes everything.

Bring it the hell ON.

We go back to the alcove because Eden insists we need rest if we're going to do this. I really want to jump into it, but I resist the urge to argue or run off. Eden knows what she's talking about, after all.

When the suns rise, we share the rest of the water along with the food in her pack. "So obviously, the staff changes things," I say around a mouthful of blueberries. "What's the game plan?"

Eden nibbles on a piece of dried meat thoughtfully before answering. "The first step is to find an arena. If we do it formally, we'll be able to challenge the faeries on our terms."

"For the treasure."

"Yes."

"And my family?"

Eden frowns. "If we're careful, yes. I thought about it a lot last night. The clue only promised we'd be able to win the final treasure, but there are other ways to get what we want, and the staff gives us leverage."

"How?"

"Well . . . when faeries give their word, they can't go back on it. Our best chance is to challenge them with the staff but only agree to play if they give their word they'll release your mom and grandma if we win." Her frown deepens a little, though.

"It will work." It *has* to.

Eden nods, looking a little more confident. "We'll just have to be careful and really think our words through."

"Okay. Careful and thoughtful wording. I'll leave it to you. Got it." I shoot her a thumbs-up.

Eden laughs, and for a second it feels kind of like we're back to normal, just goofing around and hunting for treasure. I don't forget the stakes or anything. But being on good terms with Eden again makes everything a little less scary.

We walk through the woods. Unlike yesterday, we don't try to hide ourselves. I can't stop staring at Eden as she strides forward with her shoulders squared and head held high. She looks like a totally different person. Braver, more confident. But I feel different, too. More determined and careful.

Maybe we're rubbing off on each other.

The trees end, leaving us facing a tall, square hedge wall. Through an archway cut into it, even more hedges are visible, twisting into the distance. It's a maze.

"Is this an arena?" I don't know why I'm whispering. It just feels like the right thing to do.

Eden must think so, too, because her voice is just as quiet. "Yes. The second we go in there, the challenge will start."

I want to rush in. But I don't. Instead, I take Eden's free hand in mine and give it a squeeze. "Are you ready?"

Eden takes a deep breath, then nods. "Yes. But, Lydia—" Her dark eyes lock with mine. "This is going to be hard. And scary. Are you sure you want to? I'd do my best to get your family free. I promise."

I shake my head. "Are you crazy? Of course I'm going in, too. We have a better chance together. Don't you think?"

We might clash sometimes. And fight. But we also balance each other out. There's a reason we found those treasures so quickly.

Eden smiles a little. I wonder if she's thinking the same thing. "I do." She takes a deep breath. "Okay. Let's go."

She doesn't let go of my hand. And even though I feel different about her now, I don't want her to.

Together, we step through the archway.

I feel the difference immediately. The hairs on my arms stand on end, and my heart thumps in the good way, the way it does when I've just done something reckless and gotten away with it. It's a powerful feeling.

Eden squares her shoulders. Her voice echoes through the maze.

"I'm here to offer a challenge!"

There's a shimmer in the air, and an answering shiver runs down my spine. A faerie appears in front of us.

I brace myself for the fear that came when I heard the faeries speak earlier. But it doesn't come. Maybe it's because I can't really see this faerie. He's wearing a dark cloak with a hood that turns his face into a vague, shadowy outline. It falls to his shins, leaving only his sturdy leather boots visible.

"How good of you to show up," he says. "I was *so* hoping you would."

His voice isn't what I expected, either. It's more roguish than genuinely creepy. He almost sounds charming as he continues.

"Tell me, have you . . . Oh my. *That* is unexpected." He steps forward. Light flashes along the inside of his cloak, like he's hiding a thunderstorm in there. "What *curious* magic that old staff has. But how dreadfully incomplete it is. Were you hoping we'd help you out of the goodness of our hearts?"

Eden stares at where his face should be, so solemn and brave that a wave of pride washes over me. "Do you have the final treasure? The final piece of the staff?"

"Of course we do." His voice drops to a purr. "We found it shortly after the war. Florence, that fool, played with magic she didn't understand and ruined a perfectly good tool for it. Just look at it now. Barely capable of anything, even if it had its missing piece."

Is he implying the staff won't free us? I turn to Eden, but she's still serious, not taking the bait. "It's capable of what I need it to do. And we would like to play for its final piece. Along with the freedom of Lydia's mom and grandma. You will give your word they'll go free if we win."

"Will I now?" The hooded faerie's voice is distressingly amused. "And why will I do that?"

"Because that's the only way we'll play." Eden grips the staff tighter. "We've come here with magic beyond even your comprehension, and we will play by its rules. But only on our terms. Do you really want to risk ignoring those and unbalancing the magic that brought us here with this staff in the first place?"

She's really thought about this. I cling to her hand, trying not to bounce my foot or do anything else to show how nervous I am.

There's a long moment of silence. Then the hooded faerie starts to laugh, low like a rumble of thunder. "High stakes. But shouldn't you make them higher? Aren't you forgetting something?"

Eden stares. She grips the staff a little tighter. "What do you mean?"

"Those other two that came before you. Surely you're their daughter, the one they won't stop talking about." The faerie's voice drops low, like he's a predator luring in prey. "I'm surprised. Do you not care for them as much as they care for you?"

For a second, I'm almost sure he's lying. This must be a trick. Even if her parents are alive, why would he tell us that?

But then I look at Eden, and I understand. This has broken her. Forget confident, cool, collected—all at once, she's just a kid, so full of fear and hope and guilt and anger that she can't even begin to process it.

So I step forward. "You mean it? They're alive?" If we're going to do this, I don't want Eden to have false hope.

The hooded faerie turns to me. I expect more misdirection, but he surprises me. "Certainly, they're alive. You thought we'd kill them for good? It's not as though we could have gotten rid of them once they got boring. We didn't know when we'd get more, after all. Nothing like the old days."

The wistfulness in his voice makes my skin crawl. I push it aside. "We'll fight for them, too."

"You're a brave child, aren't you? How delightful." He hums, amusement clinging to his voice. "And if I told you it would make the game harder? Would your answer stay the same? Even knowing it might mean the difference between success and failure?"

"Yes." I don't even hesitate. If we're fighting for my family, it's only fair that we fight for Eden's, too. I wouldn't dream of leaving them behind.

"Curious." The hooded faerie leans forward, so close that I should be able to see his face. But I can't. The shadow cast by the hood is too dark. "Tell me, is it altruism that drives you? Or are you just that unattached to the people you call your own?"

Rage bubbles up in my chest, and I clench my fists. Can I punch a face that's made of shadow? I'm not sure, but I sure as hell can shout in it.

Eden breaks in before I have a chance, which is probably a good thing. "Quit wasting time." Her voice shakes, but she lifts her head and looks the faerie right in his shadowy face. "Do you agree to our terms?"

The hooded faerie sighs. "Very well. The final treasure, the freedom of our captives, new and old. Is there anything else?"

"I . . . Yes. I have conditions." Eden looks a little more comfortable. This much she planned for, and it shows in her voice. "We'll play any game you want. But if we win, you need to give us the prizes within a reasonable time frame. No

243

amount of time that would see a human starve to death or die of thirst first."

I shiver. I'm glad Eden's here to close any loopholes. I wouldn't have even thought of that. I wonder if it's even necessary with the staff, but Eden knows what she's doing.

"Fair enough." The hooded faerie shakes his head slowly. "Although that staff is a bit of a nuisance, I must admit I'm excited. It's been so long since we've had a proper challenge here. And I think you two might just be it."

Although I can't see his face, I swear his gaze lingers on me. The back of my neck feels cold.

"Here are my terms," he says. "This arena will present you with three trials. You must overcome all of them to get your prizes—lose one, and lose all of them. And if you fail, you become our captives. Our new playthings."

There's a beat of silence. Eden's probably calculating the risks. I'm just letting the words sink in. An eternity of suffering is a lot to threaten. It's more serious than any consequence I've had to face.

Eden breaks the silence. "I accept. If you give your word."

"Very well." The hooded faerie faces Eden. "I give my word. You'll get the final treasure, our captives, and the ability to leave freely with them."

"Okay." Eden nods, then turns to me. "Lydia?"

There's no judgment in her gaze. If I were to run, she probably wouldn't blame me. But I wouldn't be able to live with myself. Not with Mom and Grandma counting on me. Not with *Eden* counting on me.

"I accept, too," I say.

"How fun this will be." The hooded faerie chuckles again,

dark and ominous. "Well, far be it for me to keep you. Start forward, young ones. Your trials await inside." He fades away, leaving us alone in the hedges.

Screw you AND your creepy ass hedges, thank you very much.

We stand there at the entrance of the maze for what feels like an eternity, staring at the space where the faerie disappeared.

Finally, I break the silence. "So?"

Eden startles. Her eyes are glassy and she sort of looks sick. Whatever brave face she was able to put on after finding out about her parents is gone now.

Still, she starts forward. I follow her, silence sitting heavy between us. And what the hell am I supposed to say about all of that? It's better to let her handle this herself. I'm not good at this sort of thing.

But I'm also the only one here, and I'm not sure if Eden can do this alone.

I kick a branch out of the way, watching it skitter across the hard-packed earth and into a dark hedge. "Hey . . . you okay?"

Eden looks at me out of the corner of her eye. "Are you sure you want to know?"

"I think we're sorta past the point of pretending nothing's wrong." Eden lets out a jagged laugh. I'm not sure if that means I'm doing a good job or a bad one, but I keep going. "Look, you just found out some pretty heavy shit, you know? It's okay if you're . . . not. Okay, I mean." I sound like a totally different person.

Eden *looks* like a different person, though, so I guess we're even. She's more vulnerable than I've ever seen her, with her arms crossed and her shoulders hunched up around her ears. "I should be happy. My parents are alive. That's more than I dared to hope for."

I listen to the hedges rustling around us for several seconds before realizing she's not going to say anything else. "But?" I prod.

"But they've been suffering. Because of me." Eden's voice cracks. "They came in here because of me. It's all my fault. What if they hate me now?"

I almost run into a hedge. "What? Eden, you're crazy." She gawks at me, and I wince. Shit, talk about tact. "I just mean there's no way they could hate you. You didn't shove them through that portal. You shouldn't blame yourself."

"Why not? People around me tend to get hurt. First my parents, then you."

"I'm fine."

"You're *here*." Eden looks away, eyes scanning the hedges.

247

"And even before, I thought it would be different if . . . if it wasn't so serious for you. But you got hurt anyway."

My gut twists. Honestly, I am still stinging over all of the stuff Eden kept from me this week. Bigger problems or not, it still hurts. But it doesn't seem fair to bring those issues up now. I don't want her to compare that to this thing with her parents, which genuinely isn't her fault.

I do my best to swallow my hurt feelings. "It's not the same thing. They made the choice to go into Fierborne, not you. And they made that choice because they *love* you. I don't think anything could change that."

I've got complicated feelings for Eden right now, but I can't believe her parents would be angry at her. They care so much about her. They defied witches and faeries and basically the entire goddamned universe to give her a fighting chance.

Maybe I'm imagining things, but I think some of the tension unfurls from Eden's shoulders. "Thanks, Lydia."

It's a stupid thought, but I wonder, if I'd been more open, more willing to talk about the tough stuff like Eden's parents, what would she have told me? If I'd asked, would I have gotten more information? Would Eden have lied at all?

I almost open my mouth to say this. But before I can, there's a snapping noise behind us.

Eden and I turn around slowly. The path we came from is gone. In its place is a wall of leaves, which would look totally normal if I didn't know that it just appeared out of thin air.

"That's probably not a *great* sign, is it?" I ask.

"No," Eden replies faintly. "Probably not."

On either side, branches reach out to grab us.

Eden shouts, but I don't hesitate. I'm moving on

something like instinct, guided by impulses I don't have time to question. I shove Eden and hit the ground just in time to avoid the grabbing branches. Thorny vines shoot out from the ground, and I roll onto my stomach to avoid them. I leap to my feet and tug Eden away from a swinging hedge, pressing our backs against the wall of this quickly narrowing hallway.

"Lydia, we have to go!"

But there's nowhere *to* go. Eden must see that. No matter where we go, the hedges will catch us.

Unless we play their game.

I should be scared. It's crazy that I'm not. But while my chest burns and my heart pounds, it's not in a bad way. I'm actually grinning, the sort of grin I couldn't stop if I tried.

I grab Eden's arm. "We gotta go up."

"What?"

"Up!" The hedge in front of us tilts sideways, turning from a wall to a ramp. I run up it and leap, soaring through the air, catching myself on a ledge of surprisingly sturdy leaves. The hedges build up, stacking into a wild sort of tower. Everything in me wants to climb to the top.

This is our first challenge.

I swing on the ledge and claw myself higher. The wall tilts like it's trying to throw me off. I cling and manage to stay on. "Ha! Get wrecked, you stupid faeries."

While I'm distracted by gloating, a wall of leaves slams into my chest, flinging me into the air.

I land hard in the dirt, wind knocked out of my lungs. The hedges shift around me, but I'm not worried about them grabbing me just yet. That wouldn't be a very satisfying end to their game. Eden said their goal was to break me, and I'm not broken.

"Fair play, you bastards," I grumble, sitting up.

"Lydia!" Eden's voice hisses out at me. She's tucked away between two hedges, a small sanctuary from the shifting madness of the tower.

Part of me wants to try again. I can see the way up, I swear it. I feel it in my chest, in my blood.

But this is Eden's fight, too. It wouldn't be fair to leave her behind.

I rush to her, ducking and sliding to avoid a swinging vine covered in thorns. I roll into the sanctuary, nearly crashing into Eden's legs, and bounce to my feet. "Eden, we gotta get to the top of that tower thing."

"What?" Eden actually flings an arm out. "Lydia, that's crazy. Look at it!"

To my credit, I do. The hedges, full of moving parts, tower higher than any skyscraper. Platforms float back and forth, and vines whip around like tentacles. It sort of looks like a puzzle in a video game.

"For once, I'm not going to give you shit about your weird fixation with heights, because that thing is legit terrifying. But it's part of the challenge. We can't just ignore it."

Eden makes a high, frustrated noise. "I know that! It's just . . . I want to plan."

And I get it, or I think I do. Eden's the opposite of me in a lot of ways. This is her worst nightmare, the same way that mine is having to strategize or sit still in a silent room or something. "Eden, I don't think you *can* plan for this." I bite the inside of my cheek. "Besides, I'm feeling that . . . thing again. The blessing or whatever it is."

Honestly, now that I'm thinking about it, this happened even before we found the staff. The feeling that leads me through the hedges is the same one that led me to the treasure in the cave, only it's way stronger here. Had Florian blessed me even earlier?

It doesn't matter. Who cares where this burning in my chest came from? The point is, it's there. I'm gonna use it. I take Eden's hands in mine and squeeze. "Just follow my lead, okay?"

For a second, I think she's gonna get angry at me again. I worry she's about to call me reckless, stupid, all that stuff she said before. But she just takes a deep breath and nods. "Okay."

I turn to face the writhing hedges. And I throw myself into them.

Branches fly over my head and vines attack my ankles, all trying to pull me into the walls. I shout commands over my shoulder to Eden—"jump" and "duck" and "hit the deck"—but I don't have time to think about where they're coming from. Maybe it's a blessing. Maybe it's something else. Or maybe it's just the fact that I'm in the sort of situation I do best in—challenges one after another, where the ones in front of me and behind me don't matter. All I need to worry about is what I'm doing in the moment.

I take a running jump and hit the tower with my full weight, using a branch to swing onto a hovering platform. Eden is right behind me, and I haul her up with one arm, offering her a grin.

"You keep up good."

She shakes her head. "Keep talking. I feel . . . something

251

when you tell me what to do."

"That's what she said," I respond before I can stop myself. Eden stares at me blankly, but I'm saved from getting too far into that by a vine swinging at our heads. "Duck!"

After that, there's not too much banter. We don't have the breath for it. I have to save mine for telling Eden where the threats are and how to avoid them. And I start to understand what she meant, because every time I speak, there's a pulse from my chest, like I'm shooting little adrenaline bullets from my heart.

Whatever this gift is, I'm sharing it with Eden.

It leads us up, higher and higher. I glance down to see how far we've come, but the hedges and ground below have disappeared. An inky black void swallows everything except for maybe three feet of tower below us. It looks like it wants to swallow us, too.

I grit my teeth and turn back to what's above us. No more looking down.

At the top of the tower is a bundle of branches so thickly woven together it looks like one of those wicker chairs. Except it's less like a chair and more like an egg, with a curved opening on the front. It's hollow inside, the perfect size to fit Eden and me, and it's glowing faintly gold.

That's it. That's the finish line—it has to be.

"Jump!"

I do it even as I shout at Eden to do the same, yanking myself up on a platform below the egg thing. I have to climb using a ledge as a handhold, hoisting myself up until I'm able to grab the lip of the opening.

"Yes!" I haul myself in, relief coursing through my body

like adrenaline. "Eden, come on!" I turn around to help her up, and I'm so happy and excited we made it that I'm focusing a little less on the power in my chest. And maybe that's why Eden slips.

She tries to pull herself up the way I did, only when she gets an arm over the lip of the opening, she tries to use her foot for leverage and misses the ledge. The force shoves her backward so her grasp on the branches slips. She starts to fall.

"Eden!" I lurch forward, and my hand finds her flailing, reaching one. I grab her wrist and have to brace myself on the edge of the opening to keep from falling out, my free hand wedging in the woven branches.

She grips the lip of the opening again with her free hand to pull herself up, but her toes brush the inky void below. She yelps, trying to jerk her feet up, but it's too late. Vines shoot from the darkness, wrapping around her ankles.

"Oh, hell no!" I try to pull her in, but the vines tug back. Eden looks up at me, eyes dark and pained.

"Let go. Maybe they'll still let you compete. You can get my parents free, at least."

"What? Screw that!" I pull harder. The vines pull back, and I almost get tugged over the side with her.

"No!" Eden actually tries to pull out of my grip. "No, I won't let anyone else get hurt because of me!"

The vines give an even harder yank, and I stop thinking. I hold out a hand and I *scream*. My fingertips burn, there's a pulse, and the vines shrivel and fall back into the darkness.

Eden and I both stare. Then the branches of the cocoon start to shift, closing me in. "Oh, shit." I yank her inside right as they close completely.

We're left in darkness, both breathing heavy, as the egg starts to slowly lower to the ground.

Eden's the first one to speak. "What was that?"

"Us winning the first challenge, I'm pretty sure?"

"Lydia."

I look at her. Small pinpricks of light filter through the branches, enough for me to make out the shock on her face.

"I don't know," I admit. "Maybe Florian's blessing again?"

"Faerie blessings don't do that."

I shrug. "I don't know what to tell you. Does it matter? We can focus on finding answers once we're back home."

"I *guess*." Eden sighs, shaking her head. "And . . . thank you. For helping me."

I bite the inside of my cheek. There are a million things I should tell her. Something about guilt, or the unfair expectations she has for herself. But I don't know how to even begin to talk about that stuff.

Instead, I say, "Just consider it returning the favor? I mean, you did save my ass from falling off a cliff when we met."

Although it's hard to tell in the limited light, I think Eden smiles.

What's next? Extreme hide-and-seek?

The branches slither back into the earth, leaving Eden and me on the ground. The sky is black and the moon is out again, even though it hardly took a minute to bring us down. This place is so weird. At least the hedges around us are back to normal.

I pull a twig out of my curls and examine it. "So is that what faerie magic does? Plant shit?"

"Fae magic can do a lot," Eden says. "Especially here. It's more subdued when they go into our world."

I guess that explains why Florian didn't do anything this crazy. Shit, I hope he made it. I push that thought out of my mind. "But their magic is more powerful here?"

Eden nods. "They can do almost anything. Except break

the barrier, of course."

A thought smacks into me like a freight train. "Eden, when we use the staff to break the barrier, can faeries follow us?"

"No. No, I'd never even try it if that were the case." Eden pauses for a long moment, then starts to talk like she's giving a lecture. "There are two barriers, essentially. The fae staff only affects the first one, the one that's always been there to keep the kidnapped humans in. But humans made the second barrier to seal away the faeries. *That* barrier is immune to fae magic, so the staff won't break it."

I guess that makes sense. "Can anything break that barrier? I'm not really thrilled about the idea of these creepy assholes just showing up one day."

Eden shivers as we start to walk. "I'm not sure. One of the witches who created the second barrier wrote a little about it. It was created in the first place by harnessing blood shed by both humans and faeries during the war. Breaking it would take something of equal power."

"Like what?"

"It's hard to say. But war is a massive thing. There's nothing the faeries could get here, or from us, to equal it."

"Oh. That's good."

Eden nods. On this, at least, we're in total agreement.

We continue through the hedge maze. Except it isn't really a maze anymore. More of a hedge hallway, with only the occasional turn.

It ends in a wide-open space. Hedges create walls in graceful arcs and swoops, and a little stream, its water as clear as ice, winds across the ground. Round gray stones create a path.

The hooded faerie sits on a stone chair in the center of it, checking a silver pocket watch. "You made good time. Well done." He looks up. His face is still invisible under the hood, but there's a smile in his voice. "I must admit, I'm almost proud."

I cross my arms over my chest. "Whatever, we beat your first challenge. What's next?"

A shiver worms its way up my spine as I recall Eden's words. *First they'll try to break your body, and if they can't do that, they'll break your spirit.* They had their fair crack at the first one, so will the next challenge try doing the second?

The hooded faerie stands, circling Eden and me. A sharp smell wafts from his cloak, like the scent of earth after a rainstorm. "I planned a truly fun challenge for you two next. It involves my fellows, and I thought it only fair to warn you. After all, they will not be as politely covered as I am. But do you need the warning? There's something different about you now."

The power gives a weak pulse in my chest. I curl a hand instinctively against my heart, like I can hide it behind my palm. If this blessing or whatever is an advantage, I don't want to give it away.

Eden steps forward, her voice steady. "Are you going to let us continue or not?"

"So *impatient*." The hooded faerie sighs. "I suppose it is no matter. Here is how the next challenge will go. You will be met by a number of faeries as you continue forward. They will ask you one question each. You must answer truthfully, and you can't ask any questions in return."

There's a long pause before I realize he's done. "Is that it?"

The hooded faerie laughs his low, rumbling laugh. "I'm interested to see how you do." And with that, he fades away.

I turn to Eden. "I've gotta admit, when I heard about fae torture games, I was not expecting obstacle courses and truth-or-dare minus the dare."

"Don't underestimate faeries, Lydia." Eden clenches her fists and squares her shoulders. There's genuine fear in her eyes.

Maybe the idea of being totally honest freaks her out. God knows she's not very good at it.

The thought isn't exactly fair, but it beats in my temples anyway, a thundercloud over my head. I grit my teeth against it. Eden and I can work out all that nonsense once actual lives aren't on the line. Us getting all pissy with each other is the last thing we need right now.

I stomp forward, hoping this will read as confidence instead of anything too petty. "Let's go."

There's a pause, but Eden does follow me. Honesty or not, she knows we have to keep going.

The clearing ends in a hedge archway, and it doesn't take a genius to figure out that's where we're supposed to go. The leaves look like velvet in this light, a dark green that seems like it would be soft to the touch. I actually have to stop myself from rubbing the leaves like a weirdo as we pass through them.

A faerie appears in front of us almost immediately. She's got the same sparkle in her eyes and the same pointed ears as Florian, but that's where the similarities end. Because unlike him, she's not even trying to look human. She's tall and too skinny. Her irises are wide and yellow. Her pointed ears twitch with interest, and when she circles around us too gracefully, her back arches and her legs bend in a way that shouldn't be possible.

She should terrify me. It should be like when I heard those fae voices. But the power in my chest flickers comfortingly, like a candle. It makes looking at this woman feel almost natural. Better than natural. I feel powerful.

I try to push some of that power to Eden. Maybe it works, because she looks the faerie in the eye and speaks in a steady voice. "Ask your question."

The faerie hums. Her voice is a raspy purr, more feline than human. "Do you think you're a good person?"

What the hell kind of question is that? I open my mouth to snap at her, but Eden beats me to it.

"No."

That catches me off guard. I've got some unresolved issues with her, sure. But do I think she's a bad person? That's going a little far. Can Eden seriously answer that question without even hesitating?

The faerie smiles, greed in her too-bright eyes. "Why?"

"You're allowed one question only," Eden replies.

That's smart. I wouldn't have even thought to say something like that. I heard the hooded faerie explain the rules, but I didn't think about them in-depth because they seemed so straightforward. One question only. No questions back.

Icy dread stabs me in the gut. I almost screwed everything up by blurting, *What the hell kind of question is that?* Which is, technically, a question. I could have thrown away our lives, our families' lives, in an instant of impulse.

Eden is right. I should not underestimate faeries.

The faerie turns her gaze on me. "You still have to answer my first question. Do you think you're a good person?"

I actually stop and consider my answer, after all that. "I don't know. I've never thought about it."

"That's disappointing."

"It's the most honest answer I can give you."

The faerie sighs, like wind through spindly branches. "I know." She vanishes before our eyes.

Eden clenches her fists and starts forward. Part of me wants to ask her if she really thinks she's a bad person. But is asking Eden a question against the rules? I'm not sure, and I don't want to risk it.

Another faerie appears out of thin air, blocking our path. He's built like a grizzly bear, broad and wide. When he smiles, it's with too-sharp teeth. I feel myself baring my own before I can help myself.

Bring it on.

It goes on like that. Faeries appear one after another, each with their own questions.

"What is the meaning of life?"

"Does your life have more meaning than others?"

"Would you kill to save yourself?"

Honestly, these questions don't bother me. Like, sure, it's hard to be careful with my words and think things through, but I'm not having an existential crisis or anything.

I can see they're getting to Eden, though. She chews over them for minutes sometimes, teeth clenched and hands shaking. But she always answers honestly, or at least I assume she does, because we're allowed to keep going. Even though it must feel like she's getting her chest ripped open and shown to me.

Now, me, I've always worn my heart on my sleeve. But this is new for her.

Another faerie appears, his smile as slimy as an oil slick. "Do the rewards of your actions outweigh your regrets?"

What sort of bullshit question is that? I don't even consider asking that for real, of course. Instead, I roll my eyes. "You'd have to be more specific, but generally, sure." That's as close to the truth as I can get. I'm not perfect, I know that, but I don't get the point of dwelling on regrets.

Eden's thought about it, though. I can see it in the way her face twists, the way her fists clench, the way she hesitates before answering. Her voice actually cracks when she finally speaks.

"Sometimes they do. And sometimes they don't."

The faerie fades away, and we continue on.

"Eden . . ." I'm not sure what I want to say. What I'm allowed to say. I only know that Eden's face looks pinched and tortured in the moonlight, and I'm not sure she deserves to feel that way. Finally, I squeeze her shoulder. "Hey. Don't let these assholes get to you."

Eden smiles. The tension doesn't leave her face all at once, but it gets a little better. "Right. Okay."

Another faerie appears in front of us, her skin so pale it almost looks like stone. She stares at us with impassive eyes. "Do you hold bitterness for each other in your hearts?"

Eden is the one who answers first, not even hesitating this time. "No."

My gut twists. For once, I wish I could lie. I know my

answer is unfair. Eden's reasons for lying to me were probably super complicated. I don't think she meant to hurt me as much as she did.

But she still lied. And I can't think of our kiss, which should have been such a nice moment, without feeling sick to my stomach.

"I do," I admit. And I sort of get how Eden felt, all those questions before. This is awful.

The faerie grins and fades away. For a long moment, we stay standing in that spot. I'm afraid to look at Eden, afraid of what I'll see on her face.

Eventually, she starts forward, and it's like a spell breaks. I hurry after her. "Eden—"

"It's fine."

"No." I grab her by the wrist. "It's not. I know you're . . . It's not your fault I can't let go of shit so easy. I'm upset, but I don't *want* to be."

It's true. Let the fae magic come confirm it.

Eden sighs, patting my hand. "I can't blame you. It's like I told the other faerie. There's a lot I regret. A lot I'd do differently, if I could. Especially in regard to you."

Before I can say anything—before I can even process that—a branch coils around my shoulders.

I snap it in half with a yelp, but it's too late. Eden's already struggling against vines that have wrapped around her waist. I try to send out Florian's blessing to her again, and one of the vines withers, but five more take its place.

"Eden!"

"Lydia!"

She's pulled into the hedges.

"Bastards!" I spin around, snapping vines and twigs in the process. "This isn't part of your stupid game!"

"Yes, it is."

The hooded faerie stands in the distance. His voice rumbles across the space between us like thunder to match the stormy interior of his cloak.

"This is your final question. And you need to answer it alone."

I stomp forward. If we're going to do this, I want to do it face to face. But the distance between us stays the same, no matter how much I walk. More fae bullshit. I finally give up, scowling.

"Well, ask it quick then."

I'm over this. He's clearly not, though. He tilts his face toward the sky, his hood staying perfectly positioned over his face. "You're a curious little creature. Fascinating to watch. I can imagine you back in that world you call home. I'm sure it can't contain you, in all your boundless energy. And I'm sure it feels nothing like *this* world."

Under my annoyance, a darker sort of discomfort lurks. There's a ring of truth around what he's saying. This world is different than what I'm used to, but I'm not sure I'd call it bad. Other than the asshole faeries, it's sort of exciting. And the power in my chest? That's exhilarating.

The hooded faerie nods like I spoke out loud. "So you *have* felt it. I knew you would. Which brings me to my question." He stretches out one pale hand from beneath his cloak, palm up. "If I told you it could feel even better, even more exciting—if I promised you that you'd never experience another day of dullness in your life—would you join us here?"

It's the last thing I expected, and it makes my thoughts jam up like a car crash. I almost screw the whole thing up by screaming, *What?* Is he seriously implying I'd give up people's lives just to avoid *boredom?*

I might not be a perfect person. But I'm not that bad.

"Hell fucking no," I snap. And I tell myself it's the most truthful answer I've given yet.

The hooded faerie sighs like he's actually disappointed. "How dreadfully predictable." And before I can say anything else, he fades away.

I hate everything about this.

Where did that asshole get off? Did he really expect me to want to join them just because I sort of like the way this place feels? Or did he think I was stupid enough to not realize what that would mean for Eden and our families?

I stomp through the hedges, the hooded faerie's amused tone rattling around my head. I can't get over how he acted so sure, so in control. Like he knew my every move before I was going to make it.

Like he knew *me*.

And with all that self-assurance, he asked *that* question.

"Eden!" I cup my hands around my mouth, shouting into the hedges. I'd feel better with her by my side. She'd be sure, determined, focused on our goal and nothing else.

I could use that right now. My head is a mess.

"Eden!"

This time, there's a muffled response. I hurry forward through the twisting path, and then, all at once, Eden is there, right in front of me. Relief washes away my anger, which I'm only now realizing was half worry for her. Without thinking, I rush forward and hug her.

"Eden! Are you alright?"

She stiffens in my arms. Did I startle her? She doesn't relax, even as she pats my arm. "I'm fine."

I pull away. Eden steps backward as soon as she can, turning away from me to look into the maze.

"We should keep going."

"Yeah. But, like, are you *sure* you're okay?" I reach out to grab her shoulder but stop. Maybe she doesn't want to be touched right now, and that's why she's acting so weird?

Eden lets out a short sigh that sounds almost annoyed. "I said I'm *fine*. I got my final question. We're ready to move on. Are you coming or not?"

"Of course." I start to follow her, trying to ignore the way my gut sinks. "Was it the hooded faerie for you, too?"

"No."

"Huh." I guess even faeries can't be in two places at once. "The asshole actually asked if I wanted to *join* him."

"Oh."

"Yeah." There's a pregnant pause while I wait for her to say something. She doesn't, but I continue anyway. "I said no."

"Good for you."

"What is your *deal*, Eden?" I bite the inside of my cheek. "Wait. I'm sorry. That was uncalled for." Snapping at her and

266

getting angry won't do any good. "Seriously, though, what did they ask you? No offense, but I'm sort of worried about you."

Eden sighs, finally glancing over her shoulder. Her eyes are hard in the moonlight, and a shiver runs up my spine for some reason. "That's none of your business, Lydia."

Yeah, because keeping secrets has worked so well for you, I want to snap. But I don't. Something's not right here, and I want to get to the bottom of what it is. "I mean, I heard the rest of it. What's one more? We're friends, aren't we?"

Eden stops walking so abruptly I nearly walk into her. She spins to face me, her mouth set in a hard line. "Is *that* what you think?"

"What do you mean?"

"Lydia, look." Eden pinches the bridge of her nose, and her tone makes me feel about two feet tall. "It's good that we're working together. But you and I are never going to be friends."

Punching me in the gut would feel about the same as this. As much as the faerie's question upset me, this is a thousand times worse. This is *Eden.* "Is this about me still feeling bitter or whatever? Because—"

"It's not that." Eden presses her palms together, taking a deep breath. "Look. We're working together to get our families free. That's fine. But after this, do you really want to hang out?"

"Don't you? I mean, I know we fought, but we had some fun this week—"

"Yes. And I thought we both understood it wouldn't go further than that. You're the one who wanted to make it longer with letters. I never did."

"Yeah, because you had to go to Fierborne!"

"Did I ever say that?"

She didn't. She didn't even apologize for that night with the starflies. She just got angry, turned it back on me like my feelings didn't matter. And sure, we had bigger problems.

But maybe she didn't apologize because she wasn't sorry.

"Lydia," Eden says, and it's the pity in her voice that hurts more than anything. "Did you really think this was ever going to be anything more? Why would I like someone like you?"

My ears ring, tears threatening the backs of my eyes. I open my mouth to scream at her, because I'd rather be angry at her than admit to those tears.

But . . . none of this makes sense. Eden feels bad. She said so when she answered the faeries' questions, and those answers had to be honest.

The more I actually stop and think, the more I realize. If she didn't like hanging out with me, why would she have waited for me by the bridge every day? Why would she have laughed at my jokes? Why would she have held my hand?

If she didn't like me, why would she have said all those nice things in the treehouse? We weren't entertaining each other there. We weren't on some grand adventure. We just sat there. We were comfortable with each other.

There was no way that was a lie.

I look at Eden's face. And I realize her eyes aren't shining like that because of the moonlight or emotion. Eden's eyes are so dark they're almost black, not this strange silver-brown.

Those aren't Eden's eyes.

"You aren't Eden at all, are you?"

My voice comes out surprisingly calm. Shock steals all my anger. My brain feels like that point in a movie where the music cuts out suddenly, creating a silence so complete it manages to be louder than any noise.

For a second, "Eden" stares at me with an expression so blank it's disturbing. Then a crooked grin curls up the side of her face. It transforms her, leaves me wondering how I could have ever thought this was Eden.

She grows taller, paler. Her hair lightens to a bright orange and shrinks until it frames her face. The tips of her ears twist into points. And then it's not her at all, but a creepy-looking fae guy with corkscrew curls and silver eyes.

He claps twice, the sound muffled by white gloves. "Well done." His grin widens until it's more of a grimace, and he fades away.

I watch him go. "I'm so sick of goddamned faeries."

With a shivery sound, an opening appears in the hedge to my right. Eden is on the other side with her back to me. Her shoulders tremble, and she looks oddly fragile in the moonlight.

"Eden!" I break into a run.

She turns. Her eyes are as dark as they've always been.

They're also damp.

I crash into her before I think about it, sweeping her up in a hug. Everything that pissed me off before suddenly seems smaller. Not gone away, necessarily. But even though she lied, there are things I'm sure she didn't lie about.

She didn't lie about liking me.

She didn't lie about wanting me around.

And I don't think she lied when she kissed me.

All the rest of it feels less important now that I've got those facts straight. It feels manageable, less unforgivable, and more like something we can talk out. I'm not sure why I didn't feel that way before.

Eden's arms wrap around me slowly. "It's really you?" Her voice is wispy, nearly gone.

I hug her tighter. How did I ever think that faerie was her? Eden is so warm. "Yeah. Yeah, it's me." I pull away, looking her in the eyes. She's studying mine, too. "Did those assholes try to trick you, too? Pretended to be me?"

"Yeah." She swipes a palm across her cheek, even though the glassiness hasn't actually spilled over into tears. "Yeah, they did."

"Shit." I want to do something stupidly tender, like cupping her cheek in my hand. I settle for putting it on her shoulder instead. "You didn't believe them, did you? Like, you figured out it wasn't me?"

"She did."

The voice makes us both jump. The hooded faerie leans against one of the hedges, arms crossed over his chest. He bows when he sees us looking.

"Congratulations. That was your third and final trial."

It takes a moment for me to process his words. Considering how pissed I got the last time we talked, it's hard for me to register what he says now as anything good. But if that was our final trial and Eden and I both figured out we were being tricked . . .

"Wait. We *won*?"

The hooded faerie inclines his head in a nod. "So you did. Well done."

I don't even care if he's being sarcastic right now. I throw my arms around Eden, letting out a whoop. "Eden! We did it."

She blinks rapidly, like she half expects to wake up. "We did it?" She turns to me, and joy explodes across her face like fireworks. "We *did* it!"

My heart does a little somersault. And I don't think all of that is happiness over winning.

I spin to the hooded faerie, because if I'm gonna work out my complicated feelings for Eden, it won't be with him looming over us like a creep. "Well? Are you gonna take us to our families or what?"

The hooded faerie sighs. "You *are* eager to leave, aren't you? It's a pity. You'll never burn brighter than you do here, child. Do you realize that?"

Florian's blessing flutters in my chest, like it's agreeing. I clench my teeth. "I'll live. Quit wasting time."

"I'm not wasting time." He holds up his hands, palms facing us. "There's a protocol for this, you know. We faeries are graceful losers, even though it happens so very rarely. But that doesn't mean we'll allow you to trample all over our traditions."

"What do you mean?" There's an edge to Eden's voice that echoes in my own nerves.

The hooded faerie sighs. "Humans. You have such *poor* memories." He spreads his arms. "Whenever faeries are bested in a challenge, we throw a celebration to honor the winners. It's short, a few hours, nothing that will impede your human lives. It's just our way of sending you off."

"I guess that makes sense." Eden nods slowly. "I never read

about a human winning a challenge, but it lines up with other things."

"We faeries do enjoy our celebrations." I get the sense the hooded faerie is smiling.

"When will it be?" Eden demands.

"Tomorrow. We'll give you a place to spend the evening, where you can get clean and have some rest. Then you'll be presented with your prizes and will be free to go."

Eden is quiet for a long moment before she finally speaks. "I'll accept—if you give your word that our families are done with your games starting now. We *won*. They're not your captives anymore."

Anymore. A shiver claws up my spine.

The hooded faerie smiles. "Of course. It would not be a very cheerful celebration if we didn't give them the rest and recuperation they needed, too. I give you my word."

Eden relaxes, her entire body untensing. I relax, too. If Eden thinks it's okay, if she believes this is all according to plan, then I trust her.

I *trust* her. It's a realization, but not a very shocking one.

"Okay," she says and turns to me.

I take her hand, the action as natural as breathing. When she doesn't pull away, I smile at her. She smiles back.

"Okay."

The future is bright. Your smile is brighter.

Everything happens very quickly after that. We're led to a tower that looms in the darkness, guided up a staircase, and deposited into a suite that puts every hotel I've ever seen to shame. The main room is dominated by a large bed under a glossy white canopy laced with golden thread, and the carpet is a light cream color so pristine I take off my muddy boots before Eden even gets her sneakers unlaced. A door on the far wall leads to a bathroom that looks just as fancy. The faerie who led us here tells us to ring a bell if we need anything, then leaves Eden and me alone.

Eden inspects the room and finds two nightgowns. She also discovers that the bathroom is large and private enough for both of us, separated into two with a thick sand-colored curtain. Eden takes the side with a large bathtub, and I take the side with a shower that patters down from the ceiling like a waterfall.

As I stand under the spray, I try to make sense of the past few days. Not to mention the week before it. I picture driving into Fairbrooke with Mom, and it's like I'm imagining a totally different person. It was before I knew about magic, faeries, and treasures. And before I knew about Eden.

I'm still not sure what she means to me. I know I don't feel the same way I did before the challenges. I know her better now. I've seen her at her worst, she's seen me at mine, and still, when I hugged her, she hugged me back.

No matter what else is going on, that feels like it means something.

I hear Eden exit the bathroom, but I wait a few minutes to make sure she's dressed. It reminds me a little bit of that afternoon in the treehouse. Even with the shower going full blast, I can still imagine the little sounds of shifting clothes.

Eventually, I turn off the spray and change into the nightgown left on the bathroom counter. It fits surprisingly well, even if the long hemline and gauzy half sleeves aren't my usual style.

It looks good on Eden, though. She's sitting on the edge of the bed when I walk out, combing her damp hair with her fingers. My heart stutters, and I go to sit next to her.

"Hey," I say. Which, you know, really communicates the depth of my emotions.

Eden half turns to me, her face fresh and clean in the room's cozy light. "Hi."

I swing my bare feet back and forth. I feel exposed in a

weird way, either because of the unfamiliar clothes or the unfamiliar place. "So . . . we won."

"We did." Eden smiles. It's tired and it's relieved and it's *beautiful*. This must mean so much to her. She worked so hard to get here, and now she's getting even more than she thought she would. She's going to see her parents tomorrow, even though she thought they were dead.

"What are your parents like?"

Eden blinks rapidly. "What?"

"I just—" I wave a hand. "I never asked about them before because I knew it would make you sad. But now?"

"Oh. I see." Eden looks down, her smile soft and fond. "Well, if I had to describe my mother in one word, it would be strong. She knows all different kinds of fighting styles."

"Badass."

"She's also stubborn." Eden laughs. "The most stubborn person you'd ever meet. But that's not always a bad thing— she's also the most determined."

"Sounds like you." I nudge her with my shoulder.

Eden grins wide. "Then there's my father. He's really smart. He knows *so* many languages and has an amazing memory. I don't know how he does it. And he's great with words—he always knows the right thing to say." She laughs again, but it's more bitter this time. "*Unlike* me."

Silence falls, and I don't know how to break it.

Finally, Eden does. "They're both just . . . such good people, Lydia. They're so good, and they always try to do the right thing."

"Now, that does sound like you," I say.

Eden looks away, fists curling against the cream-colored

bedspread. "I don't always do the right thing. I can be selfish. Like lying to someone for a week because it's easier for me, even when I should have told the truth." She turns to face me again. "That's what the faeries used against you, isn't it? When they pretended to be me."

"Kind of," I admit. "That and they tried to get me to believe what I thought after we kissed. That you didn't care, that you never cared."

"I shouldn't have ever let you think that. And I shouldn't have lied."

She just looks so sad. I put a hand on her shoulder. "Well, you weren't the only one. My mom lied to me. And my grandma. They both had their reasons."

"That's part of why I kept it hidden, too." Eden speaks slowly. "I kind of knew what happened with your mom. Not the whole story, but enough to put the pieces together when I heard your grandma talk. Only she wasn't telling you everything, and you didn't even seem to want to hear it. I didn't know how to deal with it, and I had so much else going on, so I just . . . didn't."

"That's fair." My insides twist at the memory, and I still don't like that she lied. But, hell, that's a heavy situation. Would I have handled it any better? "I mean, we didn't even know each other."

"Yeah." Eden looks at me, and her smile plucks at the insides of my ribs like butterfly wings. "Lydia, you shocked me from the start. You know that?"

"Well . . ." This feels almost too sincere to handle, but I push down the urge to make a dumb joke. Eden's trying to be serious.

"I'd been alone for so long. I hardly remembered what it was like to interact with people. I didn't want to let anyone in. I didn't want anyone's help. I didn't want anyone else getting hurt because of me. But you were so insistent. And you were having fun." Eden laughs, the sound so small it's almost a breath. "I'd forgotten what that felt like, honestly."

All I can do is stare. She basically said all this to me already, but that was before I knew everything. Now, the full weight of it hits me.

"I think that's why, even after I knew you and trusted you, I kept lying," she continues. "I wanted you to keep having fun. I wanted to keep having fun *with* you. For as long as I could, I wanted to pretend to be normal. I thought it would be safe. You were leaving soon, so there wasn't any danger of you getting too involved."

"And that's why you freaked out so hard that night with the starflies?"

"Yes." She looks at me, serious. "But that doesn't make it right. Lydia, I'm sorry. I'm sorry for lying and I'm sorry for letting you get involved in this without knowing the whole story. Mostly, I'm sorry for letting you think you aren't important to me." She shakes her head. "With Fierborne hanging over me, I panicked, and I handled it poorly."

Did she just say I'm important to her? Part of me wants to unpack that, but I have more urgent things to say. "I forgive you. And, hell, I'm not the poster child for handling things perfectly." I take a deep breath. "I'm sorry, too. It's not all your fault. I mean, I know I wasn't super receptive to, you know, heavier stuff. And I could've gotten my head out of my ass a little sooner. I mean, shit, I didn't even *try* to see things from your side, even before the fire. I just wanted to be mad."

Eden looks at me. "Are you still mad?"

"No." I mean it. "But still, I'm sorry."

She breaks into the softest smile, one so warm I'm surprised I don't melt on the spot. "I forgive you."

We're quiet for a while after that. But it isn't uncomfortable. The silence isn't full of words we aren't saying. Everything's out in the open, and there are no more lies between us.

Eden's the one who finally speaks. "You know, I've been dedicated to finishing the treasure hunt. But I never really thought about what would come after." She lets out the smallest laugh. "At least, not until you asked me. Isn't that weird?"

I tap my fingertips against my knee. "Nah. I mean, that's a lot to think about."

"It is a lot," Eden agrees. "But I think I need to. I'm getting more than I ever thought possible. It's time for me to think about what I want in my life now." She looks at me, and suddenly it feels like we're back in the treehouse or surrounded by starflies before everything went bad. "*Who* I want in it."

My heart races like I've just run a marathon. This feels big, but not big like magic or treasures or secrets. Not the kind of big that makes me want to run away. "Oh? And who do you want in it?"

She takes both of my hands in hers. We're close enough that I can see where her dark eyes separate from her pupils, which are just barely a shade lighter. I can see a thin scar on her cheek that's so faded it's not noticeable. I can see little hairs on her forehead right where her hairline is.

"You," she says, like it's simple, like it's easy, like it's right. And maybe it is. Maybe it can be.

"Okay," I say.

Her lips twitch up in a smile. I expect her to back away a little, but she doesn't. She doesn't let go of my hands, either. "Okay?"

I take a deep breath. I want to say a million things about lies and honesty and how she's proven herself a thousand times over. About treehouses and starflies and how I'm a little obsessed with the way she hides her giggle behind her hand. About magic, about family, and about the rest of our lives.

But those are big things, complicated things. And maybe this, the space between us that's getting smaller every second, doesn't have to be.

"I really like you a lot."

That's all I manage to say before I'm moving forward, or maybe she's moving forward, or probably we both are—it doesn't matter. What matters is that suddenly the space between us is gone, and Eden's arms are wrapped around me, her fist curled into the nightgown fabric at my waist. I press a hand to the back of her neck and thread my fingers through her damp hair.

Some things remind me of our first kiss—her lips are just as warm, her hair glossy and soft. But it's also more intense. Neither of us are holding back now, fueled by relief and victory. We won. We made it through and we're getting everything we wanted. The future sparkles ahead of us, bright and endless.

So why do I want to experience *everything*, as quickly as possible, right this second?

Because that's what it feels like when Eden kisses me. My entire body tingles, and this time it isn't weird fae magic pulsing through me. It's the way Eden sighs against my lips, the warmth of her body pressed against mine, the tight grip of her hands. It's the way her lips feel as they crash against mine, again and again, like she's as hungry as I am.

When we finally break apart, my head is spinning and Eden's gasping for breath. She actually looks a little disheveled, but she's never looked happier. "Wow."

"Yeah." My reply comes out winded. "Wow." I grab her hand, not wanting to be separated for even a second. "So, okay, I'm gonna toss it out there. How do you feel about labels?"

"Labels?"

"Sure. Girlfriend is common, but I'm flexible. You can also be the light of my life. My muse. My dearest and darlingest." I'm making absolutely no sense. I can't stop grinning, all wide and giddy. I want to kiss her again. I also kind of want to stare at her forever.

Eden giggles, pressing a hand to her mouth. "Let's stick with girlfriend."

"Deal." I giggle, too. Girlfriend. Eden is my *girlfriend*. I want to say it over and over again, feeling the word on my tongue. That would probably be weird, though. Instead, I bounce a little and say, "Bed's comfy. Not sure if I'll be able to sleep, though."

Eden's mouth drops open, and her shoulders go stiff. "Um . . . I'm not sure if I . . ."

It takes me a second before I realize what she must think I'm implying, after all that kissing and girlfriend talk.

"Oooooh my god! God. No, I . . . Look, the kissing was amazing and I definitely felt . . . you know, but I'm on the same page, for sure! I mean, I'm a . . . I've never actually done that before, so, like . . . I'd totally, definitely want to at some point, if *you* want to, but . . . not ready yet, is what I'm saying. Trying to say. Hell." My face is probably bright red by the end of that awkward ramble.

But it's enough to relax Eden. "Oh. That's good. I mean, that we're on the same page. Because I'm also not ready yet, but . . . I'd also like to, someday. When we are. Okay." She looks down, a nervous smile on her lips. "Sorry for assuming."

"No, it's totally fine! I get where you thought . . . Yeah." I giggle.

Eden giggles, too, and this time it's her turn to blush. "It's just . . . the single bed and all . . . It's sort of like something out of one of the books I'd sneak off my parents' private shelf when they were out."

I'm pretty sure my jaw hits my lap, and it's a few seconds before I can reorganize my expression into something that is within the general vicinity of chill, even though the idea of Eden reading that sort of thing is . . . a lot. And I'm trying really hard not to imagine it, because making out with her *was* incredibly hot and I don't need to be adding fuel to the fire right now by picturing her like that.

"Makes sense." By some miracle, my voice comes out steady. "I guess it does kind of feel like the sort of video I'd watch on an incognito window."

Eden's face goes blank. "On *what?*"

I burst into nervous giggles. "Oh my *god.* I can't wait to show you the Internet." This manages to be almost more exciting than the idea of Eden smuggling smut off her parents' shelf. The *memes* I'm going to catch this girl up on.

Eden's gaze softens, so fond I can hardly stand it. "I can't wait. I'm sure there's lots of stuff you'll get to show me."

"Yeah." I grab her hands in mine. "Yeah. I'll show you the world."

I remember before, in the treehouse, promising to show her Navy Pier and the Ferris wheel. That didn't feel serious, like a promise I would keep. It was just a silly thing to match the dreamy mood of the rain.

This is different. Because when I pull Eden in for another kiss, the world feels like it's actually within reach.

When we do finally settle down, it's with her back to me, my arm wrapped around her waist. She holds my hand in both of hers, pressed to her chest so her heart thrums steady and sure beneath my palm. I bury my face in her hair and count the beats until I fall asleep.

32

You look like a dream.

"Get up. We're on a tight schedule."

When the voice wakes me, the first thing I'm aware of is that Eden and I are a tangle of limbs, me halfway sprawled on top of her. Not quite as romantic as having my hand over her heart, but I always did roll around a lot in my sleep. At least I didn't drool on her.

The second thing: That voice isn't Eden's. It's not familiar at all.

I roll away and Eden sits up immediately. I'm right behind her.

A faerie stands in the doorway. *Posh* is the only word I can think of to describe him—he'd be handsome if he were less fae, with full lips and hair in an elaborate coif. But his face is too perfect, so unnatural that it circles back to creepy.

He fixes us with a stern gaze that makes me feel like I'm sitting in a principal's office. I pull a sullen *I-didn't-do-it* face on instinct.

"You have exactly five minutes to get dressed in these before your team comes in." He punctuates this by throwing white bundles of cloth at each of us. "Honestly, we spent all night putting together such a fabulous ball on such short notice. The *least* you could do is be awake on time."

I resist the urge to hurl the bundle back at him. "Gee, sorry, did you send out a goddamned agenda? Must have missed that one."

The faerie rolls his eyes. "I guess it was too much to expect that *traitor* to keep the memory of our customs alive on the other side. At any rate, your ignorance is not my problem. Five minutes." He walks out, shutting the door behind him with a firm *thud*.

My gut twists at the mention of Florian. Knowing what the other faeries think of him makes me feel closer to him, weirdly. He really was on our side, even if he didn't always show it.

Eden squeezes my shoulder. "Thinking about Florian?"

I look over at her, forcing a smile. "Hey, no fair. You've got to be a level-five girlfriend to unlock mind-reading." In spite of the weight on my heart, the word *girlfriend* thrills me.

"I'm worried about him, too." She rubs the back of my shoulder. "He could still be okay, though. We won't know for sure until we get back."

I push her hair out of her face. "Look at you, being the optimistic one." Although I want to get home as quick as possible, part of me wants to sit here with my fingertips on

Eden's cheek forever.

Eden tilts her face to kiss my palm, which does stupid little fluttery things to my chest. "Come on. Let's get dressed."

The bundles of cloth turn out to be silk slips. Eden and I get dressed in them back-to-back. It should feel like the treehouse times ten now that we're actually dating, but honestly, knowing someone could and probably will barge in at any second kind of kills the mood.

Sure enough, I don't even have time to admire her long legs and bare shoulders in her slip before a gaggle of faeries pours in. They look just as creepy as the rest, but I can't really be scared when they're all chattering excitedly and armed with makeup and fabric.

"Come on, come on! It's been *ages* since we've had a proper party!"

What follows is not the most frustrating hour of my life— nothing beats standardized tests—but it's definitely up there. First, the faeries spend what feels like an eternity on my makeup. Then they lace me up in a dress made of luxurious green fabric speckled with colors like a watercolor meadow, tugging it this way and that until it sits with a hem that stops above my knees in the front and a little below them in the back. They fuss with my bleached curls for a while before plopping down a crown of thick green vines dotted with pink and blue flowers on top of them.

This all wouldn't be so bad if they didn't chatter through it in shrill, loud voices. I can't even see Eden through her own team, and talking to her is out of the question. They won't let me get a word in edgewise.

It's sort of a relief to listen to them, though. I thought

they'd be at least a little pissed at us for taking their captives away, but mostly, they just sound excited. This is something new for them, and they haven't had that in a while. It makes our victory sink in all over again.

We really won. We get to go home.

Finally, we're left alone with promises of an escort arriving soon. As the whirlwind dies down, I have a moment to actually look at Eden.

And holy *shit*, am I glad I did. While my dress is shorter, Eden's wearing a proper ballgown starting with a tight, dark blue bodice speckled with silver jewels. But it gets lighter and fuller the farther down it goes, ending with the palest blue fading into white lace that froths around her feet like clouds. Her golden skin shimmers just a little in the light.

"So this party is bullshit and I kind of wish we could skip it, but . . ." I reach out and touch a tiny silver flower that sparkles like a star in Eden's hair. "You look really pretty."

Eden lets out a breathless, almost exasperated laugh. "Yeah, you too." She reaches out and adjusts one of the flowers braided into my crown. "You always look pretty, though."

Heat rushes to my face. "Oh, shit, yeah, you too. I didn't mean it like that?"

"I know how you meant it." Eden gives me a smile, and I want to kiss her, press my lips to hers so I can feel its shape. I don't have the time, though, because the door slams open as we lean forward.

"Seriously?" I grumble under my breath. Eden laughs again.

It's the impatient faerie from before. He wastes no time in hurrying us out the door. "The guests are waiting for you.

Honestly, I *told* the team to hurry. No respect for schedules here."

We're hustled down a hallway and a set of stairs. I get only the quickest sense of this place—cold marble, stone walls. Fae guy walks like a man on a mission, and even Eden has to jog to keep up. I'm practically running, happy my skirt is shorter than hers. Maybe I shouldn't be so worried about impressing her, considering all the dumb shit she's seen me do, but I still don't want to faceplant like an idiot.

I guess I should be glad we're in a hurry, though. The sooner we get to the party, the sooner we see our families. The thought makes me pick up my pace.

I hear the party before I see it—the familiar sound of an excited crowd mixed with less familiar music, harps and bells and something I can't place mixing together in a dreamy waltz. Then we turn the corner.

A huge ballroom greets us, made of pale stone lined in glimmering gold. Mirrors high up on the walls reflect the faeries who dance and chatter and sip from crystal glasses. My heart races from all the movement.

I scan the crowd for Mom and Grandma, but all I see are unfamiliar faces. I don't even see the hooded faerie, although I guess he could be in the crowd without his cloak.

Eden beats me to the question. "Where are our families?"

"It would hardly be entertaining if you got them right away, would it? They'll come out when the time is right—too soon, in my opinion, but I had to abide by the time constraints." Our impatient guide shoots us a put-upon look.

"But they *will* be coming, won't they?" Honestly, I don't blame Eden for being antsy. We're so close to having them back.

"Of *course*," the faerie huffs. "We keep our word. For now, do try to enjoy the party. It's in *your* honor, after all. The least you could do is be grateful." And with that, he takes the hand of a waiting female faerie and whirls into the crowd.

Eden watches them go, brow furrowed and lips pressed into a thin line. I bump her shoulder with mine. "Well, we definitely don't have to worry about our families being late. Our friend there seems like the type to keep a pretty strict schedule." Eden laughs, and I take her hand. "Come on."

"What?"

I tug her forward. "Dance with me. Maybe if we're entertaining enough, they'll get what they're looking for and let us go sooner."

That's my main reason, but I also just want to dance with her. She's beautiful, and this place is beautiful, even if I do want to leave as soon as possible. The music and the shining gold and the movement all around us—it's overwhelming in the best way. I meant it when I told the hooded faerie I'd never want to stay here, but there's part of me that wants to enjoy it while it lasts.

Eden lets me lead her onto the dance floor, and when I put my hand on her waist, she puts hers on my shoulder. She slots her free hand into mine, and we start to turn slowly in time with the dreamy music.

"You know, the dancing is nice," I say. "Would be nicer if we were back home, though. I guess there's always prom."

Eden frowns a little. "Prom?"

"Oh! It's like a school dance. Everyone dresses up and you can bring dates who don't go to your school, too. It's sort of like this, but less fancy and no prizes."

That might be the shittiest explanation possible, but I can't think of a better one. Eden sighs. "I did my best to learn about the outside world, researching what was left in the forest before people stopped going in. But there's still a lot I don't know. I want to see everything, but the idea of actually doing it . . . it's a little overwhelming."

"Well, you don't gotta do it all at once. You can do your Eden thing—make a plan and stick to it. Think it through. All that good stuff." I lean forward, gently bonking my forehead against hers. "Besides, you'll have me. I might not be able to quote Shakespeare, but I'm an expert on modern living."

Eden laughs softly. "You'll stick by me, then? Even if I don't want to rush into an adventure tomorrow?"

I lean back and shoot her my cheesiest grin. "Every day with you is an adventure, babe."

Eden's mouth drops open, but then she giggles, which is just about the cutest goddamned noise I've ever heard.

"Seriously, though." I lock eyes with her. "The important thing is that you'll be free. And sure, maybe you won't want to tackle the city right away. But wherever you end up, I'll come visit, and when you're ready, you'll come visit me. We'll make this thing work." I lean forward to peck her on the cheek. "You're stuck with me."

Even though I can't resist tacking on a half joke there, I'm serious. If Eden can get over her fears enough to want me around, I can get over mine enough to stick with her for the long haul.

Eden gives me a soft smile. "Thanks, Lydia."

She looks like she might be about to say more, but the

song ends, and the impatient faerie's voice replaces it.

"Alright, alright. I know that we'd all prefer to keep this going longer, but a promise is a promise. Besides, we do have to take mortal lifespans into account." He rolls his eyes, and a laugh rumbles through the crowd. "So although the evening is so young, it is time to award our prizes to our esteemed guests."

Eden grips my hand, and I cling back. My heart pounds, and for a second I'm terrified that this is all a trick, that they're going to build us up only to tell us our families are dead or the trials aren't over or they'll impersonate them like they did Eden—

There's a murmur. The crowd parts.

A couple with Eden's dark hair and gold skin stands there, but honestly, I barely spare them a glance. Because next to them, Mom's in a dress with varying shades of blue like a running river, and Grandma's in a dress the color of autumn leaves. Nothing matters except the fact that they're there, and their eyes are unmistakably human.

I'm running before I even realize it, and Mom starts running, too. We crash together in the middle of the ballroom, Mom scooping me up and swinging me around like I'm a little kid again. When my feet find the ground, Grandma wraps her arms around both of us. Mom starts to cry.

I cling to her. "It's okay, it's okay. We're getting out of here. It will be okay."

Mom presses kisses to the top of my head, my forehead, everywhere she can comfortably reach. "I'm so glad you're safe. Challenging a faerie is the stupidest thing you could have ever done. I'm so glad you did it. Please never do it again."

"Hey, I told you, battles for you are always worth picking."

Mom gives a watery laugh and wipes her eyes. She still doesn't let go of me, like she's afraid I'll fade away into mist if she isn't careful.

Grandma meets my eyes. She gives me a small, fragile smile. "I'm proud of you, dear."

I smile back at her, then look over her shoulder. Eden's mom is hugging her fiercely, hand running through her hair. Her dad stands with a shell-shocked expression, but when he puts a hand on Eden's shoulder, she clutches his sleeve with a shaking hand and pulls him in. He presses his forehead to the top of her hair and murmurs something too quiet for me to hear.

Part of me wants to go over there, but for once I press down on my first impulse. This isn't about me. I wait until Eden gives me the go-ahead to walk over.

Both of Eden's parents watch as I approach. Up close, their resemblance to Eden is even more obvious. She's a perfect mix of the two, his narrow nose and her dark eyes, her sharp chin and his slim fingers.

Eden smiles, taking my hand with a meet-the-parents nervousness that's almost too normal for the setting. "Um, Mom, Dad. This is Lydia, my girlfriend. She helped me with all of this."

Her parents smile welcomingly enough at me, which is a bit of a relief. Out of the corner of my eye, I see Mom's jaw drop. *Girlfriend?* she mouths, eyes as wide as dinner plates. I grin awkwardly, making a helpless gesture with my hands.

Before we can really get the introductions going, though,

a voice echoes across the ballroom.

"What a lovely scene."

Mom's face falls. I whirl toward the entrance just in time to see the hooded faerie stride in, his stormy cloak still fastened. In one hand he carries the staff, complete with a purple crystal on top. The other faeries turn to him with knowing looks as he pulls off his hood, revealing gray eyes beneath thick curls that spill over his forehead.

Mom whimpers. Grandma holds her close. Eden clutches my hand. But all this could be happening a million miles away. I can't tear my eyes off this man. I've never seen his face, but that doesn't mean he isn't familiar.

"Who are you, really?" I already know the answer. I see it in his button nose. I see it in his pale skin, more ivory than peach. I see it in his thick curls, brown a few shades lighter than Mom's—the same shade as mine before I started dying it.

All the features I inherited from the man Mom met in the forest all those years ago.

"Xavier," Mom whispers, confirming my worst fears.

33

Go ahead. Rip the blood from my veins.

"Oh, good, you *do* remember me. This would be so very awkward if you didn't." Xavier laughs. His nose wrinkles when he grins, just like mine.

"Lydia." Eden's words are barely a breath. "Lydia, is that your . . ."

I know how she's going to finish, but I don't want her to. That man is not my dad, no matter what genes we share. I step forward, fire in my guts. "What do you want?"

Xavier's gray eyes, at least, look nothing like mine. What they look is *fae*. They shine unnaturally as they fix on me. "What's mine. And that includes you."

"Like *hell* it does," I growl. I thought I knew what it

meant to be angry. But I've never felt anything like this burning in my chest. I want to scream and scrape and rip this man into pieces until I destroy every part that reminds me of myself.

It's not anger that he reflects back at me, though. There's something in those eyes of his, but I can't figure it out, can't read it in his voice. "Yes, you've made your opinion on that *quite* clear."

"This isn't right." Mom's voice wobbles throughout the room, rippling like the smallest stone dropped in a pond. "You . . . You weren't . . ."

"Fae? Yes, I did dull my shine a bit in your world." He spreads his arms. "Such a wonderful opportunity that was, before you banished me back here."

Grandma steps forward, her frail body between Xavier and Mom. "There were no other faeries in the forest. Florian would have said . . ."

"What would that fool know of the barrier?" Xavier sneers. "The trick with the staff was simply meant to rob us of our captives. But keeping us out of your world? That was all human work." He shakes his head. "And it was good work, I have to admit. Credit where credit is due. Getting me through it—that was complex magic, the sort of thing we couldn't repeat."

His grin widens, and my gut drops. How many times have I seen that same smile in my own mirror?

"You can understand, then, why I didn't just cause as much chaos as possible. I had a much greater purpose— breaking that damned barrier for good." He turns to Mom again, fixing her with a look that should be tender but isn't, not with the way his eyes reflect the light. "And that's when I met you, my sweet."

Mom takes a step back, and I take one forward, hands snapping into fists. "Don't." I don't even know what I'm saying. Don't hurt her. Don't touch her. Don't breathe in her goddamned direction. Whatever he wants, I want him to get the opposite.

His gaze turns to me, so dark and amused I feel sick. "Do you know how rare it is for a human and a faerie to conceive a child? Things need to be very specific. Neither can force themselves on the other. The human needs to be of magic, but not magic themselves. And even then, the chances of a child are slim." He shakes his head, and the worst thing is that there's *fondness* in his tone. "You're what the humans call a miracle, my child."

I want to scream. But there's so much to say that it clogs my throat like a traffic jam of denial and swear words.

"I knew I had a unique opportunity with your mother," he continues. "After all, human and faerie blood spilled to trap us here. That's powerful magic. But human and faerie blood *mixed*, creating a child? That's just as powerful. It's what we need to break the barrier." He smiles, but the light in his eyes is flat and ruthless. "If you joined us willingly, that would have been enough. But since you won't, spilling your blood will have to do."

Everything goes silent. A thousand eyes press against me as the faeries drink in my horror and anger. Those things are on my face, but they're so big I hardly feel them. Inside I'm a pit, a black hole, all destruction.

"But you can't!" Eden's voice cuts across the ballroom.

"You gave your word we'd go free."

Xavier turns to her, grin widening into something awful and taunting. "So I did. I gave *you* my word that *you'd* go free with the prizes. Nothing about Lydia." He shakes his head. "Really, it was a simple trick. You seemed so prepared I was almost surprised you fell for it."

Panic surfaces on Eden's face in slow motion, disbelief melting into anguish. "No. I'd been so prepared to go in *alone* that I hadn't even considered . . ."

The other faeries leer around us. I guess a dance wasn't enough to entertain them, after all.

"I'll be more than happy to give you your prize." Xavier gestures to me. "We just have to deal with this first."

A faerie from the crowd flashes Eden a wink. "We'll even give you a head start."

"Value your freedom, dear," Xavier says. "Get far away from Fairbrooke, because soon we'll be free as well."

The crowd's cheers ring in my ears. They're cheering because they want to kill me. *Kill* me. I should probably be more scared than I am, but mostly, I'm angry. If they're going to take me down, I'm going to go down swinging, because there's no way I'm dying without a fight.

My muscles tense. I'm ready to do it. But then I see Eden. Her hands are over her mouth and she looks horrified, but she's making eye contact with me and her pointer finger is very deliberately resting on the tip of her nose.

She shakes her head once.

It's the dumb joke signal, the one I made up before the cave. The one telling me to step back, to not do anything yet.

When she throws herself into her mom's arms, she looks

every bit like a frightened kid needing comfort. But because I saw that signal, I notice the way she tilts her head, the way her lips move a little. She's *planning* something.

And throwing myself into a fight would wreck that plan.

Part of me wants to launch myself at Xavier anyway. Wants to see how many punches I can get in before he tries to tear me apart. Wants to try to fight my way out of this on my own.

And maybe, the tiniest part of me is scared. Scared that Eden won't help me, scared that she's going to value her freedom over my life. After all, she's been fighting for that freedom for years. She's known me for a little over a week.

No. Eden wouldn't throw my life away like that. I trust her. I trust that she cares about me as much as I care about her. And the best thing I can do for her—for us, for *me*—is to try getting the faeries' guard down.

"Wait!"

Heads turn to me, including Xavier's. I force myself to meet his eyes, thinking of his disappointment when I refused his offer, his twisted fondness. There's something I can do here.

"You should've told me," I say. "Back there in the hedge maze. My answer would've been different if I'd known."

"That the other option was killing you?" Xavier shakes his head. "No, that wouldn't do. Your power doesn't work when you're coerced."

"I don't mean it like that! This changes everything for me. It's not just about saving my life."

Xavier narrows his eyes at me. "You're lying."

But I'm not, is the thing. I'm just telling the truth from a different angle. "You said it yourself. I'm half fae." I laugh, not even bothering to hide the desperation. "That's why it feels so good to be here. I never felt like I fit in back home, you know that? I always knew I was different."

Even as I speak, I realize how true the words are. Maybe I didn't angst about it or anything, but I have always felt separate from people. I could never connect with anyone. I told myself it was what I wanted.

But what if part of it is this blood in my veins?

I don't want to believe it. But I want Xavier to believe it. So I make myself. For a few seconds, I pretend to be the type of person who would unleash these people.

Xavier raises an eyebrow. "You know what we'd do if we were free?"

"Sure. I've heard about the war. But, like, honestly? Screw the people in Fairbrooke. They're all awful anyway." They did try to kill me. If I focus on that, maybe I can ignore the fact that I don't believe for a second these assholes would stop in Fairbrooke.

Xavier steps forward. I could reach out and grab him, if I wanted. I could punch him, could launch myself at him, could claw his eyes out.

I don't.

"You'd truly join us?"

"Well." I force myself to look him in the eye. "You are my dad, aren't you?"

His gaze softens. He believes me. Over his shoulder, I see fear in Eden's eyes, and my gut twists. What if I did my job too well? What if *she* believes me, too?

Before I can think—before I can do anything—Eden's

mom full-body tackles Xavier to the floor.

The staff falls from his hands, clattering to the ground. He growls, sending out a blast of fae energy that sends Eden's mom sailing through the air like a rag doll. My own magic crackles in response as Eden cries out and her dad runs for where she fell, shouting in what I think must be Chinese.

I take that magic and I *push*.

I want to destroy the faeries, to make them wither and die like the vines in the hedge maze. But they're more powerful than a bunch of plants. All I manage to do is push them back, like there's a bubble growing around me and it only blocks them out. At least they're separated from us—and the staff.

"Eden!" I cry out.

"She's helping her mom, sweetheart." My own mom darts forward, grabbing the staff. She holds it out to Grandma. "Can you get us out of here with this?"

"I think so, but I'll need time." She looks at me. "Lydia, can you hold them?"

The faeries strain against my shield. It feels like they're pushing against me, awful and claustrophobic and crushing. I hold out my arms and grit my teeth. "For now. Hurry."

Grandma frowns, raising the staff and murmuring. The crystal at the top starts to glow with soft purple light.

"Using our powers against us?" Xavier stands at the front of the crowding faeries, baring his teeth in what barely passes for a grin. "How terribly ironic, my child."

"I am *not* your child!" The bubble shrinks while I'm distracted, and I have to plant my feet and strain to keep the faeries from getting any closer. They're awful in their rage, flinging fists and blasts of magic that hit my barrier and echo

299

against my spine.

But as awful as they are, Xavier is the worst. Because he looks too much like me. "Ah, but you are my child." He takes a painful step forward, reminding me of how I had to struggle to get the staff from Fairbrooke. I push back against him as hard as I can, but I can't get him behind the barrier entirely.

Out of the corner of my eye, I see Eden and her dad supporting her mom between them. They make a beeline for Grandma—to help, I think—but I can't really keep my attention on them for too long. I have to focus on the faeries. On Xavier.

"You *are* my child," he says again, taking another step closer. "And you're using my power. I know how it feels. And I know it won't feel like this back in the mortal world." Another step. The force of it makes my feet slide backward on the polished floor.

Mom presses a hand to my back. "I've got you, sweetheart."

Xavier doesn't even look at her. "You're going to miss this." He takes another painful step, then another. Trying to hold him back is like trying to contain a tidal wave with my bare hands. "You're never going to be able to go back to your dull, normal world." Another step. I groan with effort. "Everything will bore you now that you know what could have been."

He takes another step. Another. He's almost to me. I don't know what he'll do when he gets his hands on me. Judging by his twisted expression, I doubt he's planning on giving me a fatherly lecture.

Before he can lay his hands on me, though, Mom launches

300

herself into the space between us and punches him in the face.

"Get the *fuck* away from my daughter!"

He stumbles, distracted. I push as hard as I can and he slides across the polished floor, crashing into the other faeries. Behind us, there's a sound like fabric tearing, and wind blows against my back.

"We did it!"

I turn and see a portal back to Fairbrooke lined in light purple. Eden's father rushes through, supporting her mom. Eden follows close behind, but she pauses at the entrance, turning back to me. "Come *on*, Lydia."

I look back at Xavier. He's glaring up at me, his curly hair askew, blood dripping from his lip where Mom punched him. And it's not fair—*I* want to punch him. I want to ruin his stupid face until I can't see any of myself in it, until he takes back everything he said about me. I want him to hurt as much as I do.

A week ago, I would have done it. I wouldn't have even stopped to consider my own motivations, the consequences, any of it.

Now, I do. And I realize the important thing isn't getting the last word or throwing myself into every fight I want to. The important thing is making sure this asshole never gets what he wants. He's not getting his freedom, and he's not getting me.

I take Mom's hand, and together we run through the portal.

What comes next? I don't care, as long as you're in it.

The portal disappears as soon as we step through it.

We're surrounded by charred tree trunks and scorched earth, black branches twisting toward the sky. The lack of leaves and grass makes the stunned silence between us seem extra thick.

Then Eden's mom breaks it, uttering a string of words in Chinese that sound suspiciously like swear words.

Sure enough, Eden's dad lets out a gentle laugh. "Language, dear."

"Language, he says. Language. We're home and safe and you care about me watching my *language*?" She swings Eden into a spinning hug, both of them giggling now. "I say, I don't give a *damn* about your language!"

I turn away from her family reunion to look at my own. "I never would have joined the faeries. Not even for a second. You know that, right?"

Xavier's words haunt me. *You're my child . . . Everything will bore you.* And maybe part of me does miss the way his world felt. Not enough to want to go back, but I hate that he's even a little bit right.

Mom wraps her arms around me. "I never doubted you." Her gentle tone helps. I relax into the hug as Grandma puts a hand on my shoulder. I'm not upset with them for lying anymore. We'll have plenty of time for talking things through later. For now, I'm just glad to have them home safe.

"What happened here?"

At the sound of Eden's dad's voice, we all turn. Grandma clears her throat. "There was . . . The others started to wake up. The people in town felt threatened. They took action."

A somber silence falls over the group as guilt stabs my gut. I thought the townspeople were full of shit when they blamed me for the immortals waking up, but Mom said certain sorts of magic could interfere with the sleeping spell. And I had magic in me, even if I didn't know it.

Mom must see I'm upset, because she hugs me a little tighter. "It wasn't your fault. You didn't know. *None* of us knew Xavier was fae."

"I know." I squeeze her arm. "But still, if I hadn't come, the humans would've still been asleep. I'm the reason they—"

"You're the reason they lived, young Lydia."

A voice cuts through the trees. It's familiar, even though it's too hoarse and rough. Grandma lets out a strangled cry as Florian limps out from the charred tree trunks and fallen branches, throwing herself into his embrace.

He catches her gently, dark scars running along his arms. His skin has an ashy tinge, not unlike the blackened tree trunks, and one of his eyes is a pale, milky white. But his other eye is the same warm brown—fae, but not dangerous like those back in Fierborne. It fixes on me with tired, kind curiosity. "So. You're half fae. I wondered what made you so special. Even *I* couldn't predict . . ."

"They won't be getting through the barrier again." Grandma doesn't let go of his arm, even as she steps back. "They said as much while gloating, and I'll keep a closer eye on the doorways to make sure."

"So will we." Eden's dad steps forward. "But please, can we get back to the others? The ones trapped here?" Eden's mom folds his hand into both of hers. Of course, they're worried. They'd known the others for over a hundred years.

Florian nods. "The spell reacted to the fae magic around Lydia. That plus the fire was enough to wake them fully. I led them to the caves, where the flames couldn't reach. They're still there now."

Eden's dad relaxes, shoulders slumping in relief. "We'll go to them. But first . . ."

"We should get Eden over that damn bridge," Eden's mom finishes.

"Are you sure?" Eden looks between her parents, eyebrows pulling together. "I should help."

Eden's dad smiles down at her. "Sweetheart, you've already helped so much. You saved us."

"And you shouldn't have had to." Eden's mom cups her cheek in one calloused hand. "My baby. I'm so sorry."

"*What?*" Eden's voice cracks. "But I should be apologizing. It's my fault you left."

Her parents exchange a glance, then turn to her. Her dad starts in a gentle voice, "That's not true. We made our own choices."

"And they were bad choices. I was so stubborn—"

"And I was desperate. And in that desperation, we failed you. You never should have had to go through what you did alone."

Eden bows her head, shoulders trembling. Her mom kisses the top of her hair, and her father pats her shoulder.

I look away, because what's happening between Eden and her parents feels private somehow. And to be honest, I'm still reeling from everything I've learned. Who am I now that I know this about myself?

Florian falls into step beside me as we start toward the bridge, Eden and her family leading the way. "You seem troubled, young Lydia."

I laugh. What the hell else am I supposed to do? "Well, yeah. Nothing like finding out your dad's an immortal douchebag." I can't stop thinking about all the similarities between Xavier and me. The way he laughed. The way he never took my mom seriously. How deep does his influence in me run?

And now that I know what it feels like to wield that sort of power, will I ever be happy with anything less?

Florian smiles at me. "Your sire's actions have no reflection on you. Even faeries are capable of kindness. And if they forget, they can always learn again." He gestures at his scarred body.

I take a deep breath. "I guess if I need a role model, you're a lot better than him." I smile weakly. "What do you say? Are you up for being my fairy godfather? Or fairy godmother, if that floats your boat. I'm not picky."

Warmth crinkles in the corners of his eyes. "It would be my honor, young Lydia."

"My guest room is always open to you." Grandma pats the top of my head.

I look forward, at the back of Eden's head. Well, Eden's parents did say they'd be keeping an eye on the barrier, so they'll want to stay nearby. "Yeah. I guess I'll have a few reasons to visit, huh?"

Mom laughs and wraps an arm around my shoulder. And for just a minute, I feel like everything's going to be okay. I'll have my family—my real family. I'll have Florian. And I'll have Eden. If she can figure out the whole world, I guess I can figure this out, too.

And figuring this out starts with one thing. I turn to Florian. "So, uh, first question. Do faeries have, like, super healing?"

"Yes, we do. We're also far more durable than humans."

All this time, I thought other people were being dramatic. I bury my face in my hand and laugh, shaking my head. "Yeah, okay. That explains a lot."

The laughter dies in my throat when we hit the bridge. Two people sit in the grass just inside the forest—I recognize Dale and some other guy who looks to be about Mom's age. They scramble to their feet when they see us.

"Hell, what did I tell you? I *told* you they'd show up!"

"Wow, so good to see you, too." I glare, wishing I did

have fae powers to wither him up here.

Mom storms over to Dale, shoving him so hard he falls flat on his ass. "You bastards! You almost killed us!"

"You're the ones who ran into the forest! What were we supposed to do? Stop the spell?"

"Did you even *try*?"

"You should have tried." Grandma's grave voice carries even over Mom's loud one. "You almost doomed far more than the humans of the forest."

"Which Xavier never was. You've been blaming the wrong people all along." Mom wraps her arms around herself.

"What the hell are you on about?"

We give them the high-level stuff—Xavier was a faerie, no, Mom didn't know, and no, the other trapped humans didn't know, either. Mom scowls at both of them once we're finished. "Did you even bother telling them Xavier's name? Because they probably wouldn't have even known it."

Dale shoves his hands into his pockets. "We assumed they were lying."

"How do we know you're not?" the other one asks.

I step forward. "Oh, shove it entirely up your ass. Do you even realize what could've happened if I died? The faeries would've broken free." I grin as an awful, wonderful idea occurs to me. "You know, it's not just my blood that breaks the barrier. I can do it myself, if I really want to."

"You wouldn't."

I lean forward, trying to look as fae as possible. "Don't make me."

Yeah, okay, it's an asshole move. But if I have to live with baggage this intense, I should at least be able to get something

307

out of it.

Dale and his friend gawk at me for a second before running back over the bridge. I turn, catching more than a few disapproving looks. "What? I wasn't *actually* gonna do it."

Eden's mom cackles. "Oh, I *like* this one." She slings an arm around Eden's shoulder. "You've got good taste."

"Of course, she gets her excellent taste from me." Eden's dad reels her mom in for a kiss.

Eden wrinkles her nose and murmurs a grossed-out noise, but she's grinning. Her cheeks darken a little when she turns to face me.

I take her hand. "You ready?"

"Yes."

"Still nervous?"

"*Yes.*"

I laugh. "Me too. But it's gonna be okay, you know?"

"I do. Because we're going to make it okay."

In her voice, I hear all the determination that kept her going. When I lean in to kiss her, instead of dwelling on the lies or the future, all I can think of is how impressed I am by her. How, in spite of everything, she survived.

She smiles against my lips as I pull away. I turn to face Grandma instead. "Will you do the honors?" I nod at the staff, still in her hands.

Grandma smiles and turns to face the bridge. She waves the staff in a precise motion. Purple light seeps into the air, spreading across the grass and sinking into the trees. The branches look a little less charred, and a single leaf blooms on one of them.

The bridge is still perfectly intact, and the purple light

glows even brighter when it reaches it. It shimmers there for a moment, more beautiful than even the starflies on the night Eden and I first kissed.

Then it fades away.

The air of the forest sits different somehow, lighter. I know in my bones that it worked.

I squeeze Eden's shoulder, then urge her forward. "Go on." I know it's better this way, to let her go with her family first. They've been waiting so long. They deserve it.

Eden smiles. Her mom takes her left hand, and her dad takes her right. I lean against my mom and let her wrap an arm around me. Together, we watch as Eden and her family take their first steps onto Grandma's lawn.

There's a pregnant pause, like the entire world is holding its breath. Then Eden *whoops*. It's the most joyful sound I've heard her make yet. Her father sweeps her up into his arms and her mom crushes both of them in a hug.

My mom's arm tightens around my shoulders. We're smiling as we follow them over the bridge.

35

Time to keep some promises.

One Year Later

It's dusk when my friends and I finally say our goodbyes at the entrance to the pier.

We make a whole production of it, swapping hugs and banter and promises to see each other soon. A year ago, those might have been empty promises. Now I mean every one.

Riley hangs back long enough to flash me a wink. "It's nice to finally meet your girlfriend, Lydia. You two are really cute together."

I grin back at them. They know a little bit about Eden,

although I kept out the magical bits. I just said she's been sheltered and is easing into the world. Even that is more than I might have told them a year ago. All of us confide in each other more now, and I really appreciate having all of them in my life.

Of course, the best way to show this is by shoving Riley's arm. "Yeah, yeah. Now leave me be. I got a girl to romance."

They laugh and follow the rest of the group back into the lights of the city. I turn around to face the pier.

Eden hangs back, leaning against the railing and looking into the water. She's probably worn out by all these people. I won't keep her out too much longer, but I hope she has enough energy for one more adventure today.

I sneak up behind her and wrap my arms around her waist. She leans back into them like she expected me.

"Everyone liked you," I say.

"I'm glad." She turns to face me, arms around my neck. "This has been fun, Lydia. I can see why you love it here so much."

It took a while before she was ready to tackle the city. She and her parents settled into a small town near Fairbrooke, like I expected. Starting there was probably for the best, but I knew Eden would come here one day. She wants to experience everything the world has to offer. As determined as she still is, I think she might.

I can't say the same for the others in the forest.

Most of them still live there. Florian's going by Florence these days, and she's spent a lot of time getting the trees back into shape after the fire. They're looking a lot better, and so is she—only her eye is still hurt. Grandma says the other people in the town don't like it, but they're too afraid to do anything more.

Maybe I should feel bad about scaring them. I don't. I've gotten better about running my mouth without thinking, but sometimes my specific brand of bullshit is exactly what the situation calls for.

Anyway, most of the humans aren't ready to face the world. Maybe they never will be. Maybe they'll live in the forest until they die, because they're aging again. Eden's dad has started to lose his hair, and the lines around her mom's mouth and eyes definitely weren't there before.

I spend a lot of time in Wisconsin these days. Sometimes it's in Fairbrooke, visiting Grandma and Florence. Florence has been huge in helping me process the whole half-fae thing. And just as often, I'm visiting with Eden's family. And Eden herself, of course.

Having her here in Chicago is even better, though. Part of it is because we're on my home turf for once, where I'm comfortable. But mostly, I'm just excited by what this means for our future.

Which reminds me of why we're still here. "Hey, babe."

"Yes?"

I lean forward until my lips hover next to her ear so I can whisper, "Race you!"

I whirl and run down the boardwalk.

Eden's giggle floats over my shoulder as she chases after me, which does those silly little fluttery things to my heart even now. Some things I don't think I'll ever get used to, and having a goddamned adorable girlfriend happens to be one of them. "Your apartment is that way! What are you doing?"

I slow down enough for her to catch up, lacing our fingers together once she does. "Keeping a promise."

Eden gives me a puzzled look, but my lips are sealed. Instead, I tug her in the direction of the Ferris wheel.

"Oh!" Eden's voice is soft. When I look over, her smile practically turns my heart into a puddle of goo. "You remembered."

I stand on my tiptoes to kiss her nose. "Of course I did."

Most of the time you're just put in a plain box, but I saved up enough to rent out the private one with the glass floor. Eden stresses about seeming strange or out of place sometimes, and I didn't want her to have to worry about controlling her reactions to this.

She catches on when we step inside the small, enclosed space. "Is this one special?"

I wink at her. "Only the best for you."

Eden actually blushes, face taking on a red tint right up to her hairline. It's so cute, how I can still manage to do that to her. I take advantage of our privacy by grabbing her cheeks and pressing quick, silly kisses to her lips.

By the third one, she's giggling. "Stop! I want to see."

And that's fair—I did promise her a view all those months ago. I let go of her face and sit down beside her, letting her look.

The view of the city is beautiful; I didn't lie about that. But I've seen it a thousand times. I watch Eden instead. She's staring out at the skyline like it goes on forever, like she can't imagine anything more amazing.

I think we're going to prove that wrong, again and again. Eden's working on her GED, and hopefully we'll both be able to apply for colleges in the fall. Neither of us know what we're going to study, but my friends are confused, too. We'll figure it out.

And after that?

I'm not sure. But I promised to show her the world back in that bedroom in Fierborne. And, well, I managed to keep *this* promise. Why not try for another?

I wrap my arms around Eden's waist from behind, resting my chin on her shoulder. From the top of the Ferris wheel, we look out at the skyline, the water glittering in the sun, and the promise of our future together.

Need more sapphic books with a healthy dose of magic? I've got you covered. Learn more about my debut novel *The Songbird's Refrain* or stay up to date on my latest projects by visiting byjillianmaria.com.

Acknowledgments

On my phone's camera roll, there's a discord message I've saved for posterity. Dated 10/12/2018, it's me explaining to my writing friend group that I've been hit with a very vivid (but not particularly detailed) story idea. "i'll take the ten minutes to vomit draft it, whatever lmao," I typed, followed shortly after by, "oh shit it just....it keeps growing." I couldn't have known then just how much I'd care for this spunky city girl and her story, but now I do, and I owe the people who helped me get it to publication a whole lot of thanks.

First, to that writing friend group, aka the "Avosquado." From plot bunny to published book, you guys have helped and encouraged me every step of the way. Thank you for listening to both my endless gushing about how much I love this story, as well as my frequent plot and pacing conundrums.

This book got exponentially better each draft, and that is thanks in large part to my wonderful critique partners and beta readers. To all of you: thank you for lending your time, your enthusiasm, and your absolutely incredible brains.

I also owe a great deal of thanks to my editor, Bodie. This prose wouldn't be half as clean or readable without your careful eye.

Thank you also to Laya Rose, who designed the cover—thank you for bringing my girls to life so wonderfully! I couldn't be more thrilled with the result.

I've had so many friends support me in my life, both in and out of the writing community. Thank you for continuing to be there for me, through this journey and the next.

If you've ever shown enthusiasm for my writing, whether this project or *The Songbird's Refrain*, thank you from the bottom of my heart. Writing is a lonely job, and knowing that I was able to make even a tiny difference in someone's life (or just their day) means more to me than I can say.

Finally, thanks goes to my family, especially my grandma. A lot of this book's setting and aesthetics come directly from afternoons spent at her and Grandpa's house in the country, exploring the small forest on their property with friends or cousins (but, unfortunately, no mysterious cute girls). I'm not sure what you'd think of a book like this, Grandma, if you were still around to see it. But from one writer to another, I like to think that I'd make you proud.

 **Jillian Maria** enjoys tea, pretty dresses, and ripping out pieces of herself to put in her novels. She writes the books she wants to read, prominently featuring women who are like her in some way or another. A great lover of horror, thriller and mystery novels, most of her stories have some of her own fears lurking in the margins. When she isn't willing imaginary people into existence, she's pursuing a career in public relations and content marketing. A Michigan native, Jillian spends what little free time she has hanging out with her friends, reading too much, singing along to musical numbers, and doting on her cat.

CPSIA information can be obtained
at www.ICGtesting.com
Printed in the USA
LVHW031518131221
706054LV00005B/512